Zack was amaze ever learned him in a rush

He sent up a silent prayer to just keep it coming, keep it coming.

Then things seemed to go into slow motion.

The next pain gripped Robbie even more intensely than the others. To Zack she seemed like an angel under his hands, spreading her wings in silent, intent submission, as a tiny dark head steadily slid out against his cupped palm. With his free hand he grabbed a corner of the receiving blanket to steady the slippery baby. The head rotated, revealing a darling pinched little face, then easily, slowly, powerfully, the shoulders, one then the other, followed. The rest of the tiny body appeared as if materializing from heaven.

Perfect! She was perfect!

Dear Reader,

At the start of THE BABY DIARIES series, I observed that babies seldom arrive when it is convenient. To prove my point, I decided to have the baby in this story arrive on Zack Trueblood and Robbie Tellchick's first date!

This couple seems to have everything kind of backward. People usually fall in love, get married and *then* experience labor and delivery together. But Zack and Robbie are the kind of people who forge ahead with courage and do whatever they have to do, even if that means facing down a murderer.

By the time the two of them finally admit they can't live without each other, they've caught the murderer, and eventually they get the marrying part done, too.

So here we are again, traveling the remote winding roads of the beautiful Texas Hill Country to the historic town I've named Five Points.

And while I'm sure there are real arsonists and thugs and corrupt politicians in this world, *this* small town and *these* quirky characters are pure fiction.

As always, my best to you,

Darlene Graham

P.S. I love to hear from my readers! Drop me a line at P.O. Box 72024, Norman, OK 73070 or visit www.darlenegraham. com and send an e-mail. While you're there take a peek at the third book in THE BABY DIARIES trilogy, *Lone Star Diary*, coming July 2006 from Signature Select Saga.

LONE STAR RISING
Darlene Graham

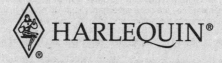

HARLEQUIN®

TORONTO • NEW YORK • LONDON
AMSTERDAM • PARIS • SYDNEY • HAMBURG
STOCKHOLM • ATHENS • TOKYO • MILAN • MADRID
PRAGUE • WARSAW • BUDAPEST • AUCKLAND

ISBN 0-373-71322-3

LONE STAR RISING

Books by Darlene Graham

HARLEQUIN SUPERROMANCE

This book is for Ray, the whistling carpenter, the original
"man from Texas" in my life.
No daughter could ask for a better father!

CHAPTER ONE

DEAR DIARY,

I feel like a fool for even writing the words Dear Diary—a woman my age (37!), a pregnant mother of three who definitely has better things to do with her time than scribbling in a diary like some teenager.

But I promised my sister Markie that I would start a diary again, just like the three of us did when we were young. Markie said to call it a journal if it made me feel better. Whatever I call it, she claims writing out my feelings will help me, heal me, give me focus, put me in touch with my deepest desires and blah, blah, blah. I don't know about all that, but God knows I could use a little diversion.

So here goes.

Dear journal, or diary or whatever, allow me to introduce myself. Roberta McBride Tellchick. Bankrupt widow. Mother of three boys with yet another on the way. Freckle-faced, redheaded middle sister. The one sandwiched in between two smart, vivid brunettes like a piece of pale cheese.

What can I possibly have to write about here? My sister has no concept of what it is like to walk in my low-heeled shoes. She's caught up in an exciting, glamorous life in Austin and has recently gotten herself blissfully married to the gorgeous man of her dreams.

Okay. That's not fair. Markie's had some serious pain to deal with in her life, and I have to say, I'm very proud of the way she handled herself. I mean, giving a baby up for adoption when she was only seventeen! And then seeing him again out of the blue when he's all grown up. Markie claims writing in her baby diary kept her sane while she endured all that pain so long ago. She says it's in our blood, this urge to write everything down. She says I'm not supposed to censor my feelings on these pages or worry about what anybody else thinks.

Okay. I have just had the day from hell.

I look like I've got a beach ball stuck under my shirt and I didn't have time to wash my hair before I went to work. I'm exhausted because I have to go to work at dark-thirty, which is the way of it when you're a lowly waitress in a diner that specializes in the monster Texas breakfast. We have to get in there and help Parson—that's been old Virgil's "real" name ever since he was in the Navy—roll out the biscuits and chop up the home fries.

Nattie Rose, the other waitress at the Hungry Aggie, told me I don't have to come in early if I don't want to. She is too kind, that Nattie Rose. Has a real heart of gold, even if she does cake on the eye makeup worse than Tammy Faye Bakker. I told her that I am grateful for the job, and I am not going to start slacking off my very first week. Especially since I'll be taking off to have the baby in only five short weeks. It's ridiculous for me to be working at all in my condition. I know that. But Danny left me and the boys with nothing, and I do mean not a thing. It looks like the farm is gone for good now, not that I'm sorry to be away from that place, away from the terrible memories.

I try my best not to relive the fire, but sometimes your mind just insists on rolling the video anyway, you know? It's been almost four months now and I still don't have the report from the local fire marshal. What's the holdup?

At least I finally started getting the social security checks, thank the Lord, but that money barely covers groceries and rent. It's not enough for those new Nike tennis shoes my oldest is suddenly needing. Not enough for the extras I'll be needing for this baby. I'm still holding out hope for the insurance money on the barn.

I don't want to waste paper and ink on my problems. I find it's actually easier to focus on something trivial like my hair. When I woke up and looked at the clock this morning, I had no choice but to twist the mess up on top of my head and clip it up into a treetop. But since my hair's the kind that has a mind of its own, by noon I'd developed a frizzy little orange halo around my face. Very, very cute.

But what does it matter how I look when—now

who on earth could be ringing my doorbell? The boys know it's too late to be having any kids over.

WHEN ROBBIE opened the door, the first thing that registered were Zack Trueblood's dark eyes, traveling over her face, then widening with what she imagined to be involuntary shock—or was it disgust?—when he came to her hair. But he rearranged his expression quickly enough. "Hello, Mrs. Tellchick."

"Hello, Zack."

"Did I catch you at a bad time?" Again his gaze slid to her hair, then slammed back down to the porch boards, then flicked up to her face, once again composed and polite. Robbie thought it was decent of him to skip her pumpkin-shaped midsection.

But when he looked once more at her hideous hair, she gave him a level gaze and patted it. "It's easy, you know. I just stick a fork in the toaster and I'm done."

The corner of his mouth lifted a little then, but he didn't actually smile. His expression said he was here on serious business. *Oh, Lord help me,* Robbie thought. She was in no mood for this. But a bad feeling in her gut told her this was some kind of follow-up visit about the fire.

"May I come in?" The way he said it was almost apologetic. Zack, she remembered from high school, had always been famously polite.

"Sure." The door of the old house Robbie had recently moved into creaked like something out of a horror movie as she opened it wider for him.

Robbie imagined a grossly pregnant widow was so not supposed to think thoughts like, *Damn, that man is hot.* But boy, was he ever. Deep-set black eyes, bronze complexion, heavy black hair. As he ambled past she couldn't help a quick glance at his muscular backside, and she caught a whiff of the most delicious aftershave she'd ever smelled.

As for herself, Robbie imagined the oniony odor of the home fries over at the Hungry Aggie mixed with the lingering aroma of the spaghetti sauce she'd made for the boys was enough to make any man retch.

She had seen Zack at the diner several times this past week with a couple of his firefighter buddies. Booth six. She suspected those big tips under the saltshaker were from him. Was that out of guilt? Pity? Robbie figured *she* was the one who should be feeling the guilt. It was *her* pleas, *her* screams that drove this man into that burning barn. Her hysteria could have cost him his life, and it had certainly done nothing to save Danny's.

These were her jumbled thoughts as Zack walked past her. That she was a mess, and that his shoulders were to die for. That his whole physique, in fact, was most impressive. He positively dwarfed her, even now, when she was fatter than a cow. Her guess was he spent a lot of time pumping iron over at that fire station.

No sooner had he stepped foot in her house than there came a scary crash from the kitchen. It sounded like glass breaking, followed by a stunningly abnormal silence, followed by the dogs' wild barking, followed by the high-pitched changeling voice of Robbie's twelve-year-old. "Now look what you've done!" he screamed. "Mom's gonna kill you!"

"Shut the hell up!" That clever retort came from Robbie's eight-year-old, who recently acquired that delightful word, along with some others she didn't want to hear in her house. If Danny were alive he'd box his son's ears for talking that way.

The pandemonium that followed—three boys yelling and two dogs barking—made Robbie wince.

"Would you excuse me?" she said sweetly to Zack. "Oh—" She turned back to him. "Please. Come on in. That is, if you think you can stand it."

This time the corners of Zack's mouth tipped up into a full-fledged grin.

ZACK TRUEBLOOD followed Robbie Tellchick down a narrow corridor that ran parallel to the stairway and ended at a high-ceilinged kitchen at the back of the house. He watched her tangled thatch of hair bounce around on the crown of her head, and wondered if this was the new style or something. Curls upon curls upon curls, and his guess was that none of it had seen a comb today.

She had always been a true redhead, he recalled. He remembered how pretty her hair was in high school, strands of spun copper mixed with streaks of blond. The rest of her looked equally disheveled. What was with the perpetual overalls? She even wore them at the diner, as if she didn't care what anybody thought of her.

The last time he'd been to her home she'd looked even frumpier, if that were possible, standing in the shadows behind the screened door of her mudporch out on the farm, cinched up in a faded pink bathrobe that looked to have seen better days. She'd grown even rounder, too. Was the poor woman having twins? He dared not let his eyes travel down to her gently swishing backside. Wouldn't that be some kind of sin against nature, to check out a pregnant woman's behind? He guessed it was those deviling memories of how cute her bottom had been in high school that made his eyes flick down there anyway.

He immediately wished they hadn't.

Despite the deterioration of her looks, he had found himself as drawn to Robbie Tellchick as ever. What was it about her? Her cheery determination to please even the grumpiest customer? Her laugh? Surely that. He could pick up the sound of it from all the way across the diner. Was it the way she'd taken hold with her boys, valiantly trying to be both mother and father? He'd seen her at a T-ball game last summer, pregnant and hot, but cheering on her youngest with all her might. And now here Zack was, about to add to her problems.

Whatever his fascination with the woman, he didn't have long to dwell on it, or his guilt, because two mutts came hurtling out of the kitchen and bumped into Robbie's legs, knocking her off balance and backward into Zack.

"Whoa!" Zack said as the dogs shot out the open front door while Zack grabbed for Robbie in several awkward places as she stumbled against him. He'd never felt anything so soft! All women were soft and, yes, he delighted in that softness, but this was a kind of softness that was unearthly, so buoyant as to be angelic, almost as if she herself were the baby. She pushed off of him like he was a brick wall and yelled, "Those dang dogs!"

Then she barreled onward into the kitchen.

The three Tellchick boys froze like little statues when they saw Zack coming up behind her. He hoped it wasn't because their young minds were flashing back to the one and only time they'd seen him before. But Zack had been in full firefighting regalia that night—turnouts, helmet, asbestos mask. Covered in black soot. Eyebrows and hair singed to brittle little filaments of scorched beige. Surely they didn't recognize him, standing here in a clean and pressed day uniform. He hoped they didn't connect him with his failure in the event that had shattered their young lives. He wondered if their mother had told them who Zack Trueblood was—the man who *hadn't* saved their father.

"Get away from that glass!" the mother shrieked.

And who could blame her? The kitchen was dim— illuminated only by a single bulb over the sink—but Zack could see shards of glass spread in a glittering array on the windowsill. In the sink, on the counter, the floor. Zack was already looking for a light switch…and for blood. "Everybody okay, fellas?" He found the switch and flipped it. No result.

They nodded mutely, these three cute kids, all obviously stamped from the same mold. Wiry and muscular the way their dad had once been, handsome and even-featured like their mother, but each distinct in coloring.

Two redheads and a lone brunette. The big one looked like one giant freckle. His hands dripped suds, and he clutched a dish rag as if he were strangling it. The middle one, nearly as dark-haired as Zack, had turned white as a sheet. The younger one had the kind of red hair that was so pale as to be almost blond. He stood hunch-shouldered like a scared little squirrel. For one second, Zack tried to remember what it felt like to be a boy, to find yourself in trouble with a stressed-out single mother. Didn't he have plenty of experience in this situation?

"What happened?" Robbie demanded as she charged forward.

"He did it!" the two younger ones said simultaneously, pointing at each other.

The older boy stepped up, careful of the glass. "Mom, these two hawnyawks were playing baseball instead of drying the dishes."

Zack had to smile. He hadn't heard anyone use the word hawnyawk since his grandfather died.

"Baseball?" Robbie's reddish mop of hair bobbled as her raised palms indicated the smallish room. "In the *kitchen?*"

"Not *real* baseball," the littlest one protested. "Mark had a golf ball and I was hittin' at it with the broomstick."

"We wasn't hurtin' anything, Mom," the middle one said. His little face was painfully sincere. "Until stupid here forgot how to bunt."

"I'm only five years old!" his little brother yelled. "I don't even get to punt yet. I just barely started T-ball!"

"It's *bunt*, twerp, not punt," the middle one yelled

back. "And ya don't swing like you're hittin' a homer in the house!"

"Do not call your brother a twerp." Robbie shot Zack an embarrassed glance. He shrugged. "Or stupid for that matter." She shoved the child's dark bangs up and zeroed in on a tiny nick above his brow. "This could have been your *eye,* young man. Is everything else okay?" she demanded.

The kids nodded solemnly.

"Mom, I'm sorry about the window." The older one moved to stand beside his brother. "But honest, I was just doing the dishes, and next thing I know a golf ball comes flying right past my head."

Robbie shoved at the boys' shoulders. "You two could have hurt your brother. Now get over by the door. Go on." Robbie's voice echoed sharply in the bare-walled kitchen. When the boys moved, she snapped open a paper bag she had snatched from under the sink and started flicking glass off the edge of the counter into it. Not carefully enough, Zack thought.

There was a right way and a wrong way to do most things. The right way being, take all necessary safety precautions.

"I'll take care of that," he said, reaching for the sack. "I have some leather work gloves out in my truck. You tend to your boys." The kids had clotted up over by the door, holding themselves in the defensive poses of boys in trouble.

She whirled on him. "Tend to them? *Tend* to them?" Her voice rose. "I ought to *tend* to their backsides.

These little incidents," she said as she plucked up some larger pieces of glass and sent them crashing into the sack with too much force, "are happening with alarming regularity around this house. A broken window, a burning dish towel." She stopped tossing glass and gave her sons a withering look. "A flooded *bathroom*. This nonsense has got to stop!" Her voice rose, threatening hysteria and tears. "Because in case nobody's noticed I've got a baby on the way in exactly five weeks!"

The younger boys cringed in guilt. The older one was blushing clear to the roots of his red hair.

"Yes, ma'am," Zack agreed quietly. Which sounded totally lame, but he didn't know what else to say. He'd given up on getting the sack out of her hands. He turned his attention to the boys. "Guys. Why don't you, uh, go in the living room while I help your mother clean this up?" He was thinking maybe it'd be better if they didn't see their mother cry.

The two younger kids seized the opportunity and shot off faster than the dogs. But the oldest one hung back. "Who are you anyway?" He was eyeing Zack's new Gall's jacket—black leather with the department shield stitched over the breast pocket.

Zack figured the kid had maybe put two and two together by now.

"I'm a, uh, a friend of your mother's. I came to talk to her about…business." Not business. Bad news.

"Were you one of the firemen that put out the fire that killed my dad?" Hearing a twelve-year-old talk about the tragedy so matter of factly nearly broke Zack's heart.

No kid should be saying words like *the fire that killed my dad.*

Robbie Tellchick's eyes widened, moist with tears. Zack had already decided that maybe this was not the night to share his news. He did not want to do anything to bring this family one more iota of pain. In fact, he had vowed to do anything in his power to help them. But in this case he didn't know how to spare them the hurt. The truth was going to come out, eventually. The fire had been determined to be arson, and the arsonist, it turned out, was the boys' father.

"Yes, I was there," he said calmly, "but that's nothing for you to worry about." He took two steps across the gritty wood floorboards, his boots clumping too loudly in the cramped space. He put his hand on the boy's shoulder and was glad that the kid didn't immediately shrug him off. "I'll help your mother clean up this mess. Why don't you go on in there with your brothers."

But the boy stood his ground, squinting at Zack with alert brown eyes. Zack dropped his hand and tried not to look guilty, though the discomfort he felt was acute.

"I'm going to learn CPR," the boy stated with conviction.

"That's good. Everybody should." Zack said it neutrally, not sure where the kid was going with this, still not sure if the kid recognized him. It occurred to Zack that he must get his grit from his mother, because he certainly hadn't gotten it from that worthless drip of a father. Zack knew he shouldn't think about a dead man with such contempt, but as far as he was concerned,

Danny Tellchick had always been a goombah of the first stripe, a guy who never appreciated or deserved a woman like Robbie McBride.

All three of the McBride sisters had been smart as whips, and beautiful to boot. Robbie's intelligence was only one of many things Zack had admired about her back when he was four grades behind her in high school.

"I expect you know CPR and all that stuff." The kid was still looking Zack up and down, his head tilting now, his gaze growing more wary.

"Yeah. I'm a firefighter." Zack stood violently still, hardly breathing, because out of the corner of his eye, he could see that Robbie's lips were pressing together, tighter and tighter.

"You're the one. Aren't you?" The kid sounded almost angry. "The one who went in and pulled my dad out of the fire and did CPR on him?"

"Yes." Zack Trueblood was indeed the one. The one who had performed pointless CPR on their father's scorched lifeless body right before these children's eyes. The one who had intensified their horror a hundred fold.

The one who had loved their mother from afar for nearly eighteen years.

CHAPTER TWO

ZACH LOOKED AT the wiry kid standing before him and felt unsure of himself for the first time in a very long time. Unsure of what the boy must be thinking. Unsure of what to say. He looked at Robbie Tellchick. Her arms were folded above her bulging tummy in a stance as closed and tight as a straight jacket. Her compressed lips indicated that she had no intention of breaking the uneasy silence.

"What's your name, son?" Zack asked the boy.

"Mark."

"Mark, would it be okay if we talked about this later? For now, why don't you go on in there with your brothers?"

The boy left quietly and Robbie proceeded to attack her task with angry purpose.

"Ma'am." Zack had to grab her arms to make her let up with the glass. "Let me do that. Really. Let me get those heavy-duty gloves from my truck. And a hammer. It would be best to break these larger pieces out." With a nod of his head he indicated the ridges of glass sticking out of the windowpane like a silhouette of the Swiss Alps. He felt her muscles tense with resistance for one second, then her arms went limp in his grip.

"I still can't talk about that night," she whispered.

"I understand. I really do," Zack assured her quietly. He still had trouble with it himself. And now he'd come with news that would only complicate the healing even further. But right now they couldn't afford to wallow in the past. There was glass to clean up and three hurting and confused children in the next room.

"Why don't you go see about your boys," he urged her again as he released her wrists.

Robbie blew out a frustrated breath and brushed back her frizzy hair. For a second, it looked like she might cry again. "Okay," she finally said. "But be careful with that glass."

"I always am," Zack said flatly. He always was. But sometimes being careful wasn't enough. Sometimes, like the night Danny Tellchick died, it was simply too late.

She turned and slowly went through a swinging door at the side of the room where he caught a glimpse of a small, dim dining room beyond.

He went back out the main doorway of the kitchen to the narrow corridor that led to the front door, which still stood open, swaying on creaky hinges in the October wind. The thing was nice and heavy, he noticed now. Solid oak. Beveled glass oval window. Probably dated back to the nineteenth century and some prosperous German immigrant who had settled in this part of Texas. He noted, too, the scarred hardwood flooring in the entry hall, the finely detailed newel post at the foot of the stairs, the weakly lit miniature chandelier overhead.

He'd never paid much attention to this house from the

street. It was one of many Victorian-era relics in Five Points, barely visible behind mounds of overgrown arbor vitae bushes. But he could see now that the place certainly had potential. Who was renting it out to Robbie Tellchick? Old man Mestor, most likely. He owned several in this part of town, all in disrepair like this one.

The living room opened off the narrow hallway with a set of double pocket doors, which stood open a crack. Walking past, he caught a glimpse of Robbie's round tummy and heard her irritated voice interrogating the boys. "Where on earth did you get a golf ball?"

A childish voice gave a defensive reply, but he couldn't make out the words.

"All right." Robbie's voice came back high and sharp. "I want you guys to go upstairs and do your homework and get your baths and put on your pajamas."

"Even me?" Zack heard Mark protest.

Zack dug the necessary items out of a toolbox mounted in the truck bed under the rear window. He'd have to ask Robbie if she had a spare cardboard box. Since she'd just moved that seemed likely.

He went back to the kitchen, and she came trundling in on his heels.

"You really don't have to do that," she said.

Of course he didn't, but he wasn't going to argue the point. "Have you got a broom and a dustpan? And a cardboard box? And maybe some duct tape?"

"I think so." She went to a door that opened to a cramped utility room, where Zack could see a washer-dryer set beyond. Thank God, Zack thought, she at least had that, with a baby coming and all. He'd never caught himself having such a purely domestic thought before. It flat out startled him.

She disappeared and flipped on a light. The room was apparently a converted porch, with a crooked old wood floor and a bank of bare windows rattling in the wind. Piles of dirty laundry and other clutter were scattered everywhere. After she rummaged around for a minute, she came back with the broom and dustpan and a sizeable cardboard box, wrestling it into the kitchen on her front like an out-of-control boat.

"Let me." He dashed to her side and took hold of it, levering the carton flat in one swift motion. At her quizzical look he said, "It's for the window."

"Ah. Good idea." She blew out a frustrated puff of air that made her frizzy bangs lift. "I guess it's too late to get anything done about replacing it tonight. The glass shop'll be closed."

"Yes, ma'am," he said as he jerked on the gloves.

She rubbed her arms, clad in the sleeves of a clingy little white T-shirt under the overalls. "The temperature's supposed to drop tonight."

He squatted to the floor and started scooping up glass with the dustpan. "Yes, ma'am."

"You know, every time you call me ma'am, it just makes everything ten times worse."

He gave her a grin over his shoulder.

"I hope you don't think that *this*—" she made a wild, frustrated gesture at the chaos around her "—is the way I usually live. I'm normally very organized, but it seems like it's taking me forever to get settled." She stuck out her bottom lip and huffed, making her bangs fly up again.

"And to top it all off, I'm cranky and pregnant. That 'ma'am' bit makes me feel like a little old lady or something. Oh, I know I'm four years older than you. I remember you from high school, at least I did once my sister reminded me about you. She claimed you got the Eagle when you were only a freshman." She gave him an assessing look. "Did you really?"

The Eagle. Zack had forgotten about it. The award stood for leadership. Integrity. Strength. Invariably the honor went to a senior, a top athlete who excelled in academics and inspired his teammates. Part of getting the Eagle entailed bench-pressing more weight than any of the other guys during football training. Even at the age of 33, Zack could still press 300.

It was that physical discipline that had enabled him to carry a heavy man like Danny Tellchick out of a burning barn with no air. Not that putting his air mask on Danny's face had done any good. The man was already dead. The fire marshal had finally confirmed that to Zack yesterday. Roy Graves had blamed the coroner for the delay. Zack just wanted to know the truth, whatever that was. When they'd held the critical stress-management session after the fire, Zack had made sure everybody clearly understood that he was the one, the only one, who would be taking any bad news to Robbie Tellchick.

Zack covered all these thoughts with another engaging grin. "Yes, ma'am."

"Cut it out. I'm not *that* much older than you, even if I do look it at the moment." She raked the frizzed hair back from her forehead. "So you can just stop the 'ma'am' stuff, okay?"

"Whatever you say...*ma'am*."

That got a perturbed little laugh out of her and Zack's heart lifted. He hadn't seen her smile, really smile, once in all the times he'd been in her presence or glimpsed her from afar in the months since her husband's death. She smiled at her customers at the diner, of course, but it was the glazed charm of a girl whose feet hurt. If they asked him, he could tell a person exactly the when, where and how of every instance when he'd seen Robbie Tellchick since the night of her husband's death. He could tell a person what she had been wearing, how her face had looked, the vivid color of her wounded green eyes.

She seemed suddenly lighter in spirit now. "Well, get busy." She flapped a hand at him as if she were bossing the boys.

He laughed and they chatted while he swept up the rest of the glass.

The house was interesting, he allowed. It had possibilities.

She agreed, filling him in on some of its odd little features.

"Your boys are sure cute kids," he said.

"A handful," she countered. "Do you have kids?"

"No," he said, "not even married."

When he'd finished duct-taping the cardboard

securely over the window opening, he said, "Okay. Have you got a flashlight?"

"Omigosh." She jerked open a drawer. "The dogs! They could get hurt. They stay out there in their doghouse at night. We'd better check for glass outside the window, too, hadn't we?"

He realized he had liked the sound of what she'd just said. She'd said *we*. There hadn't been any *we* in Zack's life in quite a while. Dates, yes. Plenty of dates. But nothing deep. Nothing lasting.

"You know, that's a good thing," Zack said as he followed her back down the hall.

She gave him a puzzled look over her shoulder.

"I mean, that you've got those dogs out there. They'll act as protection tonight—" He bit off the sentence, wishing he hadn't drawn attention to the fact that she'd be sleeping alone upstairs with nothing between her family and the outside world but a flimsy piece of cardboard.

The dogs were curled up on the porch, which was also rotting in places.

They stood up and trotted over when Robbie murmured to them. One, a fat little blond pup with sawed-off legs, looked part corgi. The other, slender of build with a long black-and-white coat, looked like he had a lot of Border collie in him.

Robbie petted them, talking baby talk as she did so, and Zack was inordinately fascinated with her long fingers as they ruffled the dogs' silky coats, and with a glimpse of maternally lush cleavage. She straightened, pushed at her back with a palm, stretching and groaning as she did, and he found himself inordinately fascinated by that, too.

"Angus, Awgie," Robbie commanded the animals, "stay."

"Angus and Awgie?" Zack grinned. "Scottish dogs, now are they?"

"McBrides." She gave her red hair a little toss that Zack found wholly endearing. "And proud of it."

Leading with the flashlight, she took Zack around to the tall side gate. It scraped pathetically on the concrete walk and Zack had to give it a shove with his shoulder to force it open.

"This place is a wreck," Robbie muttered, and led on.

The night was rapidly cooling and mist was beginning to swirl on the frost-bitten air as they made their way down a waffled and cracked sidewalk encroached by overgrown weeds and shrubs. Somewhere back in the tall trees lining the alley an owl hooted. The only other sound was the slap of Robbie's tennis shoes and the clump of Zack's boots until their steps crunched into the fallen leaves, twigs and bramble that formed drifts against the side of the house.

Outside the window in a weedy patch of mud, they found more glass, the golf ball and a cracked plastic gallon-container of ice cream—the cheap kind.

"Something tells me I didn't get the whole story." Robbie frowned at the evidence as the wind whipped tendrils of pale hair over her mouth. She brushed them away with irritation just before Zack saw a grin playing at the corners of her mouth.

"Boys will be boys," he said, trying to coax that grin upward.

"Yeah. And girls will be girls. I'm nearly as p.o.'d about the ice cream as I am about the window." Her grin materialized fully then. "I was going to have some after they went to bed."

"Ah. So you're *that* kind of girl." He grinned.

She giggled, then shivered. Without hesitating, Zack removed the new jacket he'd only recently ordered from Gall's supply. He admitted the thing was an extravagance. He had actually been glad to see the cold weather blowing in today so he had an excuse to wear it. "Here." He draped it around her shoulders.

"Thanks." She accepted his kindness without self-consciousness, he supposed on account of the baby. "Nice jacket."

"Yeah. Can I make a suggestion?" Zack didn't know why he was sticking his nose in her business. "Can you maybe let all of this go for tonight?" Maybe it was because he'd been in these boys' shoes, once. A kid that could use a little mercy.

Her eyes rose up to meet his, illuminated by a thin bar of light shining between the unbroken glass above the cardboard and the ratty window shade. She studied him briefly with a defensive look, as if to say, *What concern is it of yours?* Then her face softened, looking sad again. He felt a tightening in his chest, staring into those pretty green eyes. He'd first looked into them when he was fourteen years old and they hadn't changed a bit.

The two of them had been standing outside a school bus on a misty autumn night much like this one.

The cheerleaders and the football team had ridden the long highway home from a trouncing at the hands of the Kerrville Wolves. Throughout the whole trip, Zack had sat and studied the back of Robbie McBride's fluffy, bright hair from his seat several rows behind her, had listened to every note of her laughter as it drifted back to him in the darkened bus. Robbie McBride, the beautiful redhead, the popular senior, a girl way out of his league. In the parking lot, the kids had dispersed to their cars quickly, not wanting to linger in the atmosphere of defeat, and when Zack found himself standing alone with her, he saw his chance.

"Uh, Robbie. Are you planning on going to the dance next week?" To this day, he didn't know how he'd ever gotten up the nerve to say this.

She turned and smiled up at him. "Me? Are you talking to me?" It struck him then that she had hardly been aware of him standing there, that she was waiting on someone else, her ride most likely.

He recalled trying to be cool, glancing around the dark parking lot, up at the soft channel of light filtering down from one of the windows of the bus. He noted some of the other guys waiting for him over by Spike Porter's Mustang. "Nah. I was talking to Spike over there."

She laughed lightly. "Okay. Yeah, I'm going. I never miss a dance."

"Oh. Cool. Have you got a date?" He had never asked a girl out before.

She looked up at him, clearly astonished, as her expression grew first wide-eyed, then amused, as if some unbidden thought had caught her by surprise. That's the first time those eyes of hers had truly mesmerized him, standing there beside the bus, with the fog of their breaths mixing for one long moment. She frowned, then blinked, as if coming out of a trance. "I'm sorry. What's your name?"

"Zack. Zack Trueblood." He tilted one shoulder forward so she could see the number on his letter jacket. "Number eleven?" He arched one eyebrow at her. "And you're Robbie McBride. So now that we officially know each other, how about it? The dance?" Not only had he never asked a girl out on a date, he'd never even acted this cocky in the presence of a female before. Well, hell. He never had to do anything but stand there around most girls. Most girls got so giggly in his presence it was pathetic. Except for Jenna, his best friend Mason's little sister. But Jenna didn't count. She was a husky little imp who could land a punch to his six-pack as solidly as Mason could.

But this was Robbie McBride, senior girl extraordinaire. A real woman, who was probably used to guys acting a little more smooth.

Those beautiful eyes narrowed slightly, and the beginnings of a smile played at the corners of her gorgeous mouth. "Are you a junior? A sophomore? Or what?"

"Or what," he said with a shrug as if it didn't matter. It didn't, to him. "I'm a freshman," he finally admitted.

Her smile widened. "Well, Zack Trueblood, I am flattered. I really am. For a freshman, you really are kind of a cute, but you know—" her voice brightened "—I've got a boyfriend."

As if said boyfriend had been summoned right out of the mist, Danny Tellchick came ambling up, wearing a blue corduroy FFA jacket and stiff boot-cut jeans that swallowed his rangy frame. What does she see in this guy? Zack had wondered. Even back then, before Danny had gained fifty beer-belly pounds and managed to fail miserably at life, Zack had thought he was a tad short for the likes of Robbie McBride.

Now he wondered if Robbie Tellchick remembered that night at all.

"I think your oldest boy, especially, could use a break, don't you?" he said quietly, bringing his thoughts back to what was important in the present. The idea of a twelve-year-old being told to put on his pajamas made Zack cringe. "Maybe seeing me, when he wasn't expecting it, kind of bothered him, you know?"

She looked down at the white circle the flashlight made on the ground. After a moment she nodded.

"Mrs. Tellchick?" He swallowed. "Robbie?"

She turned her face up to him again.

"I told you this once, but I want to be sure you understand that I really meant it. I want to help you and the boys in any way I can."

She looked back down to the ground. After a long silence, without looking up at him, she said, "It wasn't your fault, you know that, don't you?"

He did know that. And he also now knew some things she didn't. But that wasn't the point. Danny Tellchick had died a horrible death, possibly a suspicious one, and now his defenseless family was thrown into turmoil and suffering through no fault of their own. If Zack could only push a giant "undo" button on the whole thing, he would. But he couldn't change anything. All he could do now was step in, be of some assistance somehow, in some way.

"Could I…would you let me come and fix this window? Tomorrow?" He wanted to add, no strings attached. He wanted to say, *I don't mean anything by offering. No pressure. It has nothing to do with the fact that I had a wild crush on you in high school. I just want to help.* But saying all that, with her so recently bereaved and being in her condition, might seem foolish—insulting, even.

Her eyes darted around, obviously tempted by the offer. "I go to work really early. The boys get themselves off to school."

"What time do you get home?"

"Around two. Then I usually try to get a little something done around here before I feed the boys supper. Sometimes I have to go back for the dinner shift if Nattie Rose needs help."

"Why don't I come over here at say, about two thirty? Tomorrow's my day off from the fire station. I'll have plenty of time to drop by and measure earlier—I can do that from the outside—and then I can have the glass all ready, so it won't take much time. I have all the other materials. I own my own carpentry and remodeling business."

"I…I don't know when I'd be able to pay you. I mean, we are finally getting a little social security income now, but…" She bit her lip and glanced at the window. "I sure don't want my landlord to see this."

Her admission tore at his heart so much that he made an involuntary move toward her and reached out to comfort with his open palm. But she shifted sideways, out of range of his touch, bringing her hands up to grasp the lapels of his jacket, clutching it tightly around her shoulders. She looked so vulnerable with her tummy protruding and her messy hair reflecting the misty yellowed light from the window that it was all Zack could do to keep from turning her toward him and wrapping his arms around her.

"Don't worry about paying me. A guy like me clears plenty in a town full of historical houses."

She nodded, then sighed dejectedly. "Okay. I think this time I'm going to just have to accept your kindness. I really appreciate it, Zack." Clutching the jacket, she bent awkwardly to retrieve the flattened carton of ice cream.

"I'll finish this. You'd better get out of the wind."

He hoped his offers of help hadn't hurt her pride. It occurred to him then that he hadn't told her what he came to say. Until now, Danny Tellchick's death certificate had read "under investigation," but soon the young widow would receive a supplementary certificate of death that revealed the truth. But for now Zack decided that bad news could just wait until a better time. Those boys weren't the only ones who needed a little mercy around here.

CHAPTER THREE

I WOKE UP at 2 a.m and couldn't go back to sleep. The wind is rattling the creaky windows of this old house worse than a hurricane.

I switched on the lamp and prowled around this room like a cranky mamma bear who'd been jolted out of hibernation, until I found this journal on the dresser. I guess it wouldn't hurt to follow my sister's advice and scribble down a few of my black little thoughts.

Markie wants me to seek counseling. But what's a counselor going to tell me? Mrs. Tellchick, you're sad? You have some very bad memories to deal with here? You've got another baby on the way, and you get to raise this one by yourself?

All summer Markie kept reminding me that this baby may seem like a burden now, but that he is a real person, who is probably going to grow up to be absolutely wonderful, a blessing. I know that. And that's not the point.

Markie is all idealistic about having children because she's recently met her beautiful all-grown-up and well-behaved son, Brandon. She forgets I've got three that I've been raising from scratch, out on a dryland farm where Danny and I barely eked out a living. I don't have any idealistic illusions about raising babies. Sleepless nights. Health worries. A steady stream of bills.

And then they become little boys, with all their antics. Like that broken window!

I have absolutely no hope of producing a girl. I'm convinced Danny didn't have any girl genes in him. None. Nada. Zip. He used to joke that we were raising our own little home-grown football team.

I just got tears in my eyes when I wrote that last part. Part of me feels like all of my hopes and dreams died with Danny in that barn. My husband wasn't perfect, but I've been with him since junior high and I don't know how to be any other way. I sure don't know how to raise these boys alone!

Seeing Zack Trueblood has got me picturing the fire in my mind all over again. It seemed like it just exploded at one point. One minute I was standing at the kitchen window, thinking I smelled smoke, and the next I was outside staring up at a whole wall of the barn engulfed in flames. I knew when I ran out there, even as I was punching 9-1-1 on the cell phone, that there was no way the fire trucks could make it from town in time. It only took me a couple of minutes to figure out where all the boys were, and that Danny was nowhere to be found.

I feel so guilty now because now I'm thinking about Zack again.

I'm thinking about him following me into the

kitchen last night. (Brave man!) That sounded a little sarcastic, even to myself, but I mean that literally. Zack Trueblood is the bravest man I know, bar none. He's so brave it takes my breath away. I'll never forget what he tried to do for me and my boys. The man plunged into a burning barn to pull out my husband's body. I get tears in my eyes every time I think about it. And here they come, right on cue. These late-night weeping sessions have got to stop. My sister's right. I am exhausting myself. I don't think I can write any more right now.

THE NEXT DAY a blast of cold Canadian air howled down from the north, making Zack's job on the window much more of a hassle than it should have been.

"You want something hot to drink?" Robbie called through the pane to him when she could see that he was almost done.

"Sounds good." His fingers were getting stiff with cold as he smoothed a seam of glazing around the glass. For more than one reason, he was glad he hadn't delayed getting this window fixed for Robbie. A stiff norther was swooping down off the Edwards plateau. The gray clouds gathering on the northwest horizon promised a cold rain later. The beginning of the fall rains was both a curse and a blessing for local firefighters.

It signaled the end of the grass fire season, but it also gave rise to the inevitable auto incidents in which folks who didn't understand how to drive the treacherous Hill

Country roads after a flash flood got swept off one of the many low water bridges in the area.

While he'd been walking the perimeter of Robbie's house earlier this afternoon, he'd noticed quite a few more things that needed repair: loose shingles, broken porch rails, a badly bent gutter spout. He was going to have a word with old man Mestor about all of that. In Zack's opinion, that old boy needed to spend more time over here fixing up his rentals and less time gabbing with his cronies over at the Hungry Aggie.

Zack knew Mestor employed pick-up loads of Mexicans out on his farm, and he could dern well put some of them to work on his shabby rental properties in town.

Zack was all about civic pride. Five Points had all the historical significance and charm of the Hill Country towns surrounding it and capitalizing on its potential was just a matter of getting old guys like Mestor to have a little more vision. Flag waving and decorating Main Street for the odd summer barbecue wasn't enough. In Zack's mind, the town's charm would have to come from more permanent improvements. But sometimes it was like pulling eyeteeth to get people to do things right.

"I hope you don't mind chamomile tea," Robbie explained when he poked his head inside the kitchen door and said, "All done."

"I'm afraid I don't have any coffee," she went on as she poured steaming water into a teapot. "Ixnay on the caffeine." She patted her tummy. "Pregnant and paranoid, that's me," she said as Zack stepped into the kitchen. "I see a potential threat to my fetus in practically everything I eat, drink, drive, breathe or even think about." She shot him an arch-browed glance as if he were in the "think about" category.

He chuckled. "Tea will be fine." He'd never cared for the herbal stuff, but he'd drink kerosene if it meant he got to sit in Robbie Tellchick's kitchen and listen to her banter—and *look* at her—while he sipped it.

He held forth the bag he'd forgotten about earlier. "Uh, hope this isn't too toxic. I guess it's a good thing this norther blew in since I left it on the front seat of my truck."

She took the insulated sack and peeked inside. The little smile he was coming to crave played around her lips. "Why thank you, Zack." She pulled it out. "Ooo. Häagen-Dazs. The good stuff."

"Ice cream probably seems kind of dumb with this cold weather setting in."

"Not to me. It's my one indulgence. And the gallon that boys destroyed was going to be all I could afford this month." The smile became full-fledged. "It was so nice of you to remember."

Knowing he'd pleased her gave him a rush of pleasure. One indulgence down, a million more to go, if he had his way.

They settled on comfortable bentwood chairs at a little white spindle-legged table near a high bow win-dow that looked out over an overgrown backyard. The narrow, bare kitchen looked slightly cheerier in the daytime, even though the skies outside were gray and threatening rain. She had lit a candle on the table and she placed the teapot on a brightly patterned quilted hot pad between them.

"And thank you again," she said, smiling as she poured his tea, "for taking all this time and trouble to fix my window."

"No trouble." He studied her in the milky afternoon light. Faint bluish circles under her eyes indicated that she was tired. Her hair was drawn back in the braid she often wore to work. She was wearing a baby blue maternity top with jeans. Watching her perform the simple task, he suddenly realized who it was she favored, at least in his mind. Nicole Kidman. Except Robbie's hair had streaks of a deeper, purer red. But there was something about the way her full rosy lips contrasted so vividly with her pale skin and her faint freckles. He wondered how she'd react if he told her she looked like the actress.

He realized he was staring at her and turned his gaze out the window. "It really wasn't any trouble," he repeated. He stole a glance at her and frowned, finding that he still couldn't tell her about the autopsy and the fire marshal's conclusions. Not now.

The heat pattern, the trailers of gasoline on concrete, the pour patterns. It all added up to one thing: arson.

It seemed abrupt to drop a bomb like that on a pregnant woman while they were just sitting here, having tea at her quaint little table. Just the two of them, alone. That's what really gave him the willies. Being alone with her, pregnant or not, gave rise to all kinds of conflicting emotions in him.

She raised her cup and sipped cautiously, noticing that he was watching her, eyeing him over the rim. She had probably already figured out he hadn't come to the house on a social call last night, and she was undoubtedly waiting for the other shoe to drop.

"How are you feeling?" he asked. Was that too personal a thing to say to a pregnant woman?

"Fine. This is my fourth, after all. There are no surprises."

That hit him with a jolt. Here he had been entertaining all these idealistic, quasi-romantic memories about the perky redheaded Robbie McBride last night, when the reality was she was pregnant Robbie Tellchick, experienced mother of three.

He sipped his tea. "This stuff's pretty good." He took another sip, stalling, angling for something to say. "So. How's your new job working out?" He'd been watching her at the café since she started waitressing there. He missed a few days when he'd worked an extra 24-hour shift and then he'd had a hardwood floor to lay for a woman over in Wildhorse. The job had taken him two solid days because the woman, a pretty-enough blonde, kept coming around to chatter. He had wondered if the other guys had tipped Robbie adequately in his absence.

"Fine. Everybody there is so nice to me. The whole town's nice to me, though I suppose there are some folks that think I'm crazy for going to work as a waitress and moving into this old rattletrap. They probably wonder why I don't take my boys out to my parents' farm and stay out there like my mother wants me to."

"Your mother and dad live out by the river, too, right?"

"Yes."

"That's a really nice farm out there."

"Not to me."

Zack gave her a quizzical look which she didn't answer. "Still," he offered sensibly, "that might have been easier on you." Though a selfish part of him was glad to have her right here in town where he had some hope of seeing her more often. It would be pretty hard to come up with excuses to drive all the way out to the McBride farm on a regular basis, and he had already taken to eating breakfast at the Hungry Aggie as often as possible. Lunch, too. Even dinner if she was doing that shift. Why not? Who was to question the eating habits of a bachelor firefighter?

He was making a regular pest of himself, probably, being too obvious about laying down those huge tips under the saltshaker. Occasionally he'd gotten that pretty smile of hers to emerge. "Why did you move into town, if I may ask? That's a pretty little farm you've got out there, too." Zack knew the property well. He'd coveted it, truth be told.

"It's a pretty little place that was falling down around my ears." She sighed heavily, and Zack didn't like the sound of it. "It's a long story. In any case I couldn't keep the farm up by myself, and there were…ugly circumstances that made it untenable to go live at my mother's house."

"*Ugly?* Like what?" He downed the remainder of his tea, and she filled his cup right away. It seemed like she was enjoying this little break, maybe even his company, he hoped.

"I don't want to bore a man like you with the McBride family's dramas."

A man like him? What did that mean? "I'm interested." He wanted to add, "in anything having to do with
you," but thought better of it. He smiled at her. *Just a
couple of minutes more of this, Lord. Please. Just a little
more normal conversation.*

"Well, you knew my sister just got married?"

"Right. I saw the pictures in the paper. To Justin
Kilgore, the congressman's son, right?"

"Um. Well, she and Justin were…sweethearts as
teenagers. And my mother came between them years
ago. She lied to them."

"Oh. That *is* kind of heavy."

"Kind of, yes. I still haven't forgiven my mother for
what she did. There's a lot more to it, but I'm not sure
my sister would want me to share the details."

"I understand. Where is your sister these days, by the
way?" Last night Zack had decided that having the sister
around when he dropped his bomb might not be a bad
idea. Robbie was so vulnerable right now. Markie
McBride had seemed really levelheaded the few times
Zack had talked to her, and she seemed genuinely concerned about helping Robbie.

"She's on her honeymoon in Aruba, but she'll be
back in a couple of weeks. She promised to help me get
this place in order when she gets home." The heavy sigh
came again. "I have to admit I could sure use the help."

"I'd be glad to offer mine." He wondered if he could
get the fire marshal to keep his findings away from the
media for a little while longer. He wondered if the bad
news had to go in the papers at all, in fact. It was a

common thing. Losers torched their own worthless barns and outbuildings all the time, then called the fire department when they were ready to put out the fire. He looked Robbie up and down, not liking the look of those shadows under her eyes. How could he make this easier for her? "I mean it. I'll be glad to help. I thought about talking to your landlord for you, too. He needs to do some repairs around here."

"Oh, I couldn't ask you to do that," she said.

"I don't mind. Mestor's not somebody you should have to even be in the same room with, much less confront."

"Well, you shouldn't have to confront him, either."

Zack smiled. "Oh, but I *like* to. We've had words before. It makes my day. By the way, I meant to check when I was here last night. Has he got smoke detectors installed here?"

Robbie slapped her forehead. "Oh, man. Here I am fretting about mercury in tuna, and I didn't even think of that."

"We keep some at the fire station. I'll bring a couple over right away. And we can get started on those boxes."

"I'll take the smoke detectors. But as for the rest of this mess…" Her eyes traveled to a cluster of half-unpacked boxes in the corner. "I just couldn't ask you to use your time off helping me unpack. I'm sure you've got better things to do. Besides, I never knew of a man who could get stuff organized the way women want it, anyway. My sister and I are pretty good at this kind of thing when the two of us get going. We learned it from our mother, who's so organized it's scary. I'll just wait 'til Markie gets back."

He nodded and smiled. "Whatever makes you the most comfortable."

Waiting for the sister, both of them. Too bad she was all the way down in Aruba. With Robbie Tellchick working over at the Hungry Aggie, it would be tough to protect her from rumors for long. Still, Zack figured he had to try. He swallowed the last of his tea. "Well, I'd better get going. I don't want to tire you out. I imagine you want to put your feet up before those boys come home from school."

"Thank you, again." She pushed up from the table. He was glad she was sensible enough not to argue about needing her rest. She walked him to the front door. When they got there, she lingered, clutching the knob. "Listen, Zack," she said. "I'm sorry. I mean, I really wish I could pay you, but—"

Before he could think about it, he clasped a palm around her arm to stop her. "No." The instant he touched her he knew the feel of her would haunt him. Her skin felt like warm silk. An unbidden vision—running his hands all over her body—assailed him. He dropped his hand and cleared his throat. "Like I told you. I wanted to help."

"Well, I was going to say I'd love to cook dinner for you sometime. I mean, would you want to maybe come over and have spaghetti with me and the boys sometime?"

"Thank you, but I couldn't impose." He wasn't about to eat this woman's food when she was barely getting by.

She gave him a little wincing frown. "Zack…you don't feel…you're not…" She seemed to be struggling to find the right words. "This isn't because you're feeling guilty about what happened to Danny or something?"

Guilt? Because he'd failed to save a man with three kids and another on the way? Because he'd just touched that man's wife and immediately wanted to do more than touch—a whole lot more? Because he was lusting after a pregnant woman, for crying out loud? Guilt? Guilt was hardly a strong enough word. All of a sudden he found he couldn't look in her eyes.

Wind gusted into the open doorway and thunder rumbled across the cloudy sky as his eyes fixed on the scarred wood floor of her entry hall, then on the stairs behind her, then traveled up searching, scanning aimlessly. One of the banisters was missing. Not safe. He'd be sure to come back to fix it. He couldn't answer her question because the truth was, yes, a part of him had felt more than guilt, a gnawing helpless frustration, over his failed attempt to save Danny Tellchick's life. But that should have changed now, in light of the findings of the fire marshal and medical examiner. That wasn't why he wanted to help her.

His motives were far less pure, some might say. *I'm hopelessly attracted to you,* his heart admitted when his eyes finally came back down to meet with hers. *Always have been.* But under the circumstances, he sure couldn't tell the woman *that,* now could he?

"I was a fatherless boy myself, once," he allowed quietly. It was true, though if he were honest, he'd have to admit that that had little to do with his reasons for helping out these boys, either. "I just want to do whatever I can to make your lives easier right now."

She smiled, and the sincerity and innocence of it

went right through him. "That's really decent of you. I just…I just wanted to be sure…you know. Well…"

"I'd better get going." He stepped onto the porch.

"Yes. I'll let you go before it starts pouring." The heavy oak door creaked on its hinges as she made to close it.

He flattened a palm on the door to stop it. "Will you be working at the restaurant tomorrow?" he asked.

She nodded. "Bright and early on the breakfast shift."

"Good." He smiled. "I'll see you then."

She nodded again and closed the door.

Zack, old buddy, what are you doing? He trotted down the uneven sidewalk toward his pickup, fat, cold raindrops smacking his face and hands as he unlocked the driver's side door.

He was pursuing her, that's what. A woman so pregnant it practically hurt to look at her. A woman with three boys. A woman who was undoubtedly still in love with her dead husband. He climbed in his truck and swept his wet hair back in frustration. A woman who, it turned out, just happened to be Zack Trueblood's lifelong ideal.

CHAPTER FOUR

UP EARLY. Despite bouts of insomnia, I keep telling myself I'm doing better day by day. I only think of Danny every day now instead of every hour. I can't figure out if all widows do this, or if it's worse for me because I'm carrying Danny's child, but it's like I can still feel him with me sometimes.

Like yesterday, when Zack Trueblood was leaving. I swear, I got the funniest feeling, like a subtle presence or something. As if Danny's ghost was swirling around us or something. Danny used to get so jealous if I so much as talked to another guy. And when Zack grabbed my arm, I felt the strangest conflicting sensations. Like I was too aware of how good it felt to be touched again, and then immediately I felt sort of guilty, like I was still married or something.

Maybe it was just all this static electricity in the air. We had thunderstorms all night. I woke up about a kazillion times. Kept hearing noises. I have like a double whammy of paranoia—the usual kind that sets in when your pregnant and anxious about anything that might threaten your baby, plus a good dose of the usual widow's insecurities on top of that.

It got really windy again a minute ago and now there's lightning like crazy. Well, time to quit scribbling in this diary and get ready for work, storm or no storm.

I hate leaving the boys to get themselves off to school when the weather's like this.

And you, little baby, you just stay all tucked away safe and sound, right here inside your mommy. Whatever am I gonna do when you decide to come out?

ROBBIE CLOSED the cover on her journal—a cheap thing with a picture of a puppy on it. She tucked it under her pillow, then she swung her feet over the side of her bed. A chill ran through her as she pulled free of the soft sheets and her toes touched down on cold floorboards. She vowed again that she would find her area rugs and spread them out *tonight*. But each day her good intentions slipped through her fingers like shifting sand, where one urgent thing morphed into another and no task was ever completed until finally, each and every night, she fell into bed, exhausted.

Taking this job was probably a bad idea, but what choice did she have? If she had waited, Parson would have been forced to fill the position with somebody else. A twist of resentment curled up again as she thought how irresponsible she'd been to let Danny cut corners by dropping his life insurance. But after years of marriage she'd been worn down, arguing with the man about every single hare-brained decision he made.

In the bathroom adjoining to the cavernous, high-ceilinged master bedroom, she studied herself in the oval mirror above the pedestal sink. She'd slept a little better last night—a few hours—with that window properly repaired, but even so she was developing permanent dark circles under her eyes.

This bathroom—there were two upstairs, one downstairs, and none of them were in good repair—was dingy, as bland as clabbered milk. White on white on white, from the tile to the tub to the limp curtain someone had left hanging crookedly at the narrow window. She made some mental notes about adding color as she washed her face.

Most small towns in the Hill Country had old houses like this one: rambling nineteenth-century monstrosities that had devolved into bleak rentals, passed from hand to hand. In the towns where historic restoration caught on, these houses got rebirthed into awesome showplaces. Painted Ladies, the civic-types called them. Robbie could envision this one that way, a beauty that shone with civic pride, only three blocks off Main Street.

After she patted her face dry, she attacked her hair with a big brush. Then her fingers went to work, efficiently plaiting the masses of reddish blond curls into a neat French braid.

As she braided, Robbie continued envisioning the house through artistic eyes. What this bathroom needed was one dramatic focal point. Like a giant stained-glass window instead of that scratched-up square of frosted Plexiglas that covered the window above the tub.

And wouldn't it be cute, she thought, to find an old velvet straight-backed sofa to tuck under the high windows in the kitchen? Wouldn't it be nice to refinish all these deep window boxes in this house in a coat of purest white and just leave the panes bare and let the sun pour in? Wouldn't polished mahogany countertops set off those high kitchen cabinets?

When she caught herself thinking like this, she always brought herself up short. Number one, she wasn't living in an HGTV show. This was life on the broke side of widowhood. Number two, old man Mestor, the crook, would never consent to doing anything expensive or upbeat to the house. Number three…baby.

The little darling kicked as Robbie pulled the stretchy panel of her well-used maternity jeans up over her belly. For a top she pulled on a boxy white shirt. Yesterday, Parson had gently objected to the overalls. Whatever.

She struggled into a pair of thick white socks and slipped her feet into her athletic shoes, and when she had trouble bending to lace them, she suffered a brief sting of tears. Danny had always tied her shoes for her this late in her pregnancies. Stop it, she told herself. You have a lot to do before you go to work.

Downstairs, she chugged down a glass of orange juice. Breakfast could be grabbed at the diner later. She put out bowls and spoons for the boys' cereal, set out the sack lunches she'd made the night before and stapled a detailed note with instructions to Mark's, then put the stapler right back where it belonged in her "grand central," her super-organized lap desk. She had done the tole painting that decorated the flip top herself. Very cute, she often thought—an elaborate pattern, a sort of blend between country quilt and Mexican mandala. Inside the lap desk was the simple system she'd been using to run this family for years and it had never failed her. With her sudden move to town, she was grateful that the whole thing was portable enough to be tossed onto the seat of her minivan.

Lightning flashed, and when hard rain lashed at the window Zack Trueblood had installed only yesterday, Robbie's thoughts went back to him. She had to admit she longed to see him, if she was honest with herself. Lord, she hated this business of being alone. She had never spent one day alone in her life. Danny had asked her to go on a hayride when they were in the eighth grade and they'd stayed together like hand-in-glove ever after.

Other guys had tried to get her attention, even tried to win her affections, but Robbie was loyal to Danny, always—even later when his irresponsibility began to let her down. Now that he was gone, she felt incredibly disloyal for the way she had been thinking about Zack Trueblood. But my gosh, that firefighter had the dreamiest coal-black eyes on God's green earth. Well, this was plain silly.

She grabbed her jacket and headed out into the storm. The rain, a driving Hill Country deluge that would flood hard-packed roads and wash out rocky ravines, hit her face and wet her hair despite the hood on her little red jacket. Her front got soaked, too, because the jacket was too small to cover her belly.

She slammed the door of her van and plucked at the soaked white fabric where her belly button poked out like a gumdrop. Nice. Thank God she would slap on an apron as soon as she got to work.

The minivan had to be cranked three times before it sputtered to life. A new worry: car trouble. She couldn't afford that now. Then it hit her. Who would drive her to the hospital when the time came? She only had five weeks. The days were racing by like ticks of a second hand. Daddy would come, of course, whenever she called him, day or night. But the McBride farm was a good seven miles out of town, and with a fourth baby, labor could be shockingly rapid.

Besides, if she called Daddy, Mother would insist on coming with him. There would be no peaceful labor and delivery then. Oh, no. Mother would boss. She'd boss Daddy. The nurses. Maybe even the doctor. Most of all Marynell would boss Robbie.

Peering out the rain-sheeted windshield and thinking of her mother's pinched face, Robbie muttered aloud, "Hurry up and get back, Markie. I'll feel a darn sight safer then." She could not wait until her sister returned from her honeymoon. Everything would be all right then. None of Robbie's other babies had come early. Markie would be home in plenty of time and then her strong, competent sister would help her.

It was only three short blocks to the gravel alley that ran behind the Hungry Aggie, but still Robbie breathed a sigh of relief as she pulled into the small lot out back, amazed that she'd made it without stalling out in high water. She slammed the van door again and dashed around rivulets of water and enormous puddles to the back door, where Parson stood holding it open.

"Come on, girl!" he hollered over the din of the pattering rain. "Before you catch your death."

"You ought not to have come in on a morning like this," he scolded when Robbie got inside. He was already helping her out of her jacket. For decades, Virgil Parson had been the only black man living or working in Five Points. But Parson never mentioned that fact, and neither did anybody else. He actually lived in another town with a sweet wife and numerous kids and grandkids. He drove to work in Five Points because at the Hungry Aggie he got to do what he did best—dish up food like an old-time chuck wagon cook, though he'd actually learned the art of slinging out large quantities of food for hungry men while serving in the Navy.

"I know how these rainy mornings go," Robbie said as she smoothed back her damp, frizzy hair. "All the farmers will come into town to get away from their wives. And they'll end up sitting right here in our booths, jawing 'til the rain stops. We will be busy filling coffee cups until noon."

Parson chuckled as if that idea plumb tickled him. "That's a fact. And it's why I came in early to make some extra pies." His black eyes sparkled in a face as furrowed as a fresh-plowed field.

Virgil Parson loved nothing so much as being

prepared and making money. And he made buckets full off the regulars at the Hungry Aggie, not to mention the seasonal tourists who wandered from town to town in the Hill Country, looking for that perfect piece of chess pie. At the Hungry Aggie they found the chess pie and much more. Barbecued chicken, baked ham, sweet potato pudding, red beans and rice, hot rolls with peach peel jelly.

Robbie tied on one of the clean white aprons that the efficient old cook had already hung on hooks next to the walk-in refrigerator. Her wet shirt felt clammy against her tummy, but she was relieved that the moisture didn't soak through the starched apron.

"You're getting better at this, girl. You even beat old Nattie Rose in here this morning," Parson informed her.

Robbie gave Parson a grimace. Nattie Rose was not old. She went to high school with Robbie's younger sister, Markie. And Nattie Rose was never late. "Hope she's not trapped out on some low water bridge," Robbie said. Nattie Rose and her husband Earl lived on Earl's family's ranch, way out on a remote ranch road. Without Nattie Rose as a rudder, Robbie's job would be hell today.

She and Parson fell into the rhythm of work in the brightly lit kitchen. He cut biscuits. She filled the two big coffeemakers. Together, they laid out bacon strips onto large jelly-roll pans. Parson always slow-baked the bacon in the kitchen's huge cast-iron ovens because he claimed that was the aroma that brought in "The Boys," as he called the customers.

When they'd gotten things organized, Parson pulled

up a stool for Robbie to perch upon. "You and Hootch-eecoo better take a load off while you all can."

Parson, who made up a nickname for everybody, had taken to calling the baby *Hootcheecoo*, which amused Robbie, since she hadn't been able to come up with a proper name for the baby yet. In the same way that Frances, Roberta and Margaret McBride were named after their aunts, Robbie's three sons had been named the masculine versions of the McBride sisters. Frank after Frankie, Rob after Robbie, and Mark after Markie. Robbie supposed she would be breaking up the family rhythm with this fourth surprise baby.

Their routine had been for Parson to scramble Robbie some eggs as soon as the grill was hot. He set a pat of butter to sizzling, tossed on peppers, onions and tomatoes, poured the whipped eggs over the pile and added a handful of chopped cilantro and a dash of *picante* sauce. Robbie's mouth started to water. Parson cooked a finer omelet than any four-star chef.

"Did you get that window fixed?" He wiped his hands on his apron while the eggs started to bubble.

"Yes," Robbie said glumly. Not because she was thinking about the window, but because of the man who had fixed it. Thinking about how he was too gorgeous, and she was too frumpy. She was starting to wish Zack Trueblood had never come around to further complicate her life.

"What's wrong?" Parson eyed her, then poked a spatula at the edge of the omelet. "You needin' a little cash money for that window, child?"

"No." Well, actually she did, but that was not Parson's problem, bless his generous old heart. "Zack Trueblood fixed it for free."

"Zack Trueblood? The one that comes in here and eats up everything but the sink? That big firefighter boy that looks about half Indian?"

Robbie winced. Nobody would dare hazard the mention of race to Parson, but such matters weren't sacrosanct to the old man. His were the old ways, plain-spoken, uncomplicated by worries about such matters as political correctness.

"What's ailing you? You look like you just bit a sour pickle." The spatula halted in midair as if a thought hit him. "You ain't having pains already, are you?"

"No." Robbie smoothed the crisp white apron over her tummy then squirmed up onto the stool. "It's just…oh, it's nothing."

"It *is* too something." Parson plunked a heavy plate with the steaming omelet before her. "And you ought not to hold it in, lest you pop or somethin'."

Robbie took up the fork and slid in a mouthful of omelet. It was absolutely perfect. Parson eyed her while she chewed, so after she took a sip of the milk he'd poured for her, she conceded, "It's Zack Trueblood. He…I don't know. He makes me…uncomfortable." Robbie couldn't admit, even to herself much less to Parson, that the word she was really searching for was more like *bothered. Hot* and bothered, actually.

"Uncomfortable? He ain't pressing himself on you or something?" Plainspoken for sure, that's what Parson was.

"No! Zack would never *press* himself on anybody!" Robbie wasn't sure why she defended the man so strongly. The heroic way he'd tried to save Danny, she supposed. She took another bite of omelet.

"Then how come your cheeks is redder'n a hot chili pepper? Listen, little sister, if he's coming around all nice like, doing favors and all, you'd best watch yourself. Ain't no woman as defenseless as a widow with—"

"Woo! Lordy!" Nattie Rose's cheery voice cut off Parson's rant as the diner's other waitress burst through the back door. "It is raining pitchforks out there! Bet we'll be swamped today!" Nattie Rose Neuberger— always called by both nicknames and never by her given one, Natalie—bustled into the kitchen, perfectly groomed in tight-fitting jeans and a starched Western shirt, raring to go, as always. She was carrying a pair of immaculate white athletic shoes with fire-red laces. She plopped onto a stool and tugged off battered, rain-soaked cowgirl boots.

Robbie shoveled in the last of her eggs, grateful to be delivered from Parson's meddling lecture. From out in the restaurant came male voices, the sounds of the first customers trickling in. Robbie peeked out of the swinging door to see Zack Trueblood and his friends sliding into their usual booth.

"Can you take care of those guys?" Nattie Rose said. She was still tying her red laces.

"Somebody needs to take care of *those* guys," Robbie mumbled as she squeezed past Nattie Rose's perch on her way out with the coffee. All three of the single firefighters were well-known about town as the most eligible of the eligible bachelors in Five Points. Nobody knew, except Parson of course, that the most handsome of them had been to Robbie's house twice now. And nobody needed to know. Robbie adopted a carefully neutral expression as she approached the booth.

"I saw her in there hanging out with some guy with a popped collar," the one named Mason was saying. "I swear the dude had a *manicure*."

Zack and his two friends chuckled. Then the firefighters all turned to Robbie, mumbling, "Hey, Robbie," like they did every morning.

"Hi, fellas." Robbie angled her washtub of a belly away from the table as she poured the first mug of coffee and the men resumed their chatter. They were all good-looking guys. Not pretty boys, but handsome in a rough-cut way with easy smiles and square jaws. And Zack Trueblood was by far the best-looking of them.

"So. What's she doing with some weirdo at the bookstore," the third guy was saying. "I thought you two had a thing going."

"Nah." The resonance of Zack Trueblood's voice so near to her body sent a tiny thrill through Robbie, but she wouldn't let herself look at him, bad as she wanted to. Not in front of these men. "I don't have any claim on Lynette. She can hang out with whoever she wants."

Robbie felt a rush of heat to her cheeks as she realized they were talking about some woman Zack must be seeing. She found she had to steady her hand as she proceeded to pour the last two mugs full.

"It doesn't bother you, even if the guy's some kind of metrosexual pinko?" Mason pressed.

"Metrosexual?" the third firefighter scoffed.

"That's urban talk for girly-man." Zack grinned. The men chuckled again.

Mason waved a paw at Zack. "Ah. Right. I forget. The great Zack Trueblood doesn't have to worry about competition, especially from some girly-man. Bet you've already turned down old Lynette every night of the week."

"Mason—" Zack's tone turned the name into a warning "—cool it."

Robbie didn't look at him, but she could sense Zack giving her an embarrassed glance.

"I dunno," the third firefighter went on in a longsuffering tone. "Much as I want to see you get that award, Zack buddy, it's always a pain to round up a woman to take to these formal dress-up things. How am I supposed to find a lady who knows how to wear anything besides jeans in a town like Five Points?"

"Hey." Mason pointed at him like he'd just had a bright idea. "Maybe you could take the metrosexual." They all guffawed at the joke as Robbie started pouring the last mug.

"You've got to take 'em out a time or two beforehand," Mason advised. "Give 'em time to get all excited and shop for a dress. Or you could be like Zack here and find yourself a rich divorcée." He turned to his friend. "So, you're still taking her out tonight?"

Robbie's eyes grew more alert and involuntarily cut to Zack. He was frowning up at her. And she was pouring coffee over the side of the mug and all over the table.

"Whoa!" Mason cried at the same time Robbie realized what she'd done.

"Sorry. Sorry," Robbie said as the firefighters snatched wads of napkins out of the holder.

"It's all right, sugar." The third one pressed some napkins into the mess.

As she nervously sopped up the coffee, Robbie could feel Zack Trueblood's hot black eyes examining her closely, but she refused to look directly at him. Her hands shook as the faces of all the single women in Five Points flipped through her mind like cards in a Rolodex.

"Hey, girl. You feeling okay?" Mason seemed to notice the depth of her distress for the first time. He took over with the napkins, bless him.

"I'm fine." Robbie sighed. "It's just this crazy weather. I was just thinking about my boys—hoping they don't get soaked waiting on the school bus." Oh, sure. *Now* she was thinking about her boys. Thinking how she had no business worrying about whether Zack Trueblood was dating some woman or not. She glanced at Zack's face. He was still frowning at her.

Mason peered out the window as fresh sheets of rain beat the windows. "Personally, I just love it when it does this," he said sarcastically.

"Yeah," his friend, equally sarcastic, chimed in. "You know we're gonna get called out to fish some yahoo out of a ditch." And then the men were off and running again, complaining about the weather and the constant problem of flooding roads and bridges in the Hill Country.

Except Zack was still looking at Robbie with an expression that said he was worried about her. Lightning flashed and thunder boomed outside the window as he said quietly, "Everything okay, Robbie?"

Robbie nodded, swallowed. *Don't look at me like that,* she wanted to say. *It makes me weak in the knees and I have work to do here.*

"You guys want the farmer breakfast?" Robbie said as she gathered up the last of the soggy napkins.

"Yep," Mason answered for them all.

Nattie Rose's round face popped under the pass-through space. "I've gotta help Parson back here, honey. Could you take care of those guys at table nine?" That's where the Rotary-types were and Robbie was well aware that Nattie Rose was making sure Robbie got the generous tips today.

The men at that table kept up a jovial banter about the weather as Robbie poured coffee into upturned mugs for all four.

"The usual for you guys?" Robbie said with a falsely light tone.

When the men nodded she was glad to dash off to the kitchen.

Back in the safety of Parson's domain, she nearly collapsed against the center island. She'd made a complete fool of herself, pouring tea for Zack in her slummy little kitchen yesterday, basking in the warmth of his attention, telling him how she'd *love* to cook spaghetti for him sometime, when all the time the man had a hot date lined up for tonight.

"What's wrong?" Parson asked.

Lord, Robbie was sick of people asking her what was *wrong*.

Nattie Rose zipped around, already getting flushed with the challenges of the day. "Look sharp, my lovelies. The masses are hungry."

Parson turned back to the grill.

Robbie took down three plates and started to fill them. Biscuit. Biscuit. Biscuit. She took up the ladle. Gravy. Gravy. Gravy.

Nattie Rose joined her at the island to work up some of the orders.

"Do you know who Zack Trueblood is dating these days?" Robbie asked casually, while her heart hammered with a fresh wave of humiliation.

"Some gal from over at Wildhorse. Divorced. I hear she's got a big ranch."

Robbie's hands kept working but her heart felt like it had clutched to a standstill. A rich woman with a ranch. Isn't that just what any man would want?

OUT OF THE CORNER of his eye, Zack noted Arlen Mestor's plodding progress as he lumbered into the restaurant. The old man shook off the rain, then ambled up on his usual stool like a grumpy grizzly bear.

"Excuse me a minute, fellas." Zack pushed up from the table and crossed the room.

He slid up on the stool next to Arlen at the counter. "Mestor."

"Trueblood." The two were acquainted, but had not been on friendly terms since the night some months prior when Zack had lectured the older man about the faulty wiring in a rental house that had burned to the ground. The family was not home at the time, but the sight of a baby doll with a melted face had set Zack's blood to boiling. Zack had already pulled a business card out of his shirt pocket. He snapped it onto the Formica in front of Arlen.

Zack tapped the card, which Mestor hadn't acknowledged. "I'll give you a discount if you let me do the repairs on that house Robbie Tellchick just rented from you."

"Nattie Rose!" Mestor bellowed toward the pass-through window as if Zack hadn't spoken. "What does a man have to do to get a cup of coffee in this joint?"

Finally, Mestor sneered at the card. "What repairs would that be?" The way his nostrils flared when he spoke reminded Zack of a snuffling pig.

"A few things here and there. Safety issues, mostly." Zack had said the word "safety" pointedly. He knew Mestor remembered well the fire that consumed one of his rental houses, if for no other reason than the financial ones.

Nattie Rose sashayed out of the kitchen brandishing a carafe of coffee. "You want a cup up here at the counter, too, Zack?" she said as she poured Mestor's.

"I'm fine," Zack said mildly.

"Sugar." Mestor tapped the counter with a stubby finger, his tone was demanding.

Nattie Rose shoved the sugar jar, which was all of a foot away, toward Mestor, and then gave him a poisonous parting look before she disappeared through the swinging door to the kitchen.

"Well," Zack pressed, "how about it? I'll only charge you for the materials, throw in my labor for free. You won't have to do a thing."

Mestor dumped a hideous amount of sugar into his coffee before he answered. "Why are you so all-fired up to work on that old house?"

"Because it needs it," Zack answered simply. "The place is an eyesore."

"Always poking your nose in where it don't belong, ain't you, Trueblood?" Mestor stirred his coffee slowly, frowning as if considering something. "I ain't sure I want you messin' with my property. And I'd still like to know why you even want to. It's that pretty little pregnant lady, ain't it?" Mestor asked the question loudly, so as to be addressing the whole restaurant.

Before Zack could answer, Mestor continued even louder. "Or should I say it's that prime piece of land that little pregnant lady has out there by the river?"

By an act of will, Zack kept his own voice low. "I don't know what you're implying, but—"

"I ain't *implying* nothin'. I am saying flat out that you have always wanted a piece of farmland out on the Blue River ever since your granddad lost his place. Your granddad used to tell me all the time how *blessed* he was to have a boy like you to take over his farm when he was gone."

Zack stared straight ahead, the muscles in his jaw working furiously. He could imagine *that* conversation, all right. Mestor had probably made some ill-advised crack about Zack's mother and her illegitimate kid, and Zack's granddad had defended them. He wondered if that accounted for Mestor's missing teeth.

"Well, old granddad's gone now, and so is his farm. Am I right?" Mestor was fairly bellowing now. "And now you're looking to replace it. But if you have some cockeyed notion that running around doing favors for the Tellchick woman will get her to sell you that land for a song, you're nothing but a fool, boy."

Nobody called Zack a fool, least of all a blustery out-of-shape middle-aged man who really was one. Mestor had a lived a life tainted by alcoholism, chronic foul moods and various run-ins with the law. A notorious tightwad, the man was twice divorced and made a nuisance of himself with ladies he eventually claimed were only after his money. Even the old man's own children avoided him. He ran around town acting like he had connections with the movers and shakers, but Zack remembered his granddad saying that among that crowd Arlen Mestor stood out like a goat in a flock of sheep.

Zack slid off the stool and stood to his full height. "Arlen, you talk too much."

"That's because I *know* too much."

When Mestor leaned toward Zack threateningly, Zack detected a whiff of alcohol. The residue from last night's binge maybe? Or maybe Mestor had already had his first Bloody Mary of the day.

"It is no surprise to me," Mestor went on without encouragement from anybody in particular, "that you approached the bank about taking over the loan on that farm. Seeing as how you could never afford the down payment in a million years, I expect you'll be awful disappointed to know that Congressman Kilgore has already foreclosed on it."

"What?" This truly was news to Zack.

"Oh, yes. I have it on good authority. Me and the congressman have been on a first-name basis for years. But you didn't know that, did you? I expect the place will just sit there now, going fallow. If you want it, you'll have to deal with the old man up in Washington, not some defenseless little widow."

Sensing trouble, the two firefighters with Zack had crossed the room and positioned themselves strategically near the two men at the bar.

But Mestor didn't seem to notice them. He was too busy running his gums. "Why, if I didn't know firsthand how worked up and self-righteous you like to get, I'd be of a mind to even wonder about that barn fire. That's an awful lot of gasoline to get spilt in a simple acciden—"

That's when Zack decked Arlen Mestor.

One second the old porker was twisting sideways on the barstool, sneering at Zack, and the next he was sprawled on his fleshy backside on the diner's green and white linoleum floor.

DARLENE GRAHAM · 67

People at the nearby tables yelled and jumped out of the way as Mestor crawfished backward and Zack loomed over him, fists clenched for another blow.

Parson came busting through the swinging doors of the kitchen shouting, "There'll be no fistfights in this here establishment!"

Zack's friends restrained him from doing further damage, though it took both of them to bodily remove him from the premises.

BACK IN THE KITCHEN, Robbie stood with palms pressed on the butcher block and her downcast face burning like fire. The baby had set up a panicky little dance inside of her, reacting, no doubt, to the shot of adrenaline his mommy was feeling as well.

"You okay, sweetie?" Nattie Rose asked anxiously, her hands suspended in the act of slinging home fries onto platters.

"Oh, fine. I'm fine. *Really.* I mean, hearing two men coming to blows because of me. That's cool. Kind of flattering, you know?"

"Honey, you don't believe what Mestor just said about Zack for one instant do you?"

"Of course not." Robbie straightened. "Nobody puts much stock in anything Mestor says."

"Well, then." Nattie Rose continued shoveling out home fries.

But Robbie stood stock-still, her mind still reeling with too much new information, too many new emotions. "Who is this woman he has a date with tonight?"

"Huh?" Nattie Rose stopped loading the plates and looked perplexed.

"A date. Tonight. I heard the guys talking about it earlier."

"You mean Zack?"

"No. *Mestor.*" Robbie looked sideways with a sarcastic squint.

"I told you about all I know, sweetie. She's got a lot of money, but just between you and me, not much class. Kind of a sexpot, far as I can tell. But it's no surprise if the man isn't exactly a monk. I mean, just look at him. What in the world does Zack's social life have to do with…"

"Don't you know anything else about her?" Robbie cut in sharply. "Does she have any kids or anything?"

"Why, I wouldn't know. Let's see." Nattie Rose strove to cooperate. "Her name's Lynette something or other. She's been in here a time or two, looking for Zack, but he—"

"She lives across the river?" Robbie interrupted.

"Yeah, I guess so. Over at Wildhorse."

"And she has a ranch out there?"

"Yes. That's all pretty much ranching country."

"Well, then." Robbie grabbed up some loaded plates, balancing them along her arms, against her tummy. "If he likes to mess with women who've got land, I reckon he's all done with me, now that Mr. Mestor has informed him of the sad facts about my farm."

"Oh, now, honey. That was uncalled for." Nattie Rose put her hands out in supplication. "Zack's a good guy. Not that sort at all."

But Robbie had already banged out the swing door to boldly face the murmuring customers of the Hungry Aggie, leaving Nattie Rose to stare, and poor old Parson, who she had flown past on his way back in, to sadly shake his head.

CHAPTER FIVE

HAD MYSELF a little crying jag tonight. It's the pregnancy, I expect. Along with all the physical benefits—headaches, hot flashes, leg pain, back pain, groin pain—when you're pregnant you get to ride a fun emotional roller coaster, as well.

I need to stop calling it a pregnancy! Sorry little one. I don't blame you for kicking me just now. I know you're a big boy already. Are you going to look like your brothers? You could do worse. Will you be like your daddy? Only in the looks department, let's hope. I shouldn't say that about Danny, but sometimes I get so angry at him I could scream! How dare he go and die and leave me stranded and penniless with four children out on a run-down farm?

If I think about Danny right now, I'm only going to feel worse. And Danny was not the reason I was crying anyway, I'm ashamed to say. It's everything that happened at the Hungry Aggie today.

I told Nattie Rose later, after seeing how they had to forcibly drag Zack out of the diner, that I wasn't putting up with any man with a temper. I had just about enough of that nonsense with Danny.

She gave me a funny look.

But I guess it's not too hard for Nattie Rose to figure out what's going on. Every time I look at Zack Trueblood—and I'm ashamed to admit this, too, because the truth is, I look at the man way too often—I feel the strangest mixture of euphoria and guilt. Go figure.

I also think I might be bummed because I found out he's dating someone, which is only natural. Nattie Rose is right, you can't expect a man that good-looking to be unattached. Why wouldn't he have a girlfriend? But does she have to be rich? Does she have to own a ranch? Does she have to be everything I'm not?

In an effort to cheer myself up, I've scrubbed out this old deep claw-foot tub upstairs. I filled it to the brim, the whole time praying it wouldn't crash through the old floorboards. But it was worth the risk. I needed…something. I've felt kind of tense and disappointed all day long.

The TV is blaring and every child has a book in his hands, so the Tellchick household is occupied for once. I sank down until the bubbles were up to my shoulders, and I've been soaking and scribbling in this diary. It really does help, you know? Somehow writing out my thoughts makes the loneliness go away.

Loneliness. It's a killer. Even with my crazy schedule, even with three kids swarming around me, it still closes in. Especially at night. That's the time a woman could use somebody to talk to. To cuddle with.

I'll be danged if I didn't just think about Zack Trueblood again. I caught myself wondering, imagining what he must be like in...yes I did. How come I never noticed Zack in high school? Danny, of course. Danny Tellchick, who filled my every waking moment, who had his mark on me from day one. But now there's no Danny. And now here's Zack, hunky as you please. And I am a free woman. So why do I feel so low for thinking about him this way?

ROBBIE LISTENED. Above the blare of the TV she could hear knocking. The boys yelled up the stairs, "Mom! Somebody's at the door!"

She eased herself up out of the water, quickly toweled off, threw on her robe and padded to the narrow window at the end of the hallway that overlooked the front walk. Sure enough, a now-familiar red pickup was parked at the curb.

She stepped onto the top landing and looked down into Mark's serious face. "You want me to answer it, Mom?" The boys were still so unused to a single-parent family, so unused to living in town.

The younger boys came jostling up beside their brother. "Mom! He won't let me have the remote!"

"Mom! Mark is bossing us around!"

Some days Robbie swore if she heard the word *Mom* one more time, she would tear her hair out by its red roots.

"Shut up, you guys!" Mark snapped at his quarreling brothers, then he looked back up at his mother again. "It's that firefighter guy. You want me to find out what he wants?"

"It's okay, honey. I'll come down."

She descended the stairs like a queen, gathering her dignity as she went. If he was going to see her in her ratty pink robe yet again, she was going to at least put on a calm front.

She flipped on the porch light, then opened the creaky door slowly, chin high. "Zack?" She smiled. Serenely, she hoped. "How nice to see you again." A frigid October wind gusted inside and billowed the hem of her robe.

"Robbie." His eyes flicked down to the fluttering robe before he locked his gaze respectfully back on her face. "I tried to call, but your cell phone is apparently turned off."

"Oh." She clutched at the lapels of the robe and looked back over her shoulder at the boys, as if they had something to do with it. "Sorry. What did you want?"

"I was wondering if I could take some, uh, measurements tonight." His eyes flicked downward again, but quickly trained back onto her face. "I was on my way home. It'll only take a second. Saves me the time of doubling back in the morning. That way I can go straight to the lumberyard."

"You're starting on the house in the morning?"

"Yes. I've only got two days off in the next seven, and we don't have all the time in the world to get this place in shape. I know it's a Saturday, and you'd probably like to sleep in." Again his eyes flicked down. This time, she was certain, to her gravid abdomen. "But maybe you could me call when you get up."

She laughed, not all that pleasantly. "Sleeping in on Saturdays. I seem to have some vague memory of that from a past life."

"Oh, yeah. I forgot." He looked toward the blaring TV. "I guess the boys get up early for cartoons."

"And for the test pattern and the farm report." Robbie wondered if she sounded cynical. Bitter. Unhappy. She wasn't. It was just that her life was probably so very different from his.

She had to wonder at the stunning contrast she must be to the sleek date he'd undoubtedly just left. Out of sheer cussedness, she looked past his shoulder to his empty pickup and said, "Thought you had a date tonight."

"I did. It's over." Something about the curt way he said it made her think that maybe more than the date was over. The idea that he'd chosen her and her home maintenance problems over the rich divorcée made her cheeks go hot.

"So, how about it?"

Much as she hated the thought of having Zack True-blood getting a good look at her, yet again, in her ratty pink bathrobe, she hated the thought of leaving him standing out there in the cold wind even more, especially when he was trying to do her a favor.

"Sure. Come in." She opened the door wider and stepped aside.

"I'd like to start out on the back porch."

"Okay. Boys," Robbie said to her gawking children, "go on upstairs and get ready for bed."

Robbie caught Zack's face as he gave the twelve-year-old a conspiratorial look. "Actually, I could use someone to hold the other end of the tape." He glanced at her robe, more pointedly this time, as if to say her attire was wholly inappropriate to the task out in the chill wind.

Robbie pulled the collar up under her chin. "Go with the man, then, Mark."

Mark grabbed his jacket as the two headed to the back door. The other boys started pestering her to go outside with Zack, but Robbie shooed them upstairs ahead of her.

Up in her own room she pulled on the nearest clothes at hand—an oversized denim shirt and a pair of black maternity leggings. She stopped at the mirror over her dresser and pulled her hair out of its messy topknot, swiped a brush through it, making the ringlets fluff up even bigger and messier. Unhappy with the effect, she pulled the masses of curls to her nape and secured them with a giant barrette. For one vain second she rued the fact that she didn't have time to slap on some makeup, then decided her color was so high maybe it didn't really matter. She didn't want to think about why this man had such a flustering effect on her every time she was within ten feet of him. Was it seemly at all to be developing a crush on the nearest male when she was so newly widowed? And so thoroughly pregnant? And a younger man to boot!

She slipped some Birkenstocks on her feet, stopped down the hallway long enough to give the younger boys some terse supervision, then headed to the kitchen.

The two guys were coming inside already. Something Zack was muttering was making Mark laugh, a sound Robbie realized she'd heard all too infrequently since Danny's death.

She snatched up the teakettle and held it under the faucet. "Can you stay for some tea?" she said as she looked over her shoulder at Zack. She hoped her cheeks weren't as red as they felt. "I'd like to discuss something with you, if you don't mind. Uh." She glanced at her son. "Mark, honey, do you want anything to eat before you go upstairs?"

"Upstairs?" The boy looked nonplussed. "Zack and me was gonna install some smoke detectors."

"We'll get it done later," Zack said. "I think your mom needs to talk to me first." He didn't add, *alone* but the boy seemed to catch on.

"I'll be upstairs doing my homework whenever you need me."

"I appreciate that."

Energized, Mark darted to a crockery cookie jar and dug out a granola bar. "See you later," he said as he bounded out.

"See you later, Mark. And thanks for helping me with the measurements." The child gave the man a friendly grin as he shut the door.

The room immediately fell into a weighty silence. "You need any help with that?" Zack said to Robbie.

"With *tea?*"

Feeling shiftless, he seated himself at the spindle-legged table by the window again.

"Mark seems like a good kid," he said while Robbie bustled around the small kitchen.

"He is. But this has been really hard on him. He was very close to his daddy. They did a lot of hunting and fishing and such together. And he misses his life on the farm."

"He told me." A shadow of emotion passed over Zack's face. "We talked about the night his dad died some." He jerked his head toward the back door. "When we were out there."

"You did?" She looked concerned.

"I told him we would. The other night?"

"Oh, yes. So you did." Robbie was amazed that he'd remembered his commitment to the boy. She'd forgotten it herself.

"You wanted to talk to me about something?" He seemed anxious to change the subject.

"Yeah." She paused. "So. I think we'd better discuss that…little *incident* in the restaurant today. You were interested in my farm?" Robbie knew she'd said it defensively, accusingly, but she had to know. What was this man really doing, hanging around her—and her kids—like this?

"I looked into it when you first put the place up for sale." He answered the slight reproach in her tone with quiet honesty.

"I'm surprised you're still wanting to come around here and do these repairs, now that you know I've signed the farm over to Kilgore." She kept her tone offhand, with her full attention on pouring the boiled water into the teapot.

"Surely you don't believe any of that crap Mestor was spouting today?"

She crossed the small space and set the teapot on the pretty potholder at the center of the table. Then she went to a cabinet for mugs. "He seemed to know an awful lot about you," she said with her back to him. "Knew your grandpa and all."

"He *knew* my grandfather. He didn't say they were friends. Grandpa never trusted Mestor any farther than he could throw him. Mestor is shady, and he knows I know it. He's hasn't liked me since the time I raked him over the coals—forgive my bad choice of words—about one of his rental houses that burned clear to the ground."

"Then if what he said isn't true, what is your motive? I mean, for hanging around me like this? A pregnant widow with three kids and all."

"My motives have nothing to do with your farm. Beyond that, is it anybody's business besides mine?"

"Yes. Mine! I'd like to get the cards on the table before you come over here and spend a lot of your time and energy for nothing. Before you get us—my sons—all attached to you."

"I told you, I want to do this."

"Why? Mestor told you he's not going to pay for it. And you know I sure can't afford it. I couldn't even pay you for the window."

"That doesn't matter. I'm going to do it anyway."

"Why?" Another pause. "Guilt?"

A silence stretched as Robbie waited and Zack clasped his big hands on the table in front of him. The corners of his mouth turned down while he examined his thumbnails. Finally he said, "Pour the tea, Robbie. I think you're right. Maybe we'd better get some cards on the table here."

She started to pour, glancing at him warily. Now that she'd forced his hand, she wasn't at all sure she wanted to hear what the man had to say. It didn't look like it was going to be good.

He took a nervous sip before he said, "Okay. Maybe I do feel a little protective of you and your family. But it's not guilt. The truth is, I've always kind of carried a torch for you."

Her jaw dropped. She stopped pouring her tea. "A torch? You mean like a crush or something?"

He nodded.

"You're kidding!" That was *not* what she had expected him to say.

"You asked about my date tonight? Well, I told her we wouldn't be seeing each other again."

"You did?" Robbie didn't touch her half-full cup. She couldn't have swallowed a drop if her life depended on it. "Why?" she said in a whisper.

"Because I want to spend as much time with you as I possibly can, so why would I want to go around seeing another woman?"

Her jaw dropped again. Then her shoulders wilted as if the air had been knocked out her. "Well. You certainly know your own mind, Zack Trueblood."

A small frown formed on his brow but he kept his eyes on hers as he went on. "Oh, I know what you're thinking. You're pregnant. You've got a pack of kids. And you're still grieving over your husband, I expect. But none of that matters to me. I'm a patient man, Robbie. And I've admired you for a long time. I'm not about to miss my shot now."

"Your *shot?*" she said, and sat up straighter.

"Bad choice of words again. What I mean is, you *are* single, even if you *are* pregnant. And I intend to show you that I can take care of you, and these boys, and that little one." He gave her tummy a small nod.

Robbie folded her hands over the mound protectively. "I don't even know you."

"But I know *you*. I know you're hardworking and honest and funny and just plain beautiful. And if you'll give me a chance, you'll discover those same things about me. Well, all but the beautiful part." He gave her a crooked grin.

But she could only manage the barest smile in response. No, this was certainly not what she had expected him to say. And she sure had not expected to find herself seated across the kitchen table from a man—much less a man as handsome as this one— having a conversation like this within six months of her husband's death. "I…I wasn't expecting you to say *that*," she stammered honestly.

"I know you weren't. And I wasn't expecting to tell you this way. But sometimes things happen like this. Kind of suddenly, but naturally."

He reached across the table and lifted one of her small hands from her abdomen, clasping it lightly in his.

"Robbie, listen to me. I think you're everything a man could want in a woman. I always have. And your being pregnant doesn't change that one bit. I'll prove it. I was thinking of asking Lynette to the firefighter's ball next week, but that's off now."

"You all didn't have a fight on account of *me?*" The very idea made Robbie feel disconcerted. Maybe Zack and this rancher woman would have made a great couple, maybe even developed an amicable relationship, while here she was, clearly not ready for any kind of relationship. Here she was, not ready for anything, not even the birth of her baby.

"No!" He squeezed her hand reassuringly, and he kept hold of it. "We didn't have a fight or anything like that. It was all very civilized. Lynette's pretty, charming even, and we had some fun dates, but she's not right for me. I simply told her that. She was a little upset, but she'll come to accept it. Better now than later."

Robbie had to agree. Although she had no experience in dating relationships because she and Danny had been sweethearts since junior high, it just made sense to her that it was wiser not to play around if you knew you weren't ever going to ever be serious about a person. Which brought her up short about her own behavior. "Zack, I want you to understand that I...I'm not ready—"

"I know you're not. Why don't we just take this one step at a time? Literally." He smiled. "I'll be back first thing in the morning to install the smoke detectors and start fixing those steps on your back porch."

Robbie couldn't seem to return his smile. She could

barely utter the word. "Okay." And when Zack finally did release her hand, she found that hers was trembling.

"THERE IS SOMETHING going on between Zack True-blood and that Tellchick woman," Arlen Mestor said to Roy Graves the next day over coffee at the Hungry Aggie. This time he didn't sit on his usual stool. Roy had chosen a booth well toward the back. And this time the old man kept his gravelly voice unusually quiet.

"I did not call you here to talk about them," Roy mumbled over the rim of his coffee mug. With his pro-fessional firefighter's uniform and his neatly styled shock of steel-gray hair, Roy looked the antithesis of Arlen. His blue eyes bored into Arlen's with righteous fire. When Arlen squirmed, Roy slurped a satisfying sip, then said, "We are here to talk about you, Arlen. You and your notorious big mouth."

Arlen grunted his displeasure at that affront. Who was Roy Graves to be calling him on the dadgum carpet this way? The town's fire chief had acted like he owned Arlen ever since that last rental house fire. Arlen wondered if Roy suspected anything about his methods. Roy was the town's fire marshal after all. But Arlen knew Roy couldn't prove anything.

Arlen considered himself pretty cagey, using a slow match for all of his fires, including this last one on the Tellchick farm. Such a simple thing—a lit cigarette wedged into a book of matches that made a reliable, and untraceable, fuse. Why those Mexicans had specifically wanted gasoline thrown everywhere was a mystery to

Arlen. He would have told them that a slow match plus all that hay was plenty, except Arlen was not about to reveal the extent of his fire knowledge to anybody. Roy Graves was suspicious enough of him. He eyed the man sitting across from him. It made Arlen uneasy that the Mexicans had contacted *him* when a little arson was needed. If a bunch of no-account Mexican criminals knew where to go, Roy might know who to blame as well.

But it was cash money, and so Arlen did what the men asked. It was no big deal to torch a run-down barn. But when Danny Tellchick's body had been pulled out of there, Arlen realized something really fishy was going on. First thing he wondered was, where did Mexicans get that much cash? He started to think how Congressman Kurt Kilgore was the only man in the county with that kind of money to throw around. That's when Arlen started to wonder if maybe the fire had something to do with the way Kilgore had gotten his hands on that Tellchick land, which had originally been Kilgore land. It all circled around and fit together, Arlen was sure. And it all came back to the land. In Texas, it always came back to the land—always had.

The point was, Roy Graves had no business acting all high and mighty with him. Arlen Mestor was a man who knew things, so Roy had better watch his p's and q's. Just because this old man was shy a few teeth and no longer gave a rat's ass how he dressed, didn't mean Arlen Mestor didn't know come up from sic 'em. After all, he could claim some stroke with the congressman. He had helped him jimmy up some ballot boxes back in the good old days.

Arlen started to say as much when that sassy little waitress Nattie Rose Neuberger swooped over with the coffeepot—for the third time. One never got such stellar service in the back booth. The woman was spying, which was her bent. "I don't think we should talk about this here," Arlen said after she left, wisely he thought.

"*Now* you decide that yapping your lips in a public place is stupid," Roy hissed. "*After* you've blasted your face off about gasoline and knowing the congressman and all."

Arlen had known it was a mistake to talk like that the minute the words left his mouth. It's just that Zack Trueblood got under his skin so bad. Cocky bastard. "The gasoline bit came out in the investigation anyway, did it not?" Arlen said by way of deflection.

"No, as a matter of fact, it did *not*. My final report has not been made public yet. I am letting Zack Trueblood be the one to tell the widow. She's going to take it better that way, I suspect. He has decided she's too delicate or some such thing, to hear it right now. Until then, I've only got one thing to say to you, Arlen. Shut your pie hole or we'll shut if for you."

"We? Who's *we?*" But they both knew who was the boss in Kilgore County. "Are you threatening me?" Arlen puffed up, filling his side of the booth like a fat badger. "Are you forgettin'—"

"Arlen! I am the fire marshal. I have the authority to arrest you."

"Arrest me? For what?"

"For arson, you old dirtbag."

"When you know good and well I was paid to do it?" Arlen's voice involuntarily rose. "Don't forget that I know—"

"You don't know diddly-squat," Roy hissed, hushing him again. "It's your word against mine. The Mexicans who paid you are long gone, and they can't be connected to anybody here. You've got your money. Now you need to do your part in this deal, and shut up."

Arlen fell silent and glared while Roy sneered at his disheveled appearance. "I have covered for you before, but I'm telling you, it's not too late for me to change my report. And if it will get rid of you, I will do it."

"You can't change your report now. You just told me Zack Trueblood already knows what that report says." Arlen could see that they were equally matched in this deal, even if Roy couldn't. Both of them had done work for the congressman, and Roy had best not forget it. "It's not me you need to worry about. It's him. He thinks he's some kind of white knight, and I'm telling you he's sniffin' around that woman worse than a hound in heat."

ZACK CAME BACK to Robbie's house the next morning to install the smoke detectors. Mark threw himself into the task with manly enthusiasm, even if he did bang the extension ladder into the woodwork a couple of times as they carried it up the stairs.

The little boys were watching cartoons at a window-rattling decibel down in the living room and the smell of something delicious cooking in the kitchen wafted up to Zack's nostrils. He couldn't help whistling a contented tune as he secured the smoke detector into place above his head. He could get used to the idea of living like this. He hoped maybe by the time he fixed up old man Mestor's monstrosity of a rental house Robbie would come to get used to the idea of him, too.

A practical man would wait. Until she had the baby. Until she was through grieving. Until she was ready to date again.

But she needed his help now. He wasn't about to watch the woman from some polite distance while she struggled to survive. He smiled down at Mark as he handed up the drill. Maybe he'd even teach her boys some handyman skills in the process.

Robbie came to the foot of the stairs. "Want to stay for breakfast?"

"You certainly know how to keep the hired help happy, ma'am."

"There you go, ma'aming me again." She shook her head and sauntered off to the kitchen.

She was a great cook, and he was already discovering that this woman was frugal to a fault, modest, and full of wit and easygoing humor, even when her back ached and her feet were swollen.

He let himself imagine the two of them getting closer and closer, growing in the kind of mutual trust and intimacy he had never managed with his first wife, something he had always longed for. Robbie Tellchick was the kind of warm, decent woman he could build a solid life with. He was already pretty sure of that. Now he only needed to convince her.

But Zack sensed in Robbie a vague mistrust even as she warmed up to him. Maybe she had accepted his help because she felt she had no choice—the house was a genuine wreck. First things first. He finished tightening the screws on the smoke alarm.

He sure hoped they wouldn't be dancing around stupid issues like his motives, or what the gossips over at the diner thought, or even more serious ones like the cloud of suspicion hanging over Danny's death. He wanted them to face everything together, out in the open. That was his plan, his hope.

"All done," he said to Mark. "You just push this—" he pointed at the red button on the device's belly "—to make sure it works. Cover your ears now."

He pushed the test button and at the squeal of the alarm the dogs barked and howled and the younger boys came running to the foot of the stairs.

"Make it stop, Zack!" the dark-headed middle child hollered upward. "It's hurtin' Awgie's ears!"

Zack reset the alarm and climbed down the ladder, feeling some satisfaction that he'd at least provided for the family's safety in this one regard.

He and Mark washed up for breakfast.

When they gathered around the little table for pancakes and bacon, Zack was surprised to find a grubby little hand slipping into his. He gave little Rob, who had taken hold of his hand, a questioning look.

"Time to pray, mister," Rob informed Zack in his husky little voice.

The boys and Robbie bowed their heads and Robbie

started to pray aloud. But Zack didn't close his eyes with them. He wanted to watch Robbie. With her head bowed and her brow gently creased in sincerity, she was uttering a simple and heartfelt prayer while he became fully aware that he was falling in love with her. Pregnant or not, it was just like he told her—she was exactly what he wanted in a woman.

He studied each of the boys' bowed heads while Robbie's soft voice droned on. Terrific little guys, everything a man could want in sons, even if they were acting out a bit right now.

He did find himself praying then, sort of. A lump formed in his throat as he sent up an inward plea—to where, to whom, he was not sure. *Help me be a good husband for her and good father to them, should I be lucky enough to be handed that privilege someday.*

His covert gaze scanned over the boys' bowed heads. Zack, of all men, understood the needs of fatherless boys. Whether Robbie ever wanted him as a mate or not, he hoped he could take the load off her by being a male role model for the boys. He actually couldn't wait to take them hunting and fishing. Right there at the rickety little breakfast table, he found himself briefly entertaining another fantasy—having three strapping stepsons, maybe four?—starring on the Five Points football team. It was possible. A man could wish—a man could pray— for far worse.

CHAPTER SIX

HERE'S A SUMMARY of my life for the past couple of weeks: I get up before dawn and fix a pot of herbal tea (my poison of choice for jolting my poor abused body awake). What I wouldn't give for a good old cup of coffee, but nothing even remotely suspicious gets into this bloated body.

The other day a trucker lit up a cigarette in the café, and bless his dear old heart, Parson went charging out to tell the guy that he was eating in a non-smoking establishment.

When the trucker said, Since when?, Parson told him since a pregnant mother has come to work there. I got tears in my eyes (once again) over that one. Weepyness is just par for the course, too.

And who needs to be awake? Having suffered through sleep deprivation with three babies now, plus working as Danny's little farm slave all those years, taught me how to slap the sandwiches together with one hand and fry up the bacon with the other, the whole time keeping one eye closed.

Anyway, I do all that stuff then leave a hastily scribbled note for my boys. Mark's in charge, once they get up. I try to see to it that they only have to slosh a little milk on their Cheerios, wolf down the bacon, and grab the lunch sacks before they catch the bus, but somehow something urgent always comes up. They are still little boys, after all.

Mark usually calls me by 7:30. Mom, where is my field trip permission slip? Mom, Rob just threw up. Mom, we missed the bus.

Thank God for Danny's sister Becky. She's been there for me more times than I can count now. Becky has five kids of her own to tend to, and a home daycare where the little ones start arriving at 7:00. So I won't be able to lean on her forever.

I wonder if I shouldn't have moved out to Mother and Daddy's place. But how could I look Mother in the face, or even look at the back of her kinked-up head, and not seethe over what she did to Markie? That sure wouldn't be good for the baby!

Which brings me to the subject of Markie, my so-called sister. I guess I got kind of dependent on good old Markie when she was staying out on the farm with me right after Danny died. She's my best friend, and I can hardly wait 'til she gets home! I'd rather depend on my own sister for help instead of Danny's. Becky's just a tad overbearing. If I want to put up with that, I'll go see Mother.

The kitchen windows are black as pitch when I leave the house. Daylight savings time is almost over now, which means Baby is coming soon.

Baby's coming! Baby's coming! That's my mantra

lately. I am planning to set up a nursery in this cute little alcove off my bedroom...when I get the time...and the money...and the energy. Zack True-blood said he would help me do it all. He said he would do anything I want. Anything.

Well, I could think of a few things, but pregnant women aren't supposed to have thoughts like that. But it's been four months since a man has touched me, and I'm beginning to think I'll forget how to...you know, do the deed. One thing me and Danny had going for us for sure—a healthy sex life. One thing I am missing for sure—the same.

And that brings me to the one truly bright spot in my days: Zack Trueblood. He comes to my house almost every day now. I'm getting attached, I know I am. Trouble is, I have no idea where this going.

TWO WEEKS PASSED and Zack spent every spare minute making the old Mestor house more livable for Robbie and her brood.

During those long deceptively calm and domestic days, Robbie continued to fall hard for Zack. He was definitely a fine specimen of a man, and he was definitely interested in *her*. His hardworking ways, his down-to-earth maturity and his ability to talk about his feelings were all a sharp contrast to the noncommunicative, whiney, self-centered Danny. But she had made up her mind to find out more about Zack's background. She wasn't going to make that mistake again—giving in to her feelings and getting all tied down instead of ruling with her head.

"Are you divorced or what?" she asked him on the second Sunday of their association. The boys had taken off on their bikes immediately after church.

Zack was at the top of a ladder again, putting fresh lightbulbs in the chandelier. She was handing the bulbs up one by one.

"Divorced. For quite a while now."

"How long?"

"Five years."

"Wow. Y'all must have been young. What happened?"

"My hitch in the Navy was almost up. When I announced my plans to return to Five Points to buy a farm, she ran off with another Navy man."

"Oh." Robbie was sorry she'd asked. "Sort of a flighty chick then, was she?" She hoped her sarcasm might diffuse a painful topic.

He looked down at her, his expression thoughtful. "You want to know the truth? It wasn't a huge loss. I hurt for while, but in the end, the divorce was a relief. She was a cutie from California, and I was plenty hung up on her—for all the wrong reasons. But then I finally realized that underneath all that golden beauty, Shawna was a spoiled brat who never showed an ounce of ambition, and spent every last dime I made to boot. I started to feel sorry for the other guy."

Robbie had always heard how divorced men—the deluded ones—unilaterally blamed their ex-wives for the breakup. How they always claimed their wives spent too much money, or criticized them too much, or whatever. "Hmm," she said quietly. "They always say it takes two."

"To wreck a marriage?" He looked at her sharply. "No, Robbie. It takes two to *build* it. But one person can kill a marriage all on their own, believe me. I don't care what the self-help books say. I'm not making light of divorce. It's a scourge. But sometimes it is necessary."

"But what if you had agreed to give up the idea of the farm?" Robbie challenged. She had to know if this man was inflexible. Self-righteous. Domineering, even. "What if you'd considered *her* goals, given her time to grow up? Did you ever think about that?"

"She didn't have any goals. I gave up a lot of things for Shawna, but I finally decided I could never please her. Besides, Shawna knew about my dream to have a farm from the start. I brought her out here to the Hill Country before we ever got married."

"You wanted a farm even way back then?"

"I knew I wanted a farm when I was ten years old."

Suddenly Robbie realized how serious Zack was about someday farming the land, how that might be a real problem between them since she herself never wanted to return to life on the farm again. *Between them?* There was no between them! What was she thinking?

"Look," he said, returning his attention to his task, "I joined the Navy because I didn't have many financial options. I come from poor folks, but they always worked hard to get ahead, especially my granddad. He taught me how to manage my money. I've got my remodeling business and I'm saving for my land—doing real good at it, too—and someday I'll have it."

For Robbie, hearing that kind of talk warmed her

heart more than if he'd whispered a bunch of sweet nothings. "I admire the fact that besides being a dedicated firefighter you run a prosperous business in your off-duty time. I always thought it'd be fun to do that— have my own business."

"Really?" He glanced over his shoulder at her. "Doing what?"

"I don't know. Well, I do, but it sounds crazy."

"Tell me."

"Okay." She handed him the last lightbulb and folded her hands atop her huge tummy. "I'd like to be an interior decorator. But in Five Points, that's like saying I'd like to be a movie star."

"Where there's a will there's a way." Zack attacked the task overhead with fresh energy. "The way I see it, there's a lot of people migrating outward from Austin, building big old houses that need decorating and landscaping and the whole bit."

"I'm starting to think you're a pretty smart man, Zack Trueblood." What she didn't say was that she was coming to realize that though he was younger, Zack was far more industrious and mature than her husband had ever been.

"I want you to know that I'm very grateful for these home improvements." She smiled up at him. "Seeing as how I might be stuck in this old rental house for a while."

"I actually enjoy renovating, redecorating, painting, landscaping, all that stuff."

"You're not just saying that to turn my head?" She continued to smile up at him. "'Cause I love doing all that stuff, too. I made a lot of spiffy changes to our old farmhouse," she enthused. "Sometimes I'd use the most mundane objects and materials. I used to call it my makeover magic. I wish you could see it."

"Maybe I will sometime." He started down the ladder.

They moved on to the task of removing the wobbly stair balusters. Robbie kept working steadily alongside Zack, though he urged her to rest often and wouldn't allow her to do anything too strenuous.

"Shawna and I never did stuff like this together," he admitted later in the day, and Robbie had a pang of regret that she'd ever brought up the woman—the *California cutie* with the golden beauty—to mind.

"I'm not comparing you to her, though." He seemed to be reading her face. "Just commenting that life's a lot more fun when you work side-by-side like this. I guess you wouldn't understand since you guys had such a good marriage."

"Where'd you get *that* idea?"

"Wasn't it?"

She hesitated for a moment before she answered quietly. "You were truthful with me, so I'll be truthful with you. Danny was more interested in hunting and fishing than marriage, I think. Oh, not that he couldn't be nice if he wanted to be. He sometimes complimented me for my practical outlook, or my sense of humor or how hard I worked."

"Not for your beauty?"

"My *beauty?*" she scoffed. "You didn't know my Danny. His pet name for me was 'Sport.' I'm afraid Danny was a typical tobacco-chewing, beer-swilling country boy, and just between you and me, he spent too much time playing with his buddies when he should have been facing his responsibilities."

"How come you stayed with him?"

"Call me crazy, but their names are Mark, Rob and Frank."

"A woman like you deserves to be taken care of, *and* to hear how beautiful she is. If you were my wife, I'd tell you that every day. Several times a day."

Robbie could see that the man was one hundred percent sincere. *If she were his wife.* After her years of deprivation with Danny, the idea that a man like Zack thought she was beautiful and wanted to tell her so took a little getting used to. "Keep talking like that and—"

"I know." He winked. "You'll fall in love with me. That's my wicked plan, *ma'am.*"

And it was working better than he realized. Again Robbie feared that her feelings for Zack Trueblood were escalating too quickly. He was not only the most handsome man she's ever seen, but he was also a great guy. Almost too good to be true. Steady as a rock, sensitive and funny and charming in a way that Danny never was. And she was already beginning to rely on Zack in ways that a woman turns to a husband.

By the following Tuesday night they were really making good progress on the house. The stair rails were fixed and solid as jail door bars. As soon as the boys went off to the movies with Marynell and P.J., Zack announced that now that the safety issues were taken care of, it was time for "a little beautification."

They tackled the little alcove off the master bedroom where the baby's crib would be set up. Zack ripped up the filthy, threadbare carpet and then the two of them got on hands and knees to scrub the woodwork and the varnished oak planks they had discovered under the carpet. Zack proceeded to plaster the cracks in the Sheetrock while Robbie started cleaning the window sills.

But she quickly grew fatigued.

Zack said, "Here," and grabbed two of the oversized pillows off her bed against the wall. "Just sit there and talk to me while I finish up." She arranged herself, legs akimbo, on the cushions and contentedly watched him work with the trowel.

"Talk to me," he finally said. It didn't matter what she said. He just liked the sound of her voice.

She picked at some hardened paint on the thigh of her overalls, then hooked her thumbs in the straps and said, "Bet you're getting sick of looking at these old things. I know I sure am."

"Matter of fact, I meant to ask you about that." Zack saw his opportunity to ask her something he'd been wanting to bring up for days. It was a delicate matter, though, for a lot of reasons. Her wardrobe being the least of them.

But he was getting that award and he wanted her to see him walk up to the podium and make his acceptance speech. Vanity, he admitted. But someday, if everything went well, he hoped this woman was going to be his wife, and he wanted this shared memory with her.

"Ask me what?" Robbie prompted.

"How'd you like to get dressed up for a change?"

"Dressed up? For what?"

"The Firefighters' Ball. I know I'm asking on short notice. It's next Friday."

"The Firefighters' Ball?" She said it with disgust, as if he'd asked her to a mud-wrestling match instead of a nice evening of dinner and dancing.

"Yeah. Happens every year to kick off Fire Prevention Week. We have it at a real nice hotel down in Austin. Representatives from all the small-town fire departments attend. The governor passes out a couple of awards." One would be his for outstanding pride and professionalism. "The money goes to buy smoke detectors for the needy."

"It's formal dress, I suppose?"

"We wear our dress blues, yes. And the ladies wear their long dresses, if that's what you mean."

"That is exactly what I mean." Robbie shifted her round bottom uncomfortably on the pillow. "I don't have any business going to a formal dance, for crying out loud. I happen to be, you know, a little bit pee-gee here."

"There will be other pregnant wives—women— *ladies* in the crowd, I'm sure. Other ladies who are expecting." He tried, too late, to mend his awkward wording. This was not going as smoothly as he'd like. Immediately after he'd broken it off with Lynette, the well-to-do ranch owner he was *supposed* to ask to this deal, he had begun fantasizing about having Robbie there with him. The circumstances were all wrong, of course, but a lifetime of wanting Robbie McBride by his side at an event like this had won out. There was always next year, his head had initially reasoned. But next year, his heart had argued, he wouldn't be getting the award.

"I'll bet there won't be any pregnant women there on a date," Robbie was saying, "not any on the verge of delivery, at least."

"Oh, come on, Robbie. This isn't Victorian England where women hide in their houses when they're *in a family way.*"

"I'm serious! What if I go into labor?" She started struggling to hoist herself up off the pillows.

"You're not due for three more weeks yet. And if you do start labor, you'll have your very own paramedic by your side, and believe it or not, there are a few hospitals in Austin." He smiled as he pulled her to her feet. "Heck. You'll be in a whole ballroom full of paramedics. And just think, at least with you in that condition, there's no chance of people gossiping about any hankypanky between us."

"Hanky-panky? Where'd you get that one? From your grandmother?"

"As a matter of fact." The face he pulled made them both laugh.

"Come on, Robbie," he coaxed again. "Wouldn't it be nice to do a little socializing for a change? How long's it been since you got dressed up and went somewhere just for fun? Just for yourself?"

She gave him a condescending look. "I bet if you think real hard, you can come up with the answer to that one."

"Exactly. What's it gonna hurt to go out and let me

treat you to a good time? Get your mind off your troubles just for one evening. Maybe you should get out while you can, before you get all tied down with the baby."

"I couldn't dance in this condition. Surely there's plenty of other women you could ask to a dance who could actually, like, *dance* with you."

"Maybe so. But I don't want any of them. I want *you*."

She gave him a little wide-eyed look before her face closed off again and she said, "Forget it, Zack." She turned away from him and snatched up a sponge and went back to her cleaning. "I don't even have a decent dress."

Zack pursed his lips as he studied her back, thinking that maybe there was a more serious undercurrent here. Maybe he was pushing her too fast. It hadn't occurred to him that there might be inherent risks—for *him*—in getting involved with a widow. What if he stuck by Robbie Tellchick while she rebounded from the worst of her grief and then, in the end, she just dumped him? What if she never got past losing her husband that way? What if he was setting himself up for a great big fall?

No. He knew Robbie Tellchick was not that kind. She was a woman of substance and would never use a man like that. Her hesitation tonight had been real.

Whatever was causing her reluctance, he decided not to push the matter for now. There was more than one way to skin a cat—and more than one way to get a pregnant woman into a formal dress.

CHAPTER SEVEN

ZACK TRUEBLOOD asked me to the Firefighters' Ball! It really does make feel like a teenager, writing something like that in a diary. But it's not as romantic as it sounds, because I still can't decide if the man feels sorry for me, or what.

Back to my reality. After the lunch crowd clears out at the diner, I race home and throw on a load of laundry. If I am very, very lucky, I get to put my feet up for a bit before I have to slap together something for the boys' dinner, and then I head back to the diner, where I'll slap together plates of meat loaf or fried chicken for Parson's regulars. These days my whole life is about slapping food together. Yuck. Nattie Rose usually shoos me off if the crowd's not too bad. Then it's home again. I fold laundry, water my few pitiful plants, supervise homework if I can browbeat the boys into doing any.

Then I fold more laundry while the boys grumble their way through the dishes, though I'm usually the one who has to scrub the tomatoey remains of spaghetti or what-have-you off the pots. Danny hated spaghetti, but the boys love it, so now we have it all the time. Living by Danny's old whims won't bring the man back now will it?

I let the kids watch some TV most evenings and, most evenings, I fall asleep on the couch while some dumb sitcom blares away.

Unless Zack is there. He doesn't expect me to help him do all these projects he's got lined up, but I feel guilty if I don't. The boys get underfoot, of course, but he's very sweet about it. Treats them like little men.

I am mortified over the way my house looks. But I swear to Pete, I have no time for dusting or vacuuming. Or flower beds. Or any of those other things I used to do so automatically and so well, but which now seem like pure indulgences. No time for homemaking of any kind, much less self-care like nails or hair or even pressing my jeans.

And right in the big middle of all this, Zack asked me to the Firefighters' Ball in Austin. Imagine! Waltzing around in a long dress on the arm of that man! Move over, Cinderella.

But who can afford a dress or all the stuff that goes with it? I can barely afford groceries. I really need that insurance money, but something tells me I'm not going to get it.

There are no fairy-tale endings. But what I wouldn't give for just a teensy bit of magic. Just one teeny, tiny little girly frill. Just one moment of feeling like a woman again instead of like some baby-making machine on hormonal overload.

THE NEXT DAY Zack cut out from his latest renovation job early and swung by the ATM machine in front of the Piggly Wiggly before heading to the Hungry Aggie.

"Nattie Rose?"

"Yeah?" The waitress whirled from her task behind the counter as if she'd been waiting for Zack to pronounce her name. The only other person in the restaurant at three in the afternoon was old Ned Spitzer, sitting crookedly in a back booth. Zack could see a thin curl of smoke above the high seat back, but he couldn't see the top of Ned's greasy old ball cap. He hoped the old codger hadn't dozed off, or that he had at least balanced the cigarette in an ashtray first. He made a mental note to go check on the old guy as soon as he'd talked to Nattie Rose.

"Lemme ask you something."

"Ask away. You want coffee?"

"Sure." It would probably taste like sludge this time of day, but if he bought a cup he wouldn't be totally wasting the waitress's time.

Zack slid up on a stool while Nattie Rose set a mug filled to the brim in front of him. "So. What's your question?"

Zack cleared his throat. "Do you know where a man might—" he lowered his voice, not wanting old Ned to hear what he was up to "—where a man might go to get a formal maternity dress?"

Nattie Rose, bless her, didn't even blink. She just grinned and, too loudly, said, "You mean for the Firefighters' Ball? For Robbie?"

Zack didn't even have to ask Nattie Rose how she knew all the doings in this town. She just knew. Everything. Always. "Yeah."

"eBay. That's where I get all my stuff."

Zack cocked an eyebrow at her outfit. He believed it. Today the town's favorite waitress was decked out in a neon pink shirt with sequins all over the bust and a pair of equally loud snug-fitting capris in a pink-and-green Hawaiian print.

"I don't think I've got time to order something off the Internet. The dance is Friday."

"Friday? You asked her to a deal like that on such short notice and she actually said yes?"

"Well, no. That's the problem. She hasn't actually said yes. Yet. That's why I need the dress. One more obstacle out of the way."

Nattie Rose's pudgy pink mouth dropped open, then snapped shut. "You mean to tell me *you* are buying her this dress?"

"If you'll tell me where I can get one."

Nattie Rose shook her head. "You are aiming to get your heart plumb broke, Zack Trueblood. You know that don't you?"

"It's my heart."

The waitress sighed. She shook her head while she took a couple of determined swipes at the counter with a damp rag. Finally she said, "I will get the dadblamed dress for you, but only because I'm thinking this whole deal might possibly cheer Robbie up. It's just crazy enough."

He slid off his stool. "Just make it a pretty one, okay?"

"Of course."

He regarded Nattie Rose's loud outfit skeptically. "Remember Robbie's kind of...elegant. And get her all the...you know, proper fixings. Here." He took his billfold out of his hip pocket and pulled out three hundred-dollar bills. "Will this cover it?"

Nattie Rose took the money and shook her head again, but this time she was smiling tenderly. "If anyone can mend Robbie's poor little heart, I expect it's you."

"I intend to give it my best shot. Parson doesn't allow smoking in here anymore, does he?" Zack jerked his head toward the back.

Nattie Rose frowned. "Is Ned smoking again? He's a fire hazard."

"I'll talk to him." Zack slid off the stool. He turned and aimed a finger at Nattie Rose as he backed toward Ned Spitzer's booth. "Remember...get a pretty one, okay?"

"Don't worry. It'll be gorgeous!"

THOUGH HER NYLON jogging suit was the softest, most pacific shade of blue, Marynell McBride's face was as gray and ominous as the storm clouds gathering on the horizon. "Now, where, exactly, are you going?" The perpetual crease between her brows deepened.

"Austin." Robbie, showered but still in flip-flops and her baggy pink bathrobe, was tromping around the living room gathering up the boys' stuff. "Turn off the TV, guys. Grandma's ready to go."

"And why are you going again?"

"The Firefighters' Ball. It's an annual event that kicks off Fire Prevention Week. They raise money for smoke detectors for the needy." Why was she parroting Zack's words to her nosy mother? She was an adult and she could go wherever she wanted, with whomever she wanted.

"Where in the world did you ever find a dress to wear to a formal dance?" Marynell knew well the plain, practical nature of her daughter's wardrobe. She'd criticized Robbie's attire often enough. And underneath the question was the subtle implication that Robbie could ill afford such a dress, and thus, should be sensible and move back home to her mother, and blah, blah, blah.

"Uh...Nattie Rose picked it up somewhere." Robbie was not above partial truths to keep her mother off her back. Marynell would have a blue-nosed fit if she knew Zack Trueblood had paid for Robbie's elegant dress.

"Oh. That was nice of her," Marynell said prissily. "But I am not at all certain it is a good idea for you to be traveling, Roberta. It's getting ready to storm outside."

Roberta? Her mother had never called her that before. It was Markie who got called *Margaret* when her mother was displeased, but Robbie had never felt the sting of her mother's disapproval this pointedly before. *Roberta?* "We're not *traveling,* for heaven's sake. We're just driving down the highway to Austin." Her tone was short, but turnabout was fair play, Robbie supposed. Her mother had never felt the prick of Robbie's impatience, either.

"But you're so close to your due date. You really

should stick closer to home, now of all times." Marynell was literally wringing her thin hands. Thunder boomed and shook the high windows of the old house.

"Here." Robbie fished around in the pocket of her robe.

"What's this?" Marynell took the card Robbie offered.

"Zack's card—call his cell phone if the boys need anything, or…anything."

Marynell frowned at it. "Isn't he a lot younger than you?"

"Mom!" Frank shrieked from the top of the stairs.

For once Robbie was grateful for the annoying sound of her middle son's high-pitched voice. "Yes, honey?"

"I can't find my socks!"

"Look down here between the couch cushions. And then you guys find your rain jackets. Mother, I'm sorry." She turned to her mom. "Could you please help the boys? I've really got to get upstairs and start getting ready. Oh. I brought them some chicken tenders and home fries. In the kitchen."

"Leftovers from that greasy restaurant again? I told you, Parson's cooking is far too rich for these children."

"Mother, you can take the leftovers with you or not. Or you can feed the boys at McDonald's for all I care."

"You don't have to get snippy with me. I am doing you a favor here. Come on, kids, Grandma will fix you a decent meal at my house."

Marynell's tone was so high-handed that Robbie instantly felt her gut tightening. Her mother was spoiling for a fight, and Robbie was dangerously close to giving it to her.

"The boys happen to like Parson's cooking, Mother." She shouldn't have done that. Responded. The old Robbie wouldn't have done that.

"What choice do they have as long as you insist on living hand-to-mouth in this dump? You could be content and secure right now, out on the farm with me and your daddy. But it's like I was telling P.J. the other day. I said, I don't know what's gotten into Robbie lately. She is being about as stiff-necked as Markie used to be. I swear, it must be genetic." Marynell aimed her bony finger at Robbie. "But your boys are the ones who are paying for your stubbornness."

Robbie felt the tension in her middle solidify. How dare her mother undermine her like this in front of her own children! If she didn't want to go to this dance so badly with Zack, she'd tell her mother to leave right now.

Instead she drew a calming breath. Gut-knotting anger was not good for the baby, she was sure. "Mother, the children are being well-fed. And I am enjoying my new job in town. I like this house—it's shaping up nicely. The baby isn't due for three more weeks, and there is absolutely nothing for you and Daddy to worry about." Robbie turned to go up the stairs before her mother looked into her eyes and saw that she was lying.

BY THE TIME Robbie finished her makeup and came out of the bathroom, rain was strafing the bedroom windows in heavy sheets. She closed the blinds and braced herself to start dressing. Nattie Rose had helped her try on the dress once, but it had been a long time since she'd worn

anything that actually fit and getting into it alone might
be tricky. She hoped she didn't rip the expensive silk
fabric, but she'd be danged if she'd ask her mother to
come up and help her.

She tried stepping into it, but the semi-fitted bodice
wouldn't come up over her tummy.

She checked her hair after she wiggled the dress
down over her head and shoulders. Despite the humidity
and having to pull a fitted halter neck into place, the so-
phisticated chignon at her nape remained sleek and
intact, smooth as satin, making her hair shine like bur-
nished copper.

It was a look wholly new to Robbie, and she loved
it, but she was having all kinds of doubts, very grave
doubts, despite the sleek coif Kathy at the Hair Hut had
created for her. After she had endured an hour in that
chair, practically the whole town had discovered that
Robbie Tellchick was going to the Firefighters' Ball in
Austin with Zack Trueblood tonight.

Nattie Rose and Parson had sprung for the hairdo.
She looked at her nails. And for the French manicure.
And a pedicure. She sighed.

Everything was perfect. So why was she so jittery?
All day, she'd been feeling this…unusual tension. She
told herself she had to calm down for the baby's sake.
She would just go out tonight and enjoy herself, like
Nattie Rose said. To heck with her mother. Old biddy.
She took a sip from the water glass she'd brought
upstairs with her.

She stood in profile to the dresser mirror, only able

to see herself from the waist up, which was enough, thank you very much. She made a futile attempt to adjust the deep neckline upward, trying better to cover her swollen cleavage.

The dress was a stunning thing, even if it had taken a couple of acres of fabric to make it. Folds of heavy midnight blue silk fell gracefully over her abdomen from a strategically placed point just under her bust. Tiny iridescent beading on the halter-style bodice had the effect of keeping the eyes directed upward to the expanse of creamy skin that rose to her throat, emphasizing her face, which Robbie had carefully made up. Not too bad, she had to admit, if you didn't look down. Trite as it sounded, she did seem to have a certain *glow* these days.

To enhance the elegant illusion that camouflaged her bulk, on her earlobes a pair of pearl-sized zirconias twinkled and glittered. She touched them, thinking how she couldn't have possibly said no to this event after Nattie Rose took a whole afternoon off to shop for this dress, these shoes, even the earrings? Zack Trueblood was sly indeed. She smiled at her reflection and picked up the blue velvet shawl that came with the dress and headed down the stairs.

Now that she was all ready to go, she grew paradoxically even more nervous. The distant lightning from the storm outside cast flashes of eerie light into the living room. She switched on a couple of lamps, finding it so quiet without the boys that she marched over and turned on the TV. The evening news was on and a map at the corner of the screen displayed a storm warning over the entire Hill Country.

Robbie perched on the couch, fidgeting and watching a news story that wormed into her consciousness, somehow upsetting her. Something about the ruthless activities of drug gangs along the U.S.–Mexican border. She silenced it with the remote, then got up and paced to the front window.

Standing there, looking out at the torrential rain, she felt the tiniest pang, the barest tightening in her abdomen. Braxton Hicks contractions, that's all. She had endured them late in every single pregnancy. They meant nothing. The argument with her mother had made her tense and she'd probably gotten dressed in too much of a rush. It had been a long time since she'd gone to so much trouble over her appearance. It was taxing. Probably not worth all that effort.

But she changed her mind when a car pulled up at the curb—a black Maxima that she didn't recognize— and Zack Trueblood got out, popping open an umbrella.

The sight of him caused her to unconsciously place four fingertips lightly over her heart.

He was an incredibly handsome man, even in plain T-shirts and jeans and boots, but as he strode up her sidewalk in his dress uniform, his good looks actually made her eyes go wide. Through the watery veil of rain, his body appeared to be one long, lean navy blue line with a massive wedge of shoulders anchoring the top. Even under the shadow of the umbrella, his white dress collar, the brass buttons on his double-breasted tunic and the lines of braid on his sleeves glowed. His face was half-hidden under the black visor of his dress hat, but the sight of his uniformed body moving so purposefully toward her was enough to make Robbie's heart beat faster.

Over the past week, she had become conditioned to anticipating his arrivals with more and more excitement, but tonight she was positively breathless. What was this man doing to her?

When she opened the door his hand was raised to knock. "Come in," she said, and waved him inside. "It's pouring out there."

"Is it really?" He smiled wryly as he collapsed the umbrella and shook droplets off his uniform. When he stepped over the threshold his eyes riveted on her. Or more specifically, on her cleavage. But only for a millisecond, before his gaze trained on her face. "Man," he said softly. "You look so beautiful, Robbie."

"Thank you. You look nice, too." Her right hand went up to touch her hair while the fingers of her left, again unconsciously, draped lightly over her exposed bosom.

"I like your hair like that. And *man,* just look at the rest of you."

He took one of her hands and held it lightly aloft while he made a business of looking her over head to toe. Then he actually emitted a wolfish whistle, which Robbie would have thought hokey, except that the sound of it made her cheeks go hot. "I gotta tell you, sweetheart," he said with obvious approval, "for a pregnant lady, you clean up real good."

"Yeah." Robbie tried to joke away the effect he was

having on her. "It was a real challenge, all right. This was all Nattie Rose's doing. She was so excited that she found this dress—"

"I can see why. It's perfect." Zack's eyes traveled over Robbie's figure again.

"You hadn't seen it?"

"Didn't want to. I wanted to be surprised." And his shining eyes said he surely was.

"Well…the way Nattie Rose was acting, you'd think she was my fairy godmother or something."

"Remind me to get her something nice to show my appreciation."

Robbie blushed even higher. She couldn't believe this man was willing to go to such lengths just to see that she had a good time on a date. Most guys wouldn't be caught dead on a date with a pregnant woman, much less buy a formal dress for her. But Zack wasn't like most guys. "Thank you for the dress, Zack. And the earrings and… everything." For some reason she looked down at her shoes.

He looked at her strappy little blue silk heels as well. "I don't imagine you'll want to be dodging puddles in those things."

"I guess I could change into something else."

"No way. I want to see those little pinkies. Maybe if we wait for a bit it will stop raining." Hill Country deluges were usually intense but short-lived. He checked his watch. "We've got plenty of time. It should only take us about an hour to get to Austin."

The tightening in Robbie's abdomen returned. *Calm*

down, she instructed her uncooperative body. "I'm having an ice water. You want something?"

"No, I'm good. I've got some bottled water out in the car…one for both of us."

He was so thoughtful. Robbie looked onto the street as she closed the door. "Is that car yours, by the way?"

"No. It's my friend Mason's. He's on duty and can't go to the ball. So he let me borrow it. I wanted you to be comfortable."

"That is so sweet of you!" Robbie exclaimed, but her enthusiasm was cut short by the tightening in her abdomen, now suspiciously regular, commanding her attention.

"What's wrong?" Zack frowned.

"Nothing," Robbie replied, but she was thinking, *Not now.* She felt selfish for thinking that way. Having a baby was more important than some charity ball. But please, God, *not now.* "Let's go sit down."

They situated themselves on the couch, side by side but not touching, and for a moment their attention was focused on the muted TV screen. There was a follow-up story about the murder on the border.

"The border's getting bad," Zack commented when he read the headline banner beneath the anchor's face. "Another shooting down there."

"Yes. I worry about my sister and her husband, working with illegal migrants the way they do."

Zack nodded. Neither one of them really wanted to talk about that.

But what *did* they want to talk about? Robbie's mind

flailed while another news story played. To save her life she couldn't come up with anything. All she could think about was her abdomen, which was cramping with alarming regularity now. Twice during this news story. She took a sip of her water, hoping it was something digestive, though she knew better. How was she going to tell him he was probably going to have to use that Maxima to drive her to the hospital instead of to the ball? She picked up the remote and changed the channel. Some little hotties in bikinis were eating cockroaches on a reality show.

"Nice," Zack said dryly. He took the remote from her hand and clicked the tube off. "Wouldn't want you getting sick and ruining your fancy dinner."

Robbie smiled wanly. She had to tell him. Here came another pain.

"Are you okay, sweetheart? You look a little pale. Or is that just because I've never seen you in makeup?"

Zack was so straightforward. When did he start calling her sweetheart like that? It made her smile again, and then without warning, a cramp hit her and tears sprang to her eyes. It got all mixed together, the pain and her emotions. Was she crying because Danny had never called her little endearments like that? Or because she was having the baby at long last…and she was all alone? She bit her lip to stop the emotions, but the tears spilled over anyway.

"Hey." Zack frowned and leaned toward her. "Sweetheart. What's wrong?"

"I don't know." She swiped at the tears as the pain let up. "Everything, I guess." She sniffed.

"Everything?" He reached in the pocket of his jacket and produced a small packet of Kleenex.

Robbie stopped sniveling long enough to give the Kleenex a skeptical glance. "What are you? Some kind of church lady or something?"

"Hey. If a guy's gonna hang out with a pregnant chick, he carries Kleenex." He wiggled one out of the pack and handed it to her. "Now. Tell me. What's wrong? Come on," he encouraged while she blew her nose. "I want all the gory details."

"Well, for one thing, I'm pregnant."

"You really *are* pregnant?" He feigned shock.

She shifted her enormous front away from him, but he took her arms and canted her back toward him. "Is that what's bothering you? The fact that you're pregnant? I told you, I couldn't care less. I just want to be with you."

"I believe you." Robbie sniffed. "It's just…" She wanted to say, *It's so hard to have a baby alone,* but she hedged. "I'm just so sick of being pregnant, if you must know."

"Well, being pregnant *is* only temporary. And won't you be thrilled to have a pretty little baby when it's all over?"

"Yes, of course. But I keep thinking, once the baby comes, then what? I'm afraid I'll end up falling back on my parents. And then I'll have to deal with my mother. She's punishing me because I refused to let her take over my life after Danny died. We had a fight tonight. I never used to fight with anybody, least of all her."

"Maybe you're changing, Robbie. People do. Especially after they've experienced a big loss the way you have."

Robbie dabbed her cheeks and went on. "She said she was going to fix the children a decent meal. She found out I've been bringing home leftovers from the Hungry Aggie."

"Well, what's wrong with that?"

"Exactly. Nobody ever died of Parson's cooking."

"Well, if they did, they were older'n Ned Spitzer by the time it happened."

"It's not just Mother. It's everything. The boys are having trouble at school. And I'm not even ready for the baby yet. And then there's the money."

"What about the money?"

Robbie tried to speak, but her tears choked her. It was humiliating, admitting this to him. "There isn't any. I don't think I'm even going to collect on the insurance."

Zack's expression shifted, closed off slightly, as if he was covering something, but then he said, "Why do you think that?"

"I think something was wrong about that fire. What if…what if Danny set it?"

"Ah, now, sweetheart. Don't get all freaked out about that. And as far as the money goes, I'd be more than happy to help you any way I can. I keep telling you that."

His generosity undid her emotions even more. "Oh, Zack. Let's face it." Robbie's face crumpled in anticipation of a fresh round of tears. "I'm a mess. And right now I'm—"

"Robbie." Zack cut her off. He braced his hands on

her shoulders and forced her to face him. "I won't let you talk about yourself that way. You are a great mom, restaurant leftovers or not, and you're a kind, soft-hearted, compassionate woman."

"Next you'll be telling me how *sweet* I am." She didn't want to be sweet. She wanted to be strong and competent and in control of her life.

"You *are* sweet and…" He paused, as if considering his next words carefully. "And you're very brave…and very beautiful."

The sudden emotion in his voice made Robbie blink. She stiffened under his hands.

"Look. You've had some heavy blows. You just need a little time to get on your feet. Come here. Let me hold you." He guided her into his arms and settled them back on the couch with her head on his shoulder.

"Zack—"

"Shh." She heard him swallow before he reached up and stroked her hair.

"Zack, I—" she started again.

"Robbie—" his voice sounded low, serious "—you feel so good in my arms." His arms tightened and the thrum of his heart beneath her ear grew stronger.

"Zack—"

"I know." He continued to stroke her smoothed-back hair. "I know it's too soon to talk like that. But if you could only know how long I've wanted to hold you. Let me. Just for a little while."

"Zack, I'm trying to tell you—"

"Before you say anything else, let me finish. You're

everything I could ever want in a woman. I didn't want to tell you how I feel so soon, but maybe it'll keep you from being so upset and worried about the future. If you'll let me, I'm going to do everything in my power to make that future bright—"

"Zack!" Robbie insisted. "Listen to me! My water just broke!"

"What?" His head jerked up like he'd been snakebit. Then he sat up, examining her, his hands on her everywhere, even on her rounded tummy, and ending up braced at her hips.

Sure enough, a dark stain was wetting the blue silk dress, spreading rapidly.

Zack clutched her firmly as if to stem the flow. "Okay. You just hang on, sweetheart. We'll get you to the hospital."

When Robbie did nothing to disguise the onset of the next pain, Zack twisted around on one knee to a squat in front of her with one hand on her belly, monitoring the contraction. He whipped out a cell phone and punched a speed dial number on it. He kept the hand in place while he talked. "Mason? I need a transport over here at Robbie Tellchick's house—yeah, old man Mestor's rental down here on Cypress Street. She's having the baby…no. Better not chance it, buddy. Her water's already broke and this contraction I'm feeling here's a doozy…*what?* Crap. Okay. Keep me posted."

He snapped the cell phone shut with irritation as Robbie was exhaling on the last wave of the contraction. "What is it?" she said when she could talk.

"The ambulance is out on a run, but they should be back soon." Unfortunately, the town had only one ambulance. And unfortunately, at the moment it was a long way away.

"That's okay," she breathed. "Before they get here, I'd like to change into some sweats or something. I don't want to show up at the hospital wearing this silly formal dress."

"Okay. I'll help you. Can you get up?" He clasped her hand.

"Of course. Yes. Of course I…can." Robbie made a start as if to push to her feet, but found herself suddenly awkward.

She scooted to the edge of the couch where Zack took her other hand and pulled her up, but no sooner was she standing than another pain gripped her.

"Ah!" she cried and doubled forward with her arms cradling her belly.

"Easy, easy," Zack murmured as he supported her in his strong arms. When the pain was done he guided her to sit in a more upright chair near the door. "Sit here while I go get your stuff. Where is it?"

"Upstairs. The bag's packed at the foot of my bed."

"Okay."

But as he turned to go, she reached out to grab for his hand. "Wait—" her voice was tight "—here's another one."

Zack frowned. *Already?* He hadn't checked his watch on the first few pains. But dropping to one knee with a palm on her hardening abdomen, he timed this one carefully. It was a full sixty seconds before he felt any softening of the uterine muscle. "Forget the bag," he said, making his decision. "Somebody else can bring it. We'd better get going."

"What about the ambulance?"

"I don't think we'd better wait for it, sweetheart."

"Why not?" Her eyes grew huge.

"Because it's actually out in Dunlap right now." The tiny town of Dunlap was twelve twisting miles of back roads away.

Robbie breathed a tense sigh. "I guess you're right. Rob came less than two hours after my labor started."

"Can you make it out to the car?"

"I think so."

Zack grabbed his umbrella. It was raining so hard now he could hardly see the black sedan parked at the curb. The downspouts next to the porch were streaming like freshly primed pumps. He hated to take her out in this deluge, especially in those stupid shoes. "Here," he said and grabbed a throw off the back of her couch. He wrapped it over her head and around her shoulders. "I'd better carry you."

Robbie didn't argue because, already, another pain was mounting, coming on much fiercer than the last.

Zack scooped her up in his arms. "Ready?"

She nodded, though, truth be told, she wasn't so sure about getting in the car now. She was already feeling like she might want to push. Unsure of what her body was doing, she debated about what to tell Zack.

But the way she gritted her teeth and gripped his

shoulder must have told him everything he needed to know. Instead of carrying her outside, he turned and hauled her straight up the stairs.

CHAPTER EIGHT

ROBBIE WOULD HAVE MADE some smart remark about the man's brute strength if she hadn't been so busy trying to breathe her way through the giant contraction that seized her.

Before they even made it all the way down the hall, yet another pain struck her like one of the lightning bolts cracking outside the window. "Whoa!" Robbie cried out. This one curled her forward in his arms, but Zack kept moving.

He swept into her bedroom and gently lowered her to one side of her queen-sized bed. He crossed to the other side, stripped the comforter back and stacked the pillows. Between pains, Robbie scooted herself over to lean against them, but it was an effort. She was definitely feeling the urge to push now.

"Zack, I wanted to push on that last one. I th-think he's coming already." She fell back on the pillows, panting, with her knees propped up. She adjusted her head with irritation because the low chignon was poking her neck.

"Here. Turn your head." Zack reached behind and she felt his fingers groping to unbind the pins that held the bun. Robbie helped, stripping off the elastic band that held her long shock of hair at her nape. As Zack's big hands slid under her neck, lifting the heavy hair, fanning the loosened tresses out onto the pillow, the action left Robbie with a strangely intimate feeling.

"Don't ever cut your hair off, okay?" Zack said. A somewhat misplaced statement, Robbie thought, under the circumstances.

"I won't," she said in a dry whisper.

But Zack didn't seem to hear her. He was already focused on other things.

He ripped off his dress jacket and tossed it away, then he snatched up the suitcase at the foot of her bed, unzipping it in two vicious swipes. "You have baby blankets in here?"

"Yes. And diapers and a little cotton cap. And a binky and a new bulb syringe somewhere in those pockets." Robbie nodded at the various pockets on top. "You ever delivered a baby?"

"One."

He found the cap and a couple of receiving blankets and some baby wipes and laid them beside Robbie. As he frantically unzipped more pockets, he cursed his stupidity under his breath. If his truck had been parked at the curb now, he could dash out and grab his emergency kit off the seat. He had sterile gloves and sterile cord clamps and a bulb syringe and the like in there. What was he thinking, leaving the kit behind, tonight of all nights. What was he thinking, taking this woman to a fancy dance when he should have been looking out for her safety. And the baby's. He'd have to leave the cord intact, deliver the placenta and wrap it up beside the newborn, hoping for the best...that the Wharton's jelly did its job and occluded the umbilicus naturally.

Robbie interrupted his search when she cried out, "Oh, God! Help me!" as the next pain slammed into her. Zack recognized the panic that accompanies transition. He bent over her and held her hand and coached her through it. When it was done he stroked her hair back from her brow and said, "You'll be fine, sweetheart. If the little dickens is determined to come this fast, we won't have any trouble." He looked over his shoulder where her bathroom door was ajar. "I'm just gonna run in there for a sec—to wash my hands and get some towels."

He left the door open and though he was so near Robbie could surely hear the water running, his ablutions seemed to take an eternity.

He quickly rolled up his shirt sleeves and scrubbed his hands with crazed fury while his eyes frantically scanned the bathroom for the items he needed. He was running cold water over a clean washcloth when the next sound Robbie made—part groan, part scream—jolted him worse than the thunderclaps outside. He grabbed a stack of towels and a jar of Vaseline and ran back into the bedroom in time to see Robbie's face reddened and crumpled with the exertion.

"Zack!" she cried, "I've gotta pu-ush."

He bent over her and gripped her hand. "Not yet, sweetheart! Gimme another sec to get ready." He was still hoping to find that bulb syringe.

She let out a high-pitched squeal and dug her nails into his arm as the involuntary urge gripped her. "I can't stop it," she ground out through clenched teeth.

"Okay. Push away," he said with far more confidence than he felt. "I'm here for you." He held her hand while she pushed.

When her exertion ended, he quickly scrunched the voluminous skirt of her formal dress up under her breasts, then he practically ripped her water-soaked, blood-tinged white cotton maternity panties as he tugged them over her legs.

As soon as he was done Robbie drew a huge breath and her chin tipped back down to her chest, her cheeks grew even redder with exertion and her eyes clamped shut with this push. And with this one she wasn't making a sound.

Zack propped a hip onto the bed and held her legs, angling her knees up out of the way. He could see the vulva clearly. To his amazement the top of a tiny dark head immediately crowned into view, then disappeared as soon as Robbie relaxed.

"Show time, sweetheart." His eyes grew misty as he smiled at the woman he so loved and admired. "This one's got dark hair."

"Really?" Robbie raised her head. "He was crowning already?" Her face was suddenly glowing with excitement.

Zack was busy shoving two thick towels under her hips. Then he used some of the baby wipes to gently swab her genitals clean. "Now," he crooned in a low, reassuring voice as his face hovered over hers, "I want you to push on this next one, real slow and real steady."

Robbie nodded with resolve.

Zack took a position at the ready, sitting twisted at her side on the bed. His goal was for a controlled delivery. Robbie's last push had been so powerful and efficient that he feared if he didn't help her gain control, the baby would shoot across the room. He told himself not to worry about the ultimate outcome. Some women just had the goods and when a woman like that spontaneously delivered there were seldom problems. The other baby he delivered had practically popped out into his hands.

"All my other deliveries were easy," Robbie reassured him, as if reading his mind.

"We'll be fine." Tenderly, he reached up to wipe her brow with the cool cloth again.

"Oh, man. Here it comes!" Robbie wrapped her slender fingers around Zack's thick wrist, lowered her chin and strained with all her might. Again, she hardly made a sound, and again, Zack felt his throat tightening with awe as he watched the baby's dark head crowning.

Robbie held the push steady while Zack counted, then she collapsed back on the pillows, panting. Zack reached over her abdomen and mopped her brow with the cool cloth once again. "Almost there. One more push oughtta do it. I want you to hold the next one as long as you can, okay?"

Robbie nodded, then opened her eyes. "Zack? I want you to concentrate on the baby when he comes out, not me. I can wait. You understand?"

He swallowed. "Okay. But listen. You've got some episiotomy scars…down there. I've…I think I know a way to keep you from tearing. I brought some…" Quickly, he opened the Vaseline and cleaned off the used layer with some Kleenex. "I promise this won't hurt."

She nodded again. "I understand. Go ahead."

Hoping to prevent a tear that might hemorrhage, he dug his fingers into the clean Vaseline and used the lubricant to massage and stretch Robbie's most private area, the way a midwife had taught the EMTs to do. He was amazed at how everything he'd ever learned was coming back to him in a rush. He sent up a silent prayer to just keep it coming, keep it coming. If ever he needed supernatural guidance, it was now.

Things seemed to go into slow motion then.

The next pain gripped Robbie even more intensely than the others. To Zack she seemed like an angel under his hands, spreading her wings in silent, intent submission, as a warm flow of the last of the amniotic fluid poured over his ministering fingers and a tiny dark head steadily slid out against his cupped palm. With his free hand he grabbed up a corner of the receiving blanket to steady the slippery baby. The head rotated, revealing a darling pinched little face, then, easily, slowly, powerfully, the shoulders, one then another, followed. The rest of the tiny body appeared, as if materializing from heaven.

Perfect! Perfect! Zack's heart cried out. She was perfect!

Her warm, slick little muscles, her soft round little

bottom. His hands molded around her tiny body like a sculptor's shaping clay.

He grabbed some Kleenex and wiped the precious little nose and mouth clear.

Robbie was gazing over her tummy in awe. "A girl! Oh, Zack!" The tears glimmering in her eyes told him just how much that meant to her, despite her earlier disclaimer. "I've got myself a little g-girl!"

"You sure do, sweetheart." He leaned up and quickly pressed his lips to her forehead, then turned back to the baby like he knew Robbie wanted him to. "And she's absolutely perfect."

He dried the tiny baby quickly with one of the receiving blankets and the rubbing stimulation brought forth her first breathy cry. When her tiny wail reached full decibel Robbie and Zack smiled at each other, then laughed nervously because they'd both been unconsciously holding their breath.

Zack wrapped the baby in a fresh receiving blanket and tucked the loosely swaddled child up onto Robbie's chest. Robbie circled her arms around her infant daughter.

For one timeless instant both stared in awe at the obviously healthy wailing baby, then both started to croon to her at once.

"She doesn't like it out here, Mommy," Zack said.

"Oh, my goodness!" Robbie cooed. "We are so, so upsetters." At the sound of her mother's voice, the baby instantly quieted. Her eyes popped opened, searching for her mother's face.

Robbie and Zack laughed. And then the tiny newborn

rooted for her own flailing fist and managed to capture her tiny thumb in her mouth!

"Oh, my," Robbie breathed, "none of my others did that."

"Well, I'll be," Zack beamed, "isn't she the little smartie pants?"

Zack had to focus back on his duties then. He palpated the cord, which was already firm and without a pulse. Then he gently palpated Robbie's now flaccid abdomen. "One more delivery," he said. "You doing okay?"

Robbie winced at his ministrations but said, "We're fine," as she wrapped the child in the folds of blue silk dress, which was ruined anyway.

"Sorry about this dress, Zack, I—"

"Shh." He touched another quick kiss to her temple. "I can't think of a better use for the thing than keeping that little darlin' warm."

Robbie looked into his eyes and thought her heart might melt. "Still, you missed your banquet and all, and I—" This time her words were interrupted by the aftershocks of the contractions that would bring forth the placenta.

Robbie's last vestige of pregnancy was delivered with one steady push and much relief.

Zack quickly checked it to make sure it was intact, then he took one of the towels and wrapped it securely to be transported next to the baby. He used the baby wipes to clean his hands for the next task.

"This next part might hurt a little bit." He knew that with a fourth baby and a fast delivery Robbie's uterus would be extrasensitive, and also more vulnerable to hemorrhage.

"I've been through all of this several times before, remember?" Robbie smiled at him, then at the baby. "And it's well worth it."

"That's my girl." With his big hand on Robbie's lower belly, Zack gently massaged the fundus of her uterus until he was satisfied it was firm. Though she winced and cried out once with a small "Ah," Robbie kept her eyes on the baby.

Then Zack said, "Pads?" with a raised eyebrow.

Robbie gave a weak nod toward the open suitcase before she let her head drop back onto the pillows.

He found the thick sanitary pads in one of the many zipper pockets, applied a couple snugly to Robbie's bottom, lowered her legs and covered her and the baby with the sheet and blanket, tucking it tight all around. He gave her foot a small comforting squeeze that left Robbie feeling oddly elated before he went into the bathroom to thoroughly wash his hands and find a cup to fetch her some water. When he came back he held her head up so she could drink, fluffed up the pillows, then sat on the bed, whipped out his cell phone and punched speed dial.

"Mason? We've got a healthy baby girl here." He gave a low chuckle at something his buddy said. "She's a little doll. Robbie did great. The baby's a little early. We need to get her to the hospital and warm her up. Where the heck's my transport…? Okay."

He snapped the phone shut. "They're coming. They got delayed because they had to go around a low water bridge that flooded. Anybody else you want me to call right away?"

"Not yet. We can have Mother and Daddy and the boys meet us at the hospital. Right now, I just want to savor this moment. Just you and me and…oh, my gosh! I don't even have a name for a girl picked out. I was so sure I was having another boy I didn't even have an ultrasound. Mommy's sorry, sweetheart." She gave her baby an apologetic smile and touched her face with a gentle finger.

"A good name will eventually come to you," Zack reassured her. He felt like he was speaking automatically because part of his mind was snagged back on those words Robbie had just said—*you and me.* He, too, wanted to savor this moment with Robbie, and Robbie alone. Truth be told, on some level he was wishing this moment would never end.

While they waited, Zack touched the baby's face and her little body in a feast of sensation. He allowed himself a few touches of Robbie, too—her brow, her cheek, her upper arm. Both of them were so soft! So warm and alive and so purely beautiful. On impulse he kissed Robbie's forehead again, drinking in her rich, sweet new-mother scent as he kept his lips there a heartbeat too long. "Congratulations, Mommy," he said, trying to cover his deep emotions with a quick smile.

"Thank you." Robbie swallowed. "Thank you, Zack. For being here for me."

"My pleasure." It was the trite thing to say, but for Zack wholly true. Delivering Robbie McBride Tellchick's baby was sure to be one of the high points of his entire life. His heart was bursting with gratitude at the privilege. Gratitude that the baby was such a healthy little dolly. Gratitude that Robbie had submitted to his ministrations with such womanly ease and grace. Gratitude that he had been the one chosen to help her in her time of need.

But as he studied Robbie's beautiful face, already Zack was wondering. Touching her while delivering her baby was one thing. The intimacies had been dictated by nature and necessity. But volition was another matter. Becoming lovers was another matter. Would she ever let him touch her so intimately again? Touch her the way a man touches a woman when he wants to show her how much he loves her?

THE PARAMEDICS that arrived were efficient and kind and apparently they knew Zack well enough to tease him about being a good little "midwife."

"Looks like you're not gonna make it to Austin for your award," one of the guys commented.

"Award?" Robbie craned her neck up from the gurney.

"It's nothing. Come on, guys. Let's get this mom and baby to the hospital."

They backed the ambulance up close to Robbie's high porch and whisked the stretcher through the driving rain so quickly that Robbie only felt a couple of raindrops on her face.

But maybe that was because Zack was hovering over her and the baby like an eagle protecting his nestlings.

He climbed up into the ambulance behind the stretcher and the other two guys slammed the doors and got in the cab. The ride to the hospital felt insufficiently short as Robbie sensed these were to be the last private moments she and Zack would share for a while.

And suddenly she wanted nothing so much as more time with this man. More time alone so she could process these new feelings that he had churned up inside of her. Having Zack take care of her—his expert handling of the crisis, his maturity and protectiveness—had nearly overwhelmed her. She was shocked that she was making the comparison, but Danny had never been so quick to take charge of a situation, never so capable of calming her fears, never so strong and gentle with his touch. Zack Trueblood was so different from her late husband that it was positively intoxicating. And, Robbie thought with a bittersweet pang, it was positively sobering as well. How could she be thinking this way when she'd just given birth to Danny's child? But Danny seemed far away, and long ago. And Zack Trueblood was here, now.

As she watched him hook the baby's tiny fingers over his pinky, she found herself comparing nonetheless, wondering what life would be like if *he* were the father of this baby.

His gaze came up and as they looked into each other's eyes over the tiny head of the newborn, Zack leaned forward and kissed Robbie's brow as he'd done several times now, so naturally. Robbie shocked herself when, almost as naturally, she nearly kissed him back!

She swallowed, struggling to come to her senses

before these new feelings overwhelmed her. It was too soon, way too soon, to be having these feelings about a man. Wasn't it?

AT THE HOSPITAL, P.J. and Marynell and Robbie's boys were already waiting. Zack hung back as they converged around Robbie's gurney when it rolled into the hallway of the postpartum unit.

"Ahh," Frank cooed, his nine-year-old face bright with joy. "Isn't she cute?" The other brothers chimed in with praises for their new baby sister.

"I got me a granddaughter," P.J. said, misty-eyed, as he crowded near the gurney. "Thanks for taking care of my little girl, Zack." The older man gave the firefighter a nod.

"Hey, Zack! Did you really deliver my mom's baby?" This from Rob, the youngest and most unsophisticated of the three children.

"Quiet, twerp!" Mark nudged him. "Mom doesn't want to think about that anymore. It's all over now." The twelve-year-old's cheeks were mottled red.

Robbie couldn't help but notice how tightly her mother's lips were pursed. No doubt Marynell would later have caustic words to say about the way the baby was born.

"I'll leave you with your family now," Zack said.

Robbie was disappointed to see that he was determined to make a quiet exit, but she couldn't blame him. Marynell was not acting friendly. "Thank you again, Zack, for everything you did," Robbie said softly.

"I'll call you." He patted her hand. And then he disappeared from her line of vision.

"P.J.," Marynell said in her take-charge voice, "take the boys to the cafeteria for some hot chocolate. I'll help the nurse get Robbie settled."

Inside the softly lit birthing room, the nurse checked and cleaned up the baby under a warmer while Marynell wordlessly helped Robbie into a gown. After the nurse wrapped the baby and put her on her side under the warmer, she attended Robbie and finally left.

No sooner had the door swished shut than Marynell flew at Robbie. "I *told* you, you had no business going to a dance, on a night like this, in your condition. What if the two of you had got caught out on some rainy highway somewhere?"

"Zack would have handled it. Mother, I'm sorry. I'm just exhausted. I want to see the boys one more time and then I need to rest."

Marynell emitted a martyr-like sigh. "All right, then. But tomorrow, before they release you from the hospital, we have got to make a good solid plan for your care. You have got to stop acting so stubborn, Robbie, and face your situation and the fact that you have got to let us help you. I'll go down and get your dad and the boys."

Robbie had a pretty good idea what her mother's "good solid plan" would be, and she figured that by "help" her mother actually meant "control," but at the moment she was too tired to care. She was asleep before the door swished shut a second time.

THE NEXT DAY things were going smoothly—Robbie was up early for a blissfully hot shower and the baby nursed like a little pro—until Marynell showed up.

"Have you thought about what you are going to do when they discharge you?" Marynell asked.

Robbie, still nursing, was taken off guard. "Not really. I was actually hoping I wouldn't have the baby until Markie got home from her honeymoon."

"Markie! So you and your sister had something all cooked up. Well, since I haven't heard from either one of you since…since…"

"Since she married *Justin,* Mother. You can say his name. Their marriage is a good thing. He's a great guy."

"Not in my book! And Markie is certainly not the one who should be taking care of my granddaughter! All Markie knows about babies is how to give one up for adoption!"

"Mother. Please stop yelling." Robbie adjusted the baby onto her shoulder to burp her. "You'll startle the baby. And stop being so unfair to Markie. She did the best she could back then."

"She dragged this family through an absolute knothole is what she did. And now she goes off on her honeymoon with that congressman's son—the very cad who got her pregnant in the first place—just pfft! As if nothing ever happened."

"Mother. Stop it."

Marynell flapped a hand, irritated. "I don't want to talk about Markie anyway. What's done is done. I want to talk about taking care of *this* baby." Marynell gave her granddaughter a beatific smile.

The smile faded and Marynell plowed on. "You'll come home with me, of course. Your father, I expect, will genuinely love this setup—his grandsons with him on the farm. I never planned on taking care of your brood—" there was that martyr-like sigh again "—but we have to do what we have to do."

Robbie knew that was far from true. Marynell adored her rambunctious grandsons. They were the boys she wished she'd raised on the McBride farm instead of three daughters. "Mother, the boys are just now getting settled in town. I'd like to keep us all at home."

"At home? You call that dump you're living in a home? That thing is nothing but one of old man Mestor's firetraps."

"It's not a firetrap! Zack checked out the wiring and the heating system very carefully. It's a sound structure that just needs a little cosmetic work. We've made great prog—"

"*We?* Is that what this is all about? Have you actually taken up with that firefighter the way some people are saying?"

Robbie's jaw tightened, then she recovered her composure. "Mother, I want you to go now. I'm tired."

Marynell gave her a flinty-eyed squint. "You will just have to set aside your hard feelings against me, Robbie. I'm going to go home now and prepare a room for you and the baby. I'd don't want to hear one more word of argument about it. I'll be back later this afternoon."

Marynell turned heel and left. Robbie wilted back against the bed pillows. Her survival instincts warned her that if she let her mother take control of her life at this critical juncture, her little family would permanently suffer under the woman's domination and she would never regain her independence. Yet, what could she do? No money. No resources. No husband.

Zack Trueblood's dark head popped around the door. "Hi." He held forth a fistful of red roses. "Your mom almost smashed these on her way out of here."

"She was in a hurry to get away from me. We were having another fight."

Zack studied her carefully from under a concerned brow before his mouth twisted wryly and he admitted, "I know. I was outside the door…listening in."

"For shame." Robbie shook her head and tsk-tsked. "I'll never get used to your honesty, Zack Trueblood."

"Yeah, you will." He grinned. "But you won't always find it so thoroughly refreshing." He stepped fully into the room, holding forth the roses. "I grabbed these at Ardella's."

"Very pretty," she said.

"I didn't wait for her to arrange them in a vase. Hope you don't think I'm being a cheapskate."

"You? The man who's practically rebuilding my house and bought me a three-hundred-dollar dress to boot?"

"Nattie Rose shouldn't have told you the price of that dress."

"A lot of people shouldn't tell a lot of things in this town, but apparently they do. Anyway, I'm sorry that I ruined your big night, Zack. What kind of award were you supposed to get?"

He gave her a cheesy grin. "It might please you to know, *ma'am*, that your baby was delivered by one of the most outstanding firefighters in Texas."

"Oh, really?"

His expression grew nonchalant. "The award was for pride and professionalism. One of the guys brought it back to the station for me."

Robbie could believe the pride part. Zack Trueblood could be cocky to the point of arrogance. She studied him as he crossed to the sink with the roses. Even the way the man moved was cocky. And yet he could turn around and be unbelievably sweet as well.

"You didn't ruin a thing," he was saying now as he unwrapped the flowers. "Seeing your baby girl safely born beats any old award any day."

He turned on the water in the sink, then looked around, helpless. "Do you think the nurse could bring a vase?" He grinned. "That's what they always do in the movies."

"*Right*. Here." Robbie reached for her plastic water pitcher. "Put them in this."

He did, rather artlessly.

"I heard that bit about you taking up with some firefighter. I hope that would be me."

Robbie smiled and avoided his directness by patting the edge of her bed. "Come here and tell me what a pretty baby I have."

They took a few moments to savor the sleeping newborn's beauty.

"Have you named her yet?" Zack asked softly.

"No. But I have a sneaking feeling my dad will want me to name her after his mother, and I refuse to do that."

"Why's that?"

"Grandmother McBride's name was Ora Lee."

"Yikes."

She smiled at Zack tenderly. "What was your grandmother's name?"

"Leotie."

"Goodness. What were they smoking back then?"

"You weren't considering naming her after *my* grandmother?"

"Well, I'm…" Robbie could feel herself starting to blush. Yes, she had been considering it. She was getting attached to this handsome man, fast. Giving over parts of her life, like the naming of her child—Danny's child— all too easily. She looked down at her sleeping baby to cover her bewilderment. "I'm just looking for ideas."

"I have one."

"Okay."

"Danielle."

When Robbie's eyes rose to meet Zack's, she thought her heart would stop. Looking into Zack's face she could not, for the life of her, conjure up Danny's. Pain and disloyalty suddenly overwhelmed her. "Why didn't I think of that?" she whispered as tears welled up in her eyes.

"Oh, sweetheart. Come here." Zack leaned forward and pulled her into an awkward hug, being careful of the baby. "I didn't mean to make you cry."

"No." Robbie sniffed. "I know you didn't. You were

being kind, like always. Always thinking of others, even Danny. Even when his own wife wasn't!"

"You've had a lot on your mind, remember?" He rubbed her arms reassuringly, then cupped a tender palm under the baby's head. "You should name her whatever you like. Something pretty and happy. How about—" he looked at the roses he'd brought her "—Rose?"

"No. I want Danielle. It's a great idea. Danielle just fits her somehow. I think she's going to have dark hair."

Indeed, the baby's little cap of hair was nearly as dark as Zack's. He stroked the tiny curls on her forehead tenderly, then fixed his eyes on Robbie. "Listen. I've arranged for a little leave time at the firehouse. What if I came over every day to help you with the baby?"

Robbie gave a delighted little gasp. "Oh, Zack, that would be wonderful!" She had to be honest with herself. Part of her elation was that she wanted to see a lot more of this man, no matter what the circumstances. When Zack was around she felt whole, strong…and very much like a woman again.

"Your mom might still have to spend the first couple of nights, on account of those people who insist on gossiping about you and *that firefighter,* but I could come over bright and early and get the boys off to school, and then make myself useful the rest of the day."

"You'd do that?"

"For you, yes. I keep telling you, Robbie. I'd do just about anything for you."

CHAPTER NINE

I HAVE TO ADMIT I missed having my journal while I was in the hospital. There were so many thoughts and feelings I wanted to write down! My sister, it turns out, was right. A journal is a great clarifying tool. And, man, do I need some clarity these days.

But I could hardly ask Zack to go fetch a silly diary for me after everything else he's done.

Having Zack Trueblood around is like having your own personal handyman, bellhop, bodyguard, errand boy, cook and bottle-washer. It pains me to even write this, but the contrast between Zack and Danny is increasingly obvious. I never realized how lazy and immature Danny really was until I saw Zack in action when he brought me and baby Danielle home from the hospital. He was like a human dynamo! I hardly had to do a thing. The man makes me feel totally safe and secure.

I'm doubly confused because while I was in the hospital the joy of having Danielle was overshadowed by the grief of losing Danny all over again. Maybe it was my hormones working against me.

But I kept thinking of how sweet Danny could be

sometimes and, of course, I was wishing he could see the baby. But then Zack would show up with his flowers and his candy and his jokes and his amazingly practical way of handling things, and I'd find myself forgetting my pain for a while.

If only it were five years from now and my heart was completely healed. I keep wondering how long Zack would be willing to wait for me.

I loved Danny. I did. But I think the drudgery of farm life had worn me down so bad that I could hardly see the man's good qualities anymore.

Every time we'd get the slightest bit ahead, Danny would blow money on some wild irresponsible scheme. He'd lose a bundle betting on the OU/Texas game or he'd "forget" to pay our quarterly taxes, or he'd pay too much money for some useless piece of farm equipment that he always promised to fix up, but he never did. Once he actually tried to start a worm farm! They all dried up when he forgot to water them. His foolishness broke my heart, at first, but after a few years, I got just plain worn out.

It's not that I minded working alongside Danny, trying to make a go of our farm. I actually enjoyed raising a garden and canning and sewing and the like. I even got a kick out of decorating on a shoestring. Transforming our old Victorian farmhouse was fun. And if I do say so myself, I was good at it. Too bad I had to leave the house behind when I left the farm.

But nothing could make me go back out there. Nothing. Even being a waitress is better than killing myself out on that farm. In a way it's ironic that I've ended up back at the Hungry Aggie because of Danny's death. Whenever I suggested returning to my old job to ease the family finances, Danny would get all puffed up like a banty rooster and start yelling about how no wife of his was going to wait on truckers and cowboys for a few petty tips. But the tips actually haven't been bad, mainly thanks to Zack, I suspect.

Speaking of Zack, I hear him downstairs now, whistling. I think he's putting away the groceries he bought. I cannot believe this man is willing to go to all this trouble for me and my family. How did I ever get so blessed? Sometimes I study Zack's face when he doesn't know I'm looking. I concentrate on every detail of his handsome profile, wondering why I didn't notice him in high school.

IN ZACK'S MIND, those first two days with a baby in the house were golden. For Robbie, and by extension for Danielle and the boys, he was happy to dig in and do anything and everything that needed doing.

He showed up at 7:00 a.m. and cheerfully sent the grumpy Marynell on her way, then he packed the kids off to school with the efficiency of a drill sergeant dispatching troops.

For the time being, the baby's needs were easily and simply met. Robbie was an expert at breastfeeding and the newborn slept in a bassinet next to Robbie's bed with a little, well-stocked changing table nearby. So, Zack decided his first order of business after he unpacked the groceries and saw that Robbie had everything she needed for her shower, was to get the rest of the house in order. While Robbie showered he knocked off the dishes, laundry and vacuuming. He was actually glad when he heard a mewling little cry and dashed upstairs to whisk Danielle up out of the bassinet. Robbie came out of the bathroom to find him pacing the room with the wailing baby hugged against his shoulder.

"The princess is upset," he said and smiled at her.

"She needs to nurse," Robbie said. She got settled against the pillows on the bed and Zack brought her the baby.

When he turned to leave, Robbie said quietly, "You don't have to go unless you just want to, Zack. I'd like it if you'd stay and talk to me."

She tilted her shoulder away from him, undoing the front of her robe to offer a breast to the fussy baby.

Though Robbie was careful to perform the maternal task modestly enough, as Zack sat in the rocker nearby and got glimpses of tiny cheek against curved breast he felt a fascination and a level of intimacy that he'd never felt with any woman before.

They talked about mundane things, and once or twice Robbie adjusted the receiving blanket that covered her shoulder, and Danielle made amusing satisfied noises, and Zack settled into some kind of mirage state where he imagined that this was his bedroom, his baby, his woman.

He served Robbie a late breakfast and then kept her company while she sponge-bathed Danielle. Just watching the baby stretch or sneeze or yawn delighted them both. Every time the baby did something cute, they ended up smiling into each other's eyes, and another stitch of intimacy seemed to weave its way between them.

For Zack, their relationship couldn't build fast enough. He kept thinking back to the way Robbie had broken down on the night of the Firefighters' Ball and he wanted to tell her not to worry, not ever again. He would take care of her, now and forever. But he knew she needed time. So he was content to do whatever he could for her, to prove the sincerity of his feelings with endless acts of service.

He served her soup and a sandwich for lunch and figured he'd hang the curtains in the nursery alcove off the master suite while Robbie and the baby took a nap on the couch downstairs. He actually caught himself whistling while he did all these things. Everything was going just fine, and he had a whole week off. A whole week with Robbie.

But Robbie's sister Frankie disrupted their domestic bliss on the third day when she blew into Robbie's house like a wind-driven grass fire.

"SISSY! I TOLD YOU, you didn't have to come," Robbie protested as Zack opened the front door wider to admit a tall, slender woman, only slightly older than Robbie, but far more sophisticated-looking.

"You know I couldn't stay away!" Frankie dashed right by Zack and fell to one knee in front of Robbie, who was holding the baby on the couch.

The sisters clasped in a hug.

Zack had seen this attractive lady at Danny's funeral, but they hadn't formally met.

"This is Zack Trueblood," Robbie said. "Zack, this is my big sis, Frankie."

Frankie twisted to look up at him. "Hi," they said simultaneously then shook hands.

Frankie's hands were perfectly manicured and ultra-soft. She was wearing a slick-looking pale green outfit—*moleskin* his old girlfriend Lynette had once called the suedelike fabric. All the McBride sisters were as beautiful as could be, and this one was no exception. She was workout slim, ivory-skinned, and sported a short chic-looking layered haircut. Pretty in a news-anchor sort of way, but not Zack's type. From her tiny designer glasses to her chunky gold watch, she definitely had the look of money about her. And Zack had caught a glimpse of a white Mercedes at the curb when he'd opened the front door.

"You're the firefighter then? The one who..." Frankie stopped herself.

"Yes, he's the one who tried to save Danny." Robbie, who had been having all kinds of emotional upheavals in the days since Danielle's birth, seemed placid as a doe now. "And the one who delivered Danielle."

"And the one who's been over here a lot, working on Robbie's house," Frankie added with a smile. "I talked to Mother," she explained. She and Robbie exchanged a weary, knowing look.

"She didn't pressure you to come?" Robbie asked.

"Heavens, no! I wanted to get my hands on this baby. Now let me get a good look at my little darling." Frankie pressed one palm into the couch and bent her head over the baby. "Can I hold her?"

Robbie handed the baby over and the women smiled and cooed over her while Zack watched. When he started to feel a little restless, a little useless, he said, "Do you need me to get anything out of the car for you?"

"Why, thank you!" Frankie dug her keys out a pocket. "Just hit the clicker."

"Right." Zack disappeared.

The sister had enough luggage in the car to tide her over for a year.

Zack hauled it all upstairs to Robbie's room as instructed.

He felt like he hardly got to touch the baby after that. Frankie toted her around until late afternoon, did not even put the child down once as far as Zack could tell.

The boys came in from school and acted like they hardly knew their aunt. Frankie smiled brightly and told them she was going to stay and help their mother for awhile and that she was going to cook them "yummy treats." The smiles the boys gave her in return looked, to Zack, perfunctory and uncertain.

Frankie brushed the boys' spiky hair to the side, arranged their shoes in marching rows by the door, and shook their jackets out at arm's length before hanging them, as if they were contaminated or something.

When the kids went in the kitchen for a snack, she followed and opened the fridge and cabinets and surveyed the sugary cereals and cold cuts Zack had bought and said, "Just like I thought. I'd better go get some decent groceries."

Hardly an hour had passed before Frankie was turning down the volume on the TV. "Baby's sleeping," she whispered with a perfectly straight finger pressed prissily to her lips.

Robbie, wisely, Zack thought, had held to the philosophy that the baby would have to adapt to the ambient noise of the household sooner or later and that the stimulation of her brothers' racket after school would encourage the newborn to get her nights and days straight.

Before long, Zack noticed that the boys were cutting a wide swath around Aunt Frankie whenever they were in the same room. It was plain to see that the kids tried the patience of their prissy aunt, and in turn her highfalutin ways annoyed the boys.

To avoid the tension the woman created, Zack had first busied himself fixing the porch outside. When that was done, he decided to work on the warped floorboards in Robbie's utility room.

In no time, Mark came out and joined him. While Zack worked replacing some loose floorboards, Mark perched himself up on the washing machine with his size twelve feet dangling in a pair of filthy socks.

"Does your aunt have any kids?" Zack asked. She looked old enough to maybe have grown ones.

"Heck, no. All she's got is a stupid poodle named *Charm* and that P.I.A. husband of hers."

Zack grinned at the board beneath his knee and

popped in a couple of nails with his nail gun. Mark had obviously heard someone else calling Frankie's husband a P.I.A.—Pain In the Ass. Danny, perhaps?

"Can I shoot in some?" Mark asked.

"Sure."

Mark hopped down and Zack knelt beside him and guided his hand until he was sure the boy could use the tool without hurting himself. "Just keep it level."

After Mark happily popped in a few finish nails, Zack said, "P.I.A., huh? Why do you say that?"

"He's some kind of hotshot surgeon. He's never around for long, but when he is, he always does something to spoil the fun. Like he took our sparklers away from us one Fourth of July. My dad would've never done that."

"Sparklers can be dangerous," Zack allowed, though he remembered being enamored with them as a boy.

"Whatever. Anyway, they got a fancy enough house, I guess. I've only been there a couple of times. You can't touch anything and the yard's like one giant flower bed. Mom wouldn't even let us throw the football out there. It's boring."

"I see," Zack said in a low voice. "Listen, bud. I, uh, I think your aunt's in the kitchen." Zack could hear Frankie, back from her grocery run, rustling around in the cabinets.

Rob stuck his head around the corner. "Hey, Mark. You wanna go ride bikes with me and Frank? Mom said we could, long as we're back by dark."

"Nah. I think I'll just hang around out here with Zack. If that's okay?" The boy looked up at the man.

"Sure. I can always use a good helper."

Mark turned out to be an excellent little helper, too. Like any oldest child, he applied himself maturely and seriously to the task at hand. The two guys had lost track of time when Robbie came out in the utility room to check on their progress. She had showered and twisted her clean hair up, and was wearing a soft pink cotton knit jogging suit Zack had never seen before.

"Wow!" She beamed. "This place looks great!"

"Thanks," Zack and Mark said simultaneously, grinning at each other.

"Mark, would you get on your bike and see if you can find your little brothers? Frankie's almost got supper ready."

"Are you glad your sister's here?" Zack asked Robbie when the boy was gone.

"Yes and no. She's a little overbearing. I realize that. And not the best person to deal with the kids, I'm afraid."

"I noticed. I was thinking maybe I could take the boys fishing or something on Saturday, to get them out of her hair. That is, if you think she'll still be here."

The sound of dishes clanking in the kitchen made Robbie lower her voice. "Oh, she'll be here. This afternoon she told me she's separated from her husband."

Zack frowned. "Really?"

News of any marriage in trouble bothered Zack more than most. He hated divorce. Though his father had never actually married his mother, he knew how the pain of abandonment and separation had adversely affected her. And his own divorce had been costly and painful.

"I could use some fresh air." Robbie took Zack's elbow and steered him through the back door.

They walked the parameter of the shady overgrown yard as the cool air of the October evening enveloped them. They stopped by the back fence in the arc of two giant lilac bushes where they would have enough privacy to talk at length.

"So, what's up with your sister's marriage, if it's any of my business?"

Robbie sighed. "Oh, Zack. Of course it's your business. I don't have any secrets from you now."

He was glad to hear it. With her, he wanted to share everything. Every worry. Every sorrow. Every joy. "So tell me."

Robbie sighed again. "You may have noticed that Frankie's a little…inflexible."

"Seems like she's wound a little tight, yeah."

"My sisters," Robbie said heavily, sadly, as if that explained something. "At least Markie's got her life straightened out now. My mother always maintained that I was the sensible one, since I was the one who stayed on in Five Points, but the truth is, my sisters were running away from *her*. And I should have."

"I take it your mother is…a little difficult."

"She's an absolute harridan. I don't know how my father has tolerated her all these years. I suppose Frankie thought she'd escaped when she ran to Austin and started a life there. But it turned out to be a regimented life with a regimented man. Frankie's life might look easy to some, but she's had a hard time. Her husband's a very successful surgeon, a very demanding man, a perfectionist. Kyle and I have never been close. Danny flat out couldn't stand him, and I'm afraid the boys don't like him much, either."

"I already picked up as much from Mark."

"Frankie's very lonely, I think. She stopped working as a nurse long ago so she could be Kyle's…clone. Kyle's a workaholic who neglects her, so her days are spent lunching with friends, running Kyle's office and maintaining her elegant home. But she's not happy. She's always wanted a baby of her own."

"Then why doesn't she have one?"

"She's tried. She's endured all kinds of fertility treatments and several miscarriages. I don't know the latest on that score, and now that they've separated, I'm afraid to ask."

"It must be hard on her, seeing you having one healthy child after another."

"Yes. But even worse than that, my younger sister Markie gave up a perfectly beautiful child for adoption long ago. My mother's always been controlling in the extreme, but apparently she did some really underhanded things back then. None of us knew the full truth until lately—we're still in the process of forgiving her."

"I figured something was going on. I overheard your mom—at the hospital—saying something about you having hard feelings toward her."

"My feelings don't matter. It's not about me. You see, way back when, my sister got pregnant by a boy she loved very much and—"

"Justin Kilgore?" Zack interrupted.

"Yes." Robbie shot him a surprised look. She'd apparently forgotten that she told Zack that Markie and Justin were sweethearts when they were younger.

"He's a really nice guy," Robbie went on quickly to defend her new brother-in-law. "And he's doing some really important humanitarian work, when he could just be living off his family money."

"Yeah. I know about it. He seems like a nice guy."

At her second questioning look, he added, "I met him in the Hungry Aggie a few months ago. Your sister was with him."

"Oh, I see. That must have been right before he found out about Brandon."

"Brandon?"

"The child Markie gave up for adoption—their son. He's eighteen now, and a very fine young man. We've all met him, except for Mother, who refuses to." Robbie sighed heavily as if the rift in her family weighed heavily on her. "It's all really complicated. But the long and short of it is, Mother and Congressman Kilgore struck up some kind of bizarre deal that if Markie would get a hush-hush abortion, Kilgore would let me and Danny have part of his property for practically nothing. I never knew, until a couple of months ago, why we got the land so easily."

"That *is* weird." Zack stared off to the west where a low golden October sun was limning the rolling Hill Country that stretched beyond Five Points. He had always wondered, unkindly he thought, how a loser like

Danny Tellchick had gotten his hands on a prime piece of Hill Country land next to the Kilgore ranch. He looked at Robbie. What mattered now was how all of this was affecting her. "So that's why the congressman was able to foreclose on your note."

"I signed the property over to him voluntarily. So Mother would leave the matter alone. Markie was afraid Mother would go to the media and expose Brandon to unsavory publicity."

"Why would she do that?"

"Blackmail, of sorts. To force the congressman to deed me the land free and clear. But once I signed it over, Mother's teeth were pulled."

"Wow." Zack studied her profile. The lowering sun had lit her features with an amber glow. He was sure he'd never seen anything as beautiful as Robbie Tellchick's face, or anything as pure as her heart. She gave up her farm, the place she had called home for her entire married life, to protect her sister. "That's just amazing, Robbie."

"Isn't it?" Her voice rose in indignation because she was taking his meaning wrong. "I've about decided Mother would pull almost anything to get what she wants."

"I didn't mean that. I meant—" his voice softened "—the way you gave up your farm to buy peace in your sister's life."

"Oh." She turned her head and looked up into his eyes. He wondered if his admiration showed there. He hoped so.

"Markie would have done the same for me." She gave a self-conscious little shrug. "Anyway, of the three of us, I think Frankie is having the most trouble facing up to all that's happened. She feels some guilt, too, I suspect, because she helped Markie hide the baby's birth from our mother. I mean, she took her seventeen-year-old sister to a home for unwed mothers, and that's pretty *out there* for Frankie, not to mention pretending she was taking Markie to a church camp. I'm sure all that still bothers her. And I'm sure that deep down it bothers her that even though Markie was young, she still did have a baby, and that Danny and I had three—four, now—that we could barely afford."

The whole time she'd been talking Zack had been intentionally staring at her as if she were totally adorable, which she was, but when she said the last part, his expression changed. He bracketed his palms on her delicate shoulders—shoulders that, in his opinion, should not have to carry these burdens. "Hey. You've got great kids. And no more worrying about money, okay? I thought we already decided that you're doing the best you can here. You'll get on your feet sooner or later. It's only a matter of time."

She smiled up at him, looking unconvinced. "I guess it doesn't do any good to worry about it, does it?"

"Nope. All that'll do is dry up your milk." Zack wanted to slap himself. What a stupid thing to say! They weren't a couple, however much he wished they were, and he had no business making any comment that referred to the woman's breasts. He made a goofy chagrined face to cover his embarrassment.

He was relieved when she let him off the hook with

nothing more than a shake of her head and a demure smile. "The point is, Frankie's got a bad case of baby hunger, so I think we can be pretty sure she's going to take over with Danielle for a while. I know you took off work so you could help me with the baby, but would you mind very much if we just let Frankie have her way for a while. I…I hope you understand."

"It's cool. I understand about sisters." He didn't. Not at all. He didn't even understand about siblings. He had always vowed that when he got married and started a family, he would not stop at producing a singleton, a lonely child like he had been. "I can always use the time to get some of these projects around here finished. As long as I get to hold the baby once in a while, I'll stay out of the way the rest of the time."

"Zack…" Robbie raised a palm and almost laid it on his chest. *It's okay,* Zack thought, *you can touch me.* When she stopped herself, he felt deeply deprived. "You can hold the baby anytime you can get her away from Frankie. In fact, I'll make a point of taking her off by ourselves so you can. Have I…have I told you what a great guy you are?"

Matter of fact, she hadn't. And he had to admit he longed to hear her say it. "No." He swallowed. "You haven't."

"You are. I…" She bit her lip.

"You what?"

"Nothing."

"What did you start to say? Let's not have secrets, or even anything held back between us. Okay, Robbie?

Like I told you, I can wait. I can wait, for you. I can be patient. But we've started out with so much trust between us. Let's keep it."

Her cheeks were glowing with something more than the sunset now. "I started to say that…that I've never met a man like you. I…" She stopped with her lips slightly open, taking small shallow breaths as if she didn't know what to do next.

"And I've never known a woman like you, Robbie." Zack found his voice had suddenly gone throaty. He couldn't stand it any longer. His mouth went to hers with a will of its own.

When his lips covered hers, he tried to take it slow, but his hunger made him aggressive. His tongue quickly found its way inside where hers met it with a silken tremble.

She tasted like one of her herbal teas and her skin smelled of wind and sunshine and newly mown grass. With a groan her soft lips opened wider to an even softer mouth.

A thrill of sexual power shot through him as he realized she wasn't about to resist him. Only the awareness of what her body had recently been through kept him from crushing her possessively against him.

But when her soft body yielded to him even further, he held her closer anyway, despite his caution.

She groaned again and he felt the press of her breasts, lush and full against him. His hands slid down her back. Her hips were full, too. All over she felt soft, but already he could feel signs that her body was returning to its former lean, hollow-bellied proportions. She was an amazing woman, he thought, naturally slim and athletic and, even at thirty-seven, as fresh-tasting and healthy as a newly budded rose.

This kiss went on, ravenous and lush, while some primal part of him flashed on a memory—of seeing her in town once, at one of the boys' baseball games out at the ballpark on a hot summer night. The fire-fighters were playing against another small-town station in the next game. He had recognized her in-stantly, even from a distance. She was standing off to the side of the dugout, lifting her strawberry blond hair off her neck, with one tanned leg cocked out, looking at the grass at her feet. He had stared at Robbie Tellchick's long legs in those short shorts and felt a wave of absolute desire. At the time he had told himself she was another man's wife and he had no business. But it had taken him weeks to get the image out of his mind.

But now he was holding her, and she was no longer another man's wife. His heart drummed wildly while he allowed other parts of himself to feel the urges he had suppressed so long ago.

Robbie moved against him, pressing her hips in a way that told him she must be feeling those urges, too. But no sooner had he felt her heat against him, than she broke the kiss off.

"Zack, the boys'll be back soon. They'll come up the alley to put the bikes in the backyard."

He pressed his forehead to hers. "I know. But, oh,

sweetheart—" his voice was husky "—let me just hold you a second. You really do feel so right in my arms."

They clung to each other for another moment before Zack said, "They're going to find out how we feel about each other sooner or later."

"I know. It's just…one thing at a time, okay? They already have a new baby sister to get used to right now."

The dogs charged to the gate, barking, and from the alley they heard boyish whoops and the crunch of bike tires on gravel.

"They're here," Robbie said.

Reluctantly, they let go of each other.

"Listen," Zack said quickly as he grabbed for her one last time, stealing one last touch of her arm. "Can I come upstairs, to your room, later tonight?"

"You mean to hold the baby?"

"No." A meaningful beat passed. "To hold you."

With wide, serious eyes that told him the idea thrilled her as much as it did him, she backed away, nodding. Then she turned and walked toward the house. When she looked back once, a thunderbolt of electric charge passed between them.

FOR SUPPER Frankie had made an enormous pot of spaghetti—plain sauce straight out of a jar and crumbled, thoroughly browned ground beef—not the way the boys liked it. Robbie's version had giant juicy meatballs and chunks of sautéed zucchini and onions in a sauce crafted from pureed tomatoes right out of her own garden.

The meal lurched along like a strained business meeting as the kids shoved the meat pellets around on their plates and Frankie nitpicked and minced and corrected their manners.

Robbie had disappeared upstairs, breast-feeding the baby in peace, Zack hoped. The boys eventually slumped or cowed into an unnatural silence around the little kitchen table while Frankie and Zack had an uneasy time getting acquainted.

"When do you have to report for work at the fire station?" Frankie said to Zack at one noticeably quiet point.

"I don't. I took the week off."

"Oh." She made some finicky stabs with her fork at her salad of field greens—something else that boys hadn't touched. "And so you're spending your time off helping out my sister and the boys. Is that it?"

Zack had to wonder what else *it* would be. What was this woman getting at? He wondered if she'd seen him and Robbie kissing outside. And he wondered what the mother had told her. Turned out he didn't have to wonder for long.

"Mother told me you and Robbie have been seeing a lot of each other. She said you were actually going on a date the night the baby was born." Seeming to remember the boys, Frankie smiled at them with the bright smile that had been pasted on her face most of the day.

"Yes." Zack didn't elaborate. He wanted to say, *actually* we were.

Another excruciating silence passed. "Will you be

going out to spend some time with your mother while you're in Five Points?" *Please say yes.*

"I'm not…not as long as Robbie needs me. Before I spend much time around Mother, I'd really like to talk to my sister Markie first. When she gets home from her honeymoon. Some unfortunate things have happened— has Robbie told you very much about the McBride family, Zack?"

"Not much, no." Zack was determined to keep his conversations with Robbie confidential. "But I under-stand there has been some kind of misunderstanding."

"Yes. It was actually between my mother and Markie. The trouble started a very long time ago, when Robbie was only nineteen, in fact, but we didn't know the full story until recently."

The same thing Robbie had said. Zack wondered if Justin Kilgore's return to the area to start up The Light at Five Points, the humanitarian organization that assisted undocumented migrant workers, had stirred up this old trouble.

"It's been a hard year for our family." Frankie was still talking. "First Danny's death, and then…this whole thing with *Markie*." Frankie released a long-suffering sigh. "My sister was a willful urchin when she was young, and I'm afraid she's not much better now."

Despite the disdain in Frankie's voice, Zack decided that he'd be glad when the other McBride sister returned from her honeymoon, if for no other reason than to run interference with this prissy one. The mother wasn't the only controlling one in this family.

Of course, the down side was that as soon as the younger sister returned he would have to give Robbie the bad news about her husband's death.

CHAPTER TEN

OKAY. LET'S TRY to get real here. First of all, it's been a long time since a man kissed me. Almost six months, to be exact.

So, naturally, I'd be predisposed to melt in Zack Trueblood's arms. Those arms! I cannot wait to feel them around me again.

And the way he tasted! I kept biting my lips after I went in the house, wondering if I'd imagined it. I never knew a kiss could taste so good, could leave a woman so desperately wanting more.

I think I'm falling in love.

But I keep holding back because I know something's going to happen and I'm going to have to wake up from this dream. Zack's not only the most handsome man I've ever seen, he's also a good person. In fact, he's almost too good to be true. Steady as a rock, sensitive, funny and responsible in a way that Danny never was. And he's so sexy it positively makes my teeth ache! Whenever he touches me, all I can think is, it's a good thing Mother Nature is prohibiting us from getting physically involved just yet. I don't think I'd be letting him come up to my bedroom tonight if it weren't for that. I couldn't trust myself with him.

Goodness! I don't think Miss Frankie is ever going to go to bed. She keeps folding the baby's laundry into precise little stacks and running up and down the stairs to put everything in its proper place. Here she comes now….

"FRANKIE, LISTEN, SWEETIE," Robbie said as her sister swept into her bedroom. "I appreciate your doing the laundry, but you can let the rest go until morning."

"Oh, it's no trouble," Frankie said brightly as she headed to the baby's changing table. "I like to do laundry. Makes me feel productive."

"What I mean is, the boys have to go to school in the morning." Discretely, Robbie tucked the diary into her bedside drawer. "And we need to have the house settled down now."

"Oh. Oh, I'm sorry. How insensitive of me." Frankie checked her expensive watch. "It *is* getting late. But…"

Frankie sidled over to Robbie's bed, where Robbie had begun changing the baby. "But your friend Zack is still downstairs," she said in a hushed voice.

"Yes, I know. He's finishing up the back porch."

"But how are we…I mean, we can't go to bed while he's still here. Can we?"

"You go on and get some rest." Robbie did not look up from her task of fastening the diaper tabs. "Zack moved your bags to Mark's room. Mark is bunking with his brothers."

"Mark's room?" Frankie looked disconcerted, and slightly suspicious. "I don't want to put him out."

"He doesn't mind. The bed's all made up with clean sheets."

"My goodness." Frankie looked taken aback. "When did you find time to do that?"

"Zack did it. We decided it would be better this way. I wouldn't want to keep you awake all night with the baby getting up for feedings and all."

"*Zack?* I see."

Robbie sure hoped she didn't. Quickly she dug one of her romance novels out her nightstand and handed it to Frankie as a distraction. "Here. Something to read. It's a good one."

Frankie looked at the flowery cover of the book as if Robbie was handing her a loaded gun.

"Take it, sissy. I know things are strained between you and Kyle right now and I know what it feels like to need a little escape from a bad situation."

Frankie looked crestfallen. "It shows, huh?"

"It has shown for a long time."

Frankie bit her lip. "I can't talk about it yet. I'll…I'll fall apart."

"Well, whenever you *are* ready to talk about it, I'm here for you."

"Oh, sissy." Frankie's face looked relieved. "Thank you for letting me come here."

"In the meantime, it won't hurt you to read something with a happy ending. Here." Robbie held the novel out again.

Frankie accepted it with a pinch about her mouth, as if she were accepting a dose of medicine or something. "I've never read one of these."

"Well, maybe it's high time." Robbie shooed her sister off to bed.

AROUND ELEVEN, she heard the creak of the loose step on the stairs and her heart started to race. Danielle was sleeping like a kitten, warm and toasty in her little bassinet.

Robbie switched off every lamp in the room except for the small one shaped like a lamb that Zack had bought for Danielle. She wanted him to see how nicely it lit the little alcove at night.

He tapped on the door and her throat was suddenly so dry, Robbie could hardly get the words out when she told him to come in.

He poked his head around the door, his handsome black eyes shining. "Is babydoll asleep?" he said.

She smiled and nodded. "Come look."

He opened the door fully and stepped around it into the softly lit room. He was wearing jeans, boots and his perennial plain white T-shirt. He had a slight five o'clock shadow, his hair was mussed, and Robbie thought he was the most beautiful apparition she'd ever seen. The thought of how good he looked made her suddenly aware of her own appearance—loosely bound, freshly washed hair, a baggy gray T-shirt over red-and-gray striped flannel pajama bottoms. But the way she was dressed didn't matter so much because Zack's attention was on the baby.

They tiptoed over to the little alcove and stood there adoring her for a moment.

"She really is the most gorgeous baby!" Robbie whispered. It was true. Danielle had the look of the quintessential Gerber baby. Chin, nose, eyes…all in perfect proportion. And she had the sweetest little rosebud mouth that at the moment was puckered in a tiny sucking motion. With Zack, Robbie was completely unashamed of her boasting.

"You have every right to be proud." Zack slipped his arms around Robbie's shoulders and she sank against him as naturally as if they'd been married for years. She tucked her head under his chin and felt she could have stood there forever, with him holding her against his chest like that.

Pressing into Zack's incredible solidness and warmth in the glow of the little lamp, with no sound but the tick of the old clock over on the nightstand as they watched the baby's rhythmic breathing, Robbie felt like she was enveloped in some kind of timeless dream. For a while she forgot all about not having any money or having to go back to work at the Hungry Aggie in a few weeks or whether the boys were ever going to adapt to all that had happened. For the first time since Danny had died, she felt whole and at peace.

"You smell so good," Zack said, the timbre of his voice kept low.

"Baby shampoo." Robbie smiled sheepishly up at him. "It's the only kind I have at the moment."

"I'll buy you any kind you want tomorrow," Zack murmured.

"Zack, you don't have to keep doing all this stuff for me—"

"I want to." A tiny frown formed between his brows that conveyed his frustration over her refusal to accept that.

"I know, but…"

"Was that kiss too much for you? Too fast?" But even as he said it he held her tighter.

"No. I mean, yes. It was, in a way. I don't know." She tried to pull away from him but he wouldn't let her go. She let him hold her and confessed, "I'm so confused. Ever since the baby was born, it's as if something's shifted inside of me, in my feelings, and I can't tell if it's just from having a baby, or if it's more."

He wrapped his arms even tighter, running his hands up her back, rocking her gently. He had a way of encouraging her, of gaining her trust, that didn't require words. It was something in his hands, in his eyes, in his steady breathing, that she couldn't define. But at the same time that this man was drawing her to him, something else was holding her back. That's what she decided to say. With Zack, there was no need to pretend. "Something is holding me back, I know that, but I can't explain it."

"It's okay. Just let me hold you."

And so she did. And she let him caress her, and kiss her, and lie with her face to face. Heart to heart.

OVER THE NEXT four nights their meetings followed a similar pattern. The only private time Zack and Robbie managed to grab for themselves was when Frankie finally retreated to Mark's room to read the novel she'd apparently become absorbed in. Zack would steadily keep working on his home improvement projects until he heard the upstairs go quiet, usually by ten, eleven at the latest. Then he'd steal up the stairs. He had even fixed that creaky step. No sense in making Frankie or the kids feel uncomfortable.

But even if it had, he wouldn't have missed his private time with Robbie and the baby every night for all the world. He was drawn as if by magnetic force to the master suite at the top of the stairs.

He would tap on Robbie's door. She'd be in there, in the softly lit room that smelled constantly of fresh laundry and baby powder, wearing an oversized T-shirt and baggy pajama bottoms, or she would be loosely sashed into that limp pink bathrobe that he was becoming so irrationally attached to. More than once now, he'd dreamed of loosening that sash and sliding the fluid fabric down over her milky white shoulders.

Robbie would be bustling about, arranging stuff, opening and closing drawers, or she'd be bent over the baby, diapering and cooing. Once she'd been sitting up on the bed, nursing the baby. His heart had begun to race at that tender sight. But because he feared it would make Robbie tense, he tried not to look directly at her exposed breasts, though his eyes wanted to drink in the image of the mother and baby, for many reasons.

Another night, Danielle happened to be already asleep, and Robbie was propped up on pillows on the bed, scribbling in her journal. That's how he liked to find her best. Relaxed. Smiling. With her long, freshly brushed hair flowing over her shoulders.

Each night he would go to her, to bury his face in her neck and let himself feel momentarily drunk with her scent. To hold her. Kiss her. To laugh softly and have those priceless murmuring conversations with her. They talked about so many things, big and small, that he lost track of it all, when he had intended to savor every word, to store away each newly revealed thing in his heart. The fact that she liked to lie on the grass and look up at the clouds on a sunny day or that he liked to lie up on a hill and look at the stars on a clear night.

Sometimes he envied Robbie her journal and he wondered if she was writing about him in there now that they were practically lovers. They hadn't done the actual act, but he knew, and she knew, that they surely would when her body was ready.

For Zack, these nights in the quiet, intimate confines of such a feminine woman's bedroom were as near to bliss as anything he'd ever felt.

On the fifth night, when her soft voice didn't answer his third careful knock, he opened the door and peeked in. What if something had happened to them?

To his relief—and disappointment—she was asleep with the baby tucked under one arm and her diary falling open at the fingertips of the other hand. Quietly, with extreme care, he reached across to lift the baby so he could move her to her bassinet.

Danielle arched her tiny back in a stretch, stuck out

her bottom lip and raised perfect pointy little elbows up beside her ears, but her eyes didn't open. Zack smiled at the little face he had grown to love so much. *Love.* What a mystery. How absolutely certain a man could be of his feelings when it was real.

Fortunately, Robbie barely stirred when he had removed the baby. He tucked Danielle into her bassinet, realizing he couldn't feel more tenderness toward the infant if she were his own daughter.

He went back to Robbie, thinking how lovely she looked asleep. He missed her, longed to add one more night to the storehouse of their growing intimacy, but he knew he wouldn't wake her up for anything. He wanted her to rest, to fully recover from the birth. For him. For them.

He decided to just straighten the room, tuck Robbie in and be on his way.

As he slid the diary from Robbie's fingers, he glanced at the open pages. The sight of his name in her rounded handwriting snagged his attention. He read a few lines, then a few more. His whole body strummed with jubilation as he read the words, *I think I'm falling in love.*

He took a moment to savor Robbie's words about him before he idly flipped back a few pages. He frowned as he read an entry recording Robbie's heartbreak over the loss of all her dreams with Danny. He was especially touched when he read how she had always longed to plant a field of wildflowers in a certain valley out on their farm, but in the endless days of work she had never found time for such a frivolous project.

Maybe he'd give her what she wanted someday. Maybe he'd give her that field of wildflowers. Part of him felt compelled to read more, to know her deepest sorrows, her secret dreams, her heart's desire, but integrity won out and finally he placed the diary on the nightstand. As he lifted Robbie's legs to place them under the covers, she groaned softly.

She readjusted herself onto her side as he tucked the covers around her shoulders. "'Night, Zack," she mumbled as naturally as if he were going to climb into the bed beside her.

He would, someday, he vowed. As a husband who would not disappoint her. As a husband who would adore her and take care of her in a way that her first one apparently never had.

Zack stood in the softly lamplit room for some time, watching Robbie sleep, thinking about so many things. About how she sacrificed her farm to stop their mother from exposing the son Markie gave up for adoption to public scrutiny. About how he hoped that someday the hideous memory of Danny's death would no longer haunt her—or him. About how being her lover would be his greatest joy when her body was ready and the timing was right.

With a full heart, he made his decision. When her body was ready, he would be ready in other ways. He would step up his plans to start a family life with Robbie immediately. First thing in the morning, he was putting in a call to Congressman Kurt Kilgore.

KURT KILGORE was already having a bear of a day. He hadn't even left his Alexandria town house before the line that forwarded from the Capitol had started ringing. Every time the damned thing jangled, it set his jaw on edge so bad he had trouble finishing up his shave. It didn't even help that his aide and live-in mistress intercepted the calls as faithfully as any housemaid. Because he knew what they were about.

Back on the wild grass prairies north of Austin, trouble was brewing faster than a black thundercloud. The biggest highway project underway in the U.S. was giving the local politicians headaches, and now they were trying to drag the Washington politicians into the ruckus.

Misery loves company, Kurt thought as the phone on the bathroom vanity bleeped yet again. The caller ID flashed a number with a Hill Country area code *again.* Z. J. Trueblood, the name read. Who was that? Another rancher? Some no-account city councilman?

This latest little prairie-grass fire was all about the so-called Trans-Texas Corridor usurping property rights. Kurt was familiar with a phenomenon that his advisors called the "tipping point," when constituents got all excited about one thing all at once. Unfortunately, it was happening this morning.

But the Trans-Texas Corridor was going to happen, no matter how stirred up the grass-roots groups opposing it got. And to get built, the Corridor would inevitably gobble up pristine prairie lands from the well-organized farmers and ranchers who had supported Kurt for nearly two decades.

"No help for it, Vernon," Kurt told the third rancher who had called him this morning to complain that his homestead could be "flat stolen" under the state's "quick claim" program in less than three months. "I'd take the money," Kurt had advised him. What else could he say? Land got sacrificed to sprawl.

"I cannot believe I am hearing such lame talk from a Kilgore," the steamed landowner had shouted into the phone. "From a man whose own grandfather started a ranch in 1851. How'd you like to see your ranch turned into a parking lot for a cheap motel? But I expect the Kilgore house and lands have about reached that sorry pass already, now that your son has turned it into a bleeding-heart asylum for Mexicans."

Kurt hung up…and cut himself shaving. Damn his son Justin's hide. Would that Kurt had the power to plow a road right through Justin's domain. The Light at Five Points amounted to nothing but spitting in a fire in Kurt's estimation. They would end up saving a few migrants in a cause célèbre that would generate a ton of feel-good publicity, but that was all. What was the point? Justin was wasting his life.

All Kurt cared about now was avoiding this highway flap if it threatened to erode his power base. If the thing started looking like some Texas-sized boondoggle as the private investors lined up for exclusive ownership of the super-road—and all the wealth and power that repre-sented—Kurt would have to pretend that he wanted no part of it. The big companies gave politicians the most money, naturally. But Kurt had already decided he

would rather dig into his hidden cache of Mayan artifacts to fund his next campaign, risky as that would be.

Hell, it was beyond risky. It was next to impossible now,
thanks to an ignorant little hick named Danny Tellchick.

Again, he cursed that stupid little farmer who had
actually had the audacity to try to blackmail him over
the contents of those caves. He cursed the necessary
murder. He cursed the twitchy little runaway Mexicans.
Some decoys. He cursed Marynell McBride. Her most
of all. The net result of all of it was that Kurt could not
get his hands on his artifacts. Not fast enough.

"Some guy named Zack Trueblood," his aide said,
poking her pretty blond head into the bathroom. "Wants
to talk to you about the Tellchick farm. More of this
business about the Corridor, I suppose. Want me to take
a message?"

"The Tellchick farm?" Kurt's razor halted. He swabbed
the shaving cream off his jowls and quickly hooked his
wire-rimmed glasses over his ears. "I'll talk to him." He
snapped up the phone and released the hold button. When
the aide stood there too long, he shooed her away.

"Kurt Kilgore speaking."

"Congressman, this is Zack Trueblood. Thank you
for taking my call." The voice was deep, but youngish,
and had enough of a good-old-boy drawl to tell Kurt the
man was range bred.

"How may I help you, Mr. Trueblood?" Kurt's own
resonant voice, he knew, could intimidate just about
anybody. He didn't really want to help this guy. He
wanted to keep this brief, but the Tellchick Farm, as it

had been recently called, was a property Kurt could ill afford to ignore. It was, it so happened, where the artifacts were hidden. No. He could never ignore a man who wanted to talk about that place. If there had been trouble on that farm again, he needed to hear it. And firsthand, not through his aide.

"I understand that you have repossessed Robbie Tellchick's farm."

"I didn't repossess it. She let the loan go back. There's a difference."

"Yes, sir. I understand."

"I believe it was what Mrs. Tellchick wanted. She wanted out from under the loan, the poor thing. I have no use for a broken-down farm, you understand."

"Then perhaps you'll be glad to learn you have a potential buyer."

No, Kurt was most definitely not glad to hear that. "A potential buyer? Who would that be?"

"I'd like to work out the financing to assume the note, if possible. I'd pay you for any equity, of course."

"Not interested," Kurt said abruptly.

"But—"

"Now you'll have to excuse me, Mr. Trueblood. I'm having a busy day. Thank you for calling." He hung up.

ZACK LISTENED to the dial tone in astonishment. What was that all about?

Unprepared to be shut out like that, he flipped his cell phone shut numbly and wondered what his next move should be. Then a hopeful thought hit him.

Kilgore's son Justin had seemed like a decent guy. Robbie seemed to think highly of him. Zack decided to see if maybe the son could help reason with the father. He needed to talk to him about the night of the fire anyway. One more thing that would have to wait until the couple got back from Aruba.

But he wouldn't have to wait long. Within the week, Mr. and Mrs. Justin Kilgore would be returning from their honeymoon.

CHAPTER ELEVEN

"Sissy!" Robbie threw the door open wide and gathered Markie in an enthusiastic hug. "I'm so glad you're back!"

"We got in late last night." Markie stepped around some of the boys' discarded sports equipment as she made her way into Robbie's house. Her sister's enthusiastic greeting made her glad to be home, but it tugged at her heart all the more because Markie suspected Zack Trueblood was about to break Robbie's heart.

When she and Justin returned from their honeymoon, a raft of messages had been waiting on their answering machine. Most had to do with The Light at Five Points, but five were from Zack Trueblood.

"Mrs. Kilgore—Markie—" the deep-voiced firefighter had said, "I'm sorry to disturb you so soon after your honeymoon, but I need to talk to you as soon as you and Justin get back to Five Points. It's very important."

Markie had feared, before she even returned Trueblood's call, that this had something to do with the fire. The town fire marshal must have completed his investigation long ago. The delay in getting answers was worrying her.

"Is it about the fire?" she asked him immediately

when she called back. "Is it bad news?" If Danny—that shiftless little twerp—had started the fire himself and had somehow gotten trapped in the barn, would it jeopardize Robbie's insurance money?

"I'm afraid so, but I think Robbie should be the first to hear it."

"And you want me there for support?"

"Yes, ma'am."

"I should have called last night," Markie said, trying to cover her nervousness when she saw Robbie, "but it was late when…by the time I decided to come. I'm glad you're already awake."

"Honey, I'm always awake. I've got a newborn here."

"Where is our little angel?" Markie waggled a gift bag full of pink baby outfits. Presents weren't going to soften the blow, but she wasn't about to show up empty-handed.

"Wait 'til you see her! She's gorgeous," Robbie bubbled as she pulled at her sister's arm. "So bright and alert! She sucked her thumb the minute she was born. She's only ten days old and practically ready to talk! Come in, come in! She's asleep, but we can take a peek at her. Then I'll make you some coffee and you've got to tell me all about honeymooning in Aruba. God knows I could use the diversion. My life has been anything but a vacation lately—"

The rumble of an engine pulling up at the curb interrupted Robbie's nattering. "Is that somebody pulling up outside?"

Markie turned to one of the sidelight windows by the

door and glanced out. Zack's sparkling clean red pickup was pulling up at the curb.

Now she would have to explain herself fast. She whirled to her sister. "It's Zack Trueblood. He called out to Five Points and asked if I would come over here before he started his shift today—"

"Really? So early?" Robbie went to the other side-light window.

"Yes." Beyond the door came the sound of the engine being cut, then the slam of a truck door.

"What's going on?" Robbie seemed frozen in place, staring out at Zack.

Nervously, Markie peeked out again. He was striding up the walk, looking militarily handsome in a well-pressed firefighter's uniform. Zack had been only a year behind Markie in high school. So he must have been a freshman when Robbie was a senior. *Was he married?* Markie wondered as she studied him. He had a strong, pleasant face, though he was not pretty-boy handsome, and he was tall and fit enough to be in a beefcake calendar.

The sight of him, so polished, made Markie suddenly galvanized. She had an irrational moment of regret that her appearance—predictably classic and pulled together with a crisp white cotton shirt tucked into rust-colored stretch jeans, simple loafers, flawless makeup, sleek hair—contrasted so strongly with her sister's. Robbie looked a fright with her old pink bathrobe gaping open and her hair clipped up in a tangled tree-top. She was about to take a dose of bad news from that man, and she would be mortified to be sitting there in a faded bathrobe when she heard it. Too late, Markie realized she should have prepared her better.

"Maybe you'd better run upstairs and change into something decent. I'll let him in."

"Don't be silly." Robbie closed the lapels of the robe and lifted her chin defiantly. "I look just fine. This robe covers me okay and besides, Zack's already seen me in it."

"He *has?*" Markie wanted to bite her tongue for sounding even the least little bit like her mother.

"Many times." Robbie smiled and cinched up the sash. "Have you gone and got yourself married and turned into a prude, little sister?"

"A prude? Me? Of course not, but that is one extremely good-looking man walking up your sidewalk in case you haven't noticed."

"Oh, I've noticed. Look, with this guy I have never pretended to be anything other than what I am—a pregnant farm wife."

"You're not a wife anymore, you're a widow, and you're not pregnant anymore, either. Have you thought about *that?*"

"Obviously *you're* thinking about it. So, maybe you'd better mind your own beeswax, sissy."

Markie was astounded. What had become of her milquetoast middle sister during her absence? But it was too late for psychoanalysis. Zack Trueblood's knock sounded on the door. Markie peered through the sheers and saw the edge of one massive shoulder blocking the morning sun.

"Go on up," she urged as she reached for the doorknob, but Robbie stopped her.

"The robe is fine. Would you mind putting on that coffee? Zack will probably want some, too."

As she headed back to the kitchen to make a pot of coffee, Markie heard the creak of the old door's hinges. Then she heard Robbie say, "Hi. You know you don't have to knock. Come on in."

Before Markie could get over her surprise at that, she looked back just in time to see Robbie and Zack molded to each other in a full frontal embrace. She ducked into the kitchen, mouth agape.

Murmuring followed, but from beyond the kitchen door Markie couldn't make it out. What was going on between her sister and this hunk of a firefighter? She reopened the door a crack and listened.

She heard Zack's deep voice saying, "I hope it's okay that I came by so early. Is your sister Markie here yet?"

Robbie's voice: "She's making coffee in the kitchen."

Markie hurried to start making the coffee.

More murmuring, this time sounding more agitated, even a bit querulous. Then the soft slap of Robbie's house shoes accompanied by the clump of boots coming down the hallway. Then Robbie's pink fluffiness and Trueblood's masculine energy seemed to instantly fill the small kitchen. He ran a hand through his close-cropped dark hair, nodded and said quietly, "Hello, Mrs. Kilgore."

Hearing herself called that still sent a wave of happiness through Markie, but it was overshadowed by the seriousness in Zack's eyes. "Call me Markie. Nice to see you again, Zack." She explained to Robbie that they had first become acquainted at the diner.

"I know." Robbie tugged the sash of her robe tighter above the little pouch of her tummy, then seated herself stiffly in the chair at the head of the table. Trueblood pulled out a chair near her and sat down, his posture rigid as well.

Markie proceeded with the coffee, listening with her back turned to them.

"Okay. What's this all about, Zack?" Robbie's tone was oddly cool now. *Why?* Markie wondered. After all, this was the man who had tried to save Robbie's husband's life. The man who had delivered her baby.

"I'm afraid I've got to tell you something bad, sweetheart."

Sweetheart? *Sweetheart?*

"Is that why you showed up here unannounced, that first night, when the boys broke the window?"

What on earth were these two talking about? It dawned on Markie that a lot—*a lot*—had happened while she had been honeymooning down in Aruba.

"No. I mean, yes, I did intend to tell you then. I had told the chief I wanted to come over here and tell you this myself because I thought it might go easier with you, coming from me. But that wasn't the only reason I came. I wanted to help you, too. I wanted to check on you and the kids. Then when I saw how things were—"

"You mean what a mess my life is."

"Robbie. Stop. I just decided, considering everything, that it could wait until your sister was here. I didn't know the baby would come early and all of that."

Markie peeked over her shoulder to see Robbie self-consciously smoothing her tangled ponytail into shape. "All right. Just tell it to me then."

"I want you to promise me something first." Trueblood tried to touch Robbie's hand, but she withdrew it, so he folded his large hands on the table as the coffeemaker started to emit gurgling noises. "I don't want you to get yourself all upset. You need to stay calm for the baby."

"I'll stay calm." Robbie's voice grew even colder.

"Okay. Let's wait 'til your sister sits down."

Feeling incredible apprehension, Markie set three of Robbie's better cups and saucers on the table as the incongruously pleasant aroma of freshly brewed coffee started to fill the room.

"You take anything in it?" she asked Zack.

"Nothing, thanks," Zack said.

Robbie frowned at her and slid a palm over her cup. "No caffeine for me. I'm nursing."

"I'll make you some tea then." Markie started for the tin of herbal tea on the counter.

Robbie raised a hand to stop her. "Sit down. I want to hear what Zack has to say."

"Let me pour the coffee first." Markie carried the carafe over and felt the oddest sense of detachment, as if she were Nattie Rose at the café, while she filled two cups. But it went away as soon as she lowered herself into the chair right next to Robbie and looked into her sister's accusing eyes.

"You know what this is all about?"

"No." But Markie suspected.

Robbie turned her head to Zack, calmly. "Well, are you going to tell us what it is?"

Zack cleared his throat and gave Markie a concerned glance. "The fire marshal has completed his initial report and Danny's final autopsy results are in."

"You've seen the paperwork?" Markie put in.

"No, ma'am. I just have the information the fire marshal told me in person." He paused and leaned toward Robbie, giving her his full attention. "And I'm afraid I have some bad news, sweetheart." Unselfconsciously, he grasped Robbie's small hand in his large one.

Her cool facade crumbled as Robbie reached the other hand toward Markie.

Markie took it instantly. Robbie's fingers felt like ice. "I'm here for you, sissy," Markie said.

Trueblood's gaze swept over the two women, then fixed steadily, sorrowfully, on Robbie's face. "It was ruled arson."

"Arson?" Robbie's hand tensed.

"The fire was started with an accelerant. Tractor gasoline, looks like. Poured around the concrete slab of the barn."

"But…I thought it was those giant hay bales going up?"

"That's what made the fire so hot, yes."

Robbie's posture wilted as she lowered her head.

Then Robbie started to shake. Her face seemed to go white under her freckles, her pale eyelashes fluttered against the bluish rings under her eyes, and her down-turned lips looked suddenly bloodless, parched and chapped. But Trueblood was gazing at her with an adoring, pained expression, as if she were a beautiful damsel in distress that he, personally, intended to rescue.

Markie watched in mute fascination as Trueblood's thumb worked the top of Robbie's knuckles. As if they'd been holding hands at this kitchen table all of their lives. What was the deal here? Did Zack Trueblood have a crush on her sister? And Robbie. She started to cry as he rubbed her hand, angling her head at a dependent angle toward his massive shoulder. She extracted her hand from Markie's, not Zack's, and planted it like a visor over her eyes. Zack put his other hand on Robbie's shoulder, bracketing her with Markie. Markie felt the soft fabric of the robe pull away from her fingers as the strong man rubbed Robbie's back, then pulled her firmly into his embrace.

Robbie clung to him, and he let her cry.

After a while Zack continued gently, "There's something else." His voice was full of regret. "Danny was already dead when I pulled him out of that barn. The medical examiner determined that he did not die of smoke inhalation or of his burns. There were no traces of smoke in his lungs and the burns were not that extensive."

Robbie slowly raised her head and sat up straight. Her gaze fixed on Trueblood's. "Then what…?"

"A blow to the head."

"Do you mean like foul play of some kind?"

Trueblood squeezed her hand, leaning closer. "Sweetheart. No. It was likely from a fall or some object hitting him from the hayloft."

"No." Robbie was shaking her head.

"Sweetheart."

"So you're saying Danny torched his own barn?" Robbie's voice rose. "Is that what the fire marshal thinks?"

"It looks likely, considering his financial picture."

"But there were some illegal aliens on our land," Robbie protested, "right before the fire!"

"Now hold on." Markie defended the Mexicans who had been staying at The Light at Five Points. "Those men are innocent. They had nothing to do with the fire. They indicated to Justin they were bribed to loiter around the caves by someone."

"Well, for crying out loud, then who bribed them?" Robbie's voice rose higher.

"We have no idea, Robbie," Markie explained patiently. "You know as well as I do that the Morales brothers have disappeared. They were scared to death."

"Then shouldn't the sheriff be finding out where they are? Shouldn't the sheriff be investigating this blow to the head?" Robbie's face flushed. "What if Danny was murdered?" Tears sprang to her eyes.

"Sweetheart." Zack grabbed her hand again. "You've got to stay calm. Remember? For the baby."

Robbie twisted free. "How can I sit here like some contented cow when someone might have killed my baby's father? You don't understand how I feel! And neither do you, Markie. Neither one of you has lost a spouse like that." Robbie looked ashamed the minute she'd shouted the words, for Zack and Markie both had done everything in their power to support her. And both had been through terrible pain in their lives. Zack broke the stunned silence.

"I'd do anything to undo what happened that night," he said softly, "to bring him back for you, Robbie. And for the boys. You know that. But I can't."

"I know that. You tried, in fact." Robbie swallowed and closed her eyes. "You've done so much for me. And I never even thanked you for trying to save him." A fresh tear leaked out from under her eyelashes. "For the way you…you risked your own life."

"No," he said quietly, hushing her, soothing her. "You don't have to thank me." He dug a Kleenex out of the breast pocket of his uniform and reached up and wiped away the tear. "It's going to be all right," he continued in the same hushed, reassuring tone. "I'm going to keep an eye on this situation until we get to the bottom of it."

Robbie released Zack's hand to take the Kleenex and pressed it to her eyes.

"In the meantime, if you, or your sister—" it seemed to Markie he said *sister* more pointedly "—have any information that might help in the investigation, would you come to me? Other than that, I want you to let the sheriff handle this." He ducked his head to look more directly at Robbie's downcast face. "Would you do that for me?"

Robbie nodded, staring at the table, pressing the Kleenex to her nose.

Zack turned to Markie. "I've got to report for duty now, but I'll check back with you later."

Over her Kleenex, Robbie shot Markie a determined look.

"I'll see you out." Markie got up.

When they were outside on the sidewalk, Trueblood said, "I hate to leave her like this. She didn't take that well." He looked back at the house with a worried expression.

"Well, why would she? But it's always better to know the truth. I think she suspected something was not right about that fire. Even for a barn fire, it went up so fast."

Trueblood nodded.

"Do you agree that Danny did this himself?" Markie was thinking of how bad the farm's books looked when Robbie had finally let her see them, of how Danny might have been desperate to sacrifice a dilapidated barn for the insurance money.

Zack frowned. "I've seen cases like this before. All I can say is, it's a good thing nobody else was hurt. Most times you can't stand to get within two hundred feet of a hay bale on fire. The gasoline was unnecessary, matter of fact, but it kind of cinches the arson thing."

"If Danny set the fire himself and accidentally bumped his head before he got out, that means Robbie will lose the insurance money she so desperately needs. Right?"

"I'm afraid so. I didn't tell Robbie this, because there's no reason to upset her even more, but something about the way the investigation was handled makes me uneasy. The fire marshal took a long time to reach his conclusions. And…" He hesitated.

"Tell me. I'm her sister."

"It's something I saw the night of the fire, on my way into the back side of that barn."

"What?"

"Drag marks. In the dirt. Like somebody had recently pulled something heavy into the barn. I should have had the guys take pictures that night."

"You were pretty busy that night. And according to my sister, you got pretty emotional at the scene, after you tried CPR. And didn't you get some burns that had to be treated?"

He shook his head no, though he had been burned along a tiny line on his forehead where the mask slipped. "Well, it's too late to follow up on those marks now. The site's been cleared. Even the concrete slab is gone."

"What about the first Mexican illegals Danny claims he saw out on his land? That angle seems to have been dropped."

"What do you mean the *first* ones? They're not the same ones who admitted to your husband they'd been over there, in the caves?"

"The Moraleses? I wasn't there when they talked to Justin but they indicated to him that there were some other men, coyote types, who'd been there earlier. They were scared to death the night they ran from Five Points, rattling on about getting blamed for the fire. But that's all we know. They are long gone now. Disappeared into the ether the way undocumented migrants do."

Zack dug in his shirt pocket. "I'll do some more

checking with the fire marshal. Here's my card. My home and cell phone numbers are written on the back. You can call me anytime. Anytime. But especially if you or Justin hear anything from these Morales brothers."

"I will," Markie promised.

Trueblood looked up at the second story of the old house.

"Now that you and your sister Frankie are here to help Robbie, I should have more time to do some checking around. I'd like to have a talk with the migrants living out at The Light at Five Points. And I'd like to talk to Justin, too."

"I'll tell him to call you."

When Markie went back into the kitchen she bent to wrap Robbie's shoulders in a hug. "You go ahead and cry, sweetie."

Robbie sniffed. She straightened in her chair and blew her nose. "What'd Zack say out there?"

Markie started cleaning up the coffee cups. She didn't want to worry her sister with talk of Mexican coyotes and the like. "I think Zack is genuinely concerned about you. And a blind man could see he's interested in you in more romantic ways as well."

Robbie gave Markie a look that would have curdled milk. "I hope to goodness you are listening to yourself. There's nothing romantic about this situation. I've just had a baby and now my dead husband is being accused of torching his own barn."

Markie could see no point in encouraging her sister's denial. She herself had learned firsthand the high cost of denying one's true feelings. She had, after all, seen Zack and Robbie hugging. "It's okay, you know, to let yourself fall in love again."

"Who's falling in love?" It was Frankie coming into the kitchen with the baby strapped to her stomach in a Snugli.

"Sissy!" Frankie and Markie went to each other and hugged, being careful of the baby's head, then taking a moment to coo over her.

"How was your honeymoon?" Frankie studied Markie with a wan little smile that was as sad as it was well-wishing.

Markie gave her a curious look in return, but only said, "Wonderful. Really, really wonderful."

"I'm glad you're happy." Frankie's gaze fixed on Robbie's tear-blotched face. "What's going on in here?"

Robbie shook her head and pressed the Kleenex to her nose again.

Markie spoke up. "Robbie just got some bad news from Zack Trueblood."

"I thought I heard his voice." Frankie patted the baby. "Listen. Danielle is getting fussy. She needs to nurse. But I can make her a bottle if you're too upset."

"Don't be silly. Give her to me." Robbie raised her chin and held out her arms for the baby.

"What kind of bad news?" Frankie said as she undid the Snugli.

Robbie was busy loosening her clothing for the baby so Markie answered for her. "It seems the barn fire was caused by arson."

"Arson?" Frankie handed the baby down. "I thought it was some kind of accident with the tractor gasoline."

"It was no accident," Markie informed her seriously. "Somebody used the gasoline as an…an…"

"Accelerant," Robbie supplied the word Zack had used.

"And Zack came here to inform you of that himself?" Robbie nodded.

"I can see why he wanted to be the one to give you the news." Frankie sighed.

"What does that mean?" Robbie looked up, her expression defensive.

"Everybody can see that the man is thoroughly smitten with you."

"Smitten?" Robbie intoned dryly with her eyes fixed back on the baby, but her cheeks were blazing.

"Sissy." Markie stepped in with her two cents. This was the way it had always been with the McBride sisters. No pretense. No secrets. "Wake up and smell the aftershave. The man is clearly crazy about you."

"And he's crazy about this baby," Frankie added as she looked at her niece fondly. "I could see it from that first day I came here." Frankie crossed to the window that faced the street and peeked out. Trueblood's red pickup was gone, of course. "A guy like that can have any woman he wants, and probably does. At first I thought maybe he felt sorry for Robbie because here she is—new baby, no husband."

Robbie shot her sisters a warning look. "There is nothing untoward going on between me and Zack Trueblood. We barely know each other, for crying out loud."

"Nobody said anything about anything *untoward*. I just wish you'd stop denying your own happiness." Markie couldn't help sounding exasperated. Robbie and her rule book. "You can honor Danny's memory and still have a new relationship, you know."

"It's too soon for me to be thinking about a new relationship." Robbie bit her lip and her expression became tight as she looked down at the baby. "It would be disloyal to Danny."

"Sissy, you can't go on grieving forever," Markie insisted. "Besides, what about Zack's feelings? I saw you hugging him."

"Oh, *really?*" Frankie turned from the window.

Robbie's shoulders grew tense and Danielle fussed at her breast. "I wish to goodness you two would mind your own business." She looked down at the baby. "Honestly. You two sound as nosy as Mother and Ardella. Or old man Mestor."

"Mestor?" Markie looked to Frankie. "You'll have to translate that one for me."

"He said something about Zack being sweet on Robbie during a big argument they had in the Hungry Aggie. It was raining outside, so practically the whole town was in there to witness it."

"An argument? About what?"

"Me." Robbie had resumed nursing Danielle.

"Really?" Markie's eyebrows went up.

Robbie waved off her sister's interest and focused firmly on the baby. "It doesn't matter. I don't give a flying eff what anybody in this town thinks of me.

There is nothing…romantic between me and Zack Trueblood."

"Why else would he be coming around like this, sweetie?" Frankie said.

"Mestor only talked like that because he thinks Zack was after my farm," Robbie explained to Markie, still not taking her eyes off the baby.

Frankie elaborated. "Apparently Zack expressed an interest in Robbie's farm. Inquiring at the bank about taking over the loan."

"Oh. I see," Markie said. "I guess that was before she let it go back to the congressman."

"The *congressman?*" Frankie scoffed. "The man is your father-in-law now, for Pete's sake. Can't you just call him Kurt?"

"Not really. I hardly know him. And I don't especially want to. The congressman's world is all about the congressman."

"Yeah. I thought it was strange when he couldn't even make it to his own son's wedding."

"Old man Kilgore is not the point. Our sister's situation *is*." Markie adopted a pensive expression. "Back to Zack. So, he lit into old man Mestor for accusing him of trying to get your farm?"

"No. He didn't hit him until he made some kind of crack about the fire. You know—" Finally Robbie looked up from the baby, her closed expression transformed. Eyes wide, mouth agape, she said, "That's odd. Mestor seemed to have some idea that the fire wasn't an accident. I wonder what made him say that?"

"What did he say?" Markie was still desperate to get caught up on all that had happened in her absence.

"He said something about that being an awful lot of spilt gasoline for a simple accident."

"And that's when Zack hit him?"

"He knocked him off his bar stool."

"Wow." Markie's eyebrows shot up. "I've always admired Zack Trueblood. I remember when he got the award that time. He was pretty young, too."

"The Eagle," Robbie said absently, with her gaze contentedly fixed on the baby. "When he was in the ninth grade."

Markie and Frankie exchanged a conspiratorial look their middle sister couldn't see. "Do you remember anything about Zack from high school?" Markie asked Frankie in a tone that was more innocuous than the look.

"Not at all. He was way after my time. He was only, like, in the seventh grade when I graduated. But what I've seen of him lately makes me think he's a pretty stand-up guy."

"Even if it comes from Zack Trueblood," Robbie said, looking up, "I'm not buying the so-called official explanation."

"Are you thinking you'll have to prove them wrong to get your insurance money?"

"All I know is I need some answers before I can go on with my life, and as soon as I have the strength I am going to find them. I'm planning on digging into the investigation myself as soon as the baby is past this newborn stage. I am not going to just let this go by."

"But what are you planning to do?"

"First of all, I'm going to get a copy of Danny's autopsy."

"What good will that do?" Markie argued. "You wouldn't know what any of it meant any way."

"Kyle would."

"Oh, no." Frankie put her hands up. "I'm not asking any favors of that man."

Markie looked at the oldest sister curiously. "Has something happened between you and Kyle?"

Robbie and Frankie exchanged a loaded look over the baby's head.

"Tell her." Robbie held Frankie's anxious stare with a level gaze. "It won't do you any good to hide the truth."

"Kyle is having an affair," Frankie blurted.

"What?" Markie clanked her coffee cup down on the saucer.

"With his nurse."

"Why, that sneaky little bastard!"

"Maybe it's partly my fault. I don't know." Frankie's beautiful features crumpled in misery. "After the last miscarriage, he became so distant. It seemed like I couldn't do anything to please him anymore. I have to admit, I found it easier to withdraw than to face our problems."

"You listen to me, sissy." Markie aimed a finger at Frankie. "Don't you dare take the blame for his bad behavior. *Dr. Kyle* is nothing but a freaking middle-aged cliché!"

Robbie raised the baby to her shoulder to burp her. "Markie's right. Kyle has been a little prick from the get-go, and now he's just matured into a little prick with male menopause. You've been a great wife to him, and you deserve far better. What you deserve is a real man, not some selfish little egomaniac who's always acted like he's the sun and you're his satellite."

Listening to Robbie talk like that, Markie marveled again at how much her middle sister had changed in only a few short months. "What are you going to do now?" Markie asked Frankie.

Frankie slumped back against the counter with her long legs crossed at the ankles. "I don't know. Kyle refused to break it off with her, so we're officially separated. I told him I was going back to Five Points and that I didn't know when, if ever, I'd be returning to Austin."

"You don't have to ever go back if you don't want to," Robbie offered kindly. "You can stay here with me and the boys and Danielle as long as you want to."

"That's sweet, honey, but Mark is going to want his room back sooner or later. I was thinking maybe it's time for me to go out to Mother and Daddy's for a little while."

"You'll go crazy staying up in that attic room," Robbie argued.

"Actually, I'm kind of looking forward to it. It can be peaceful out there, you know? Maybe it'll help me think."

"Mother will be breathing down your neck, trying to get you to reconcile with Kyle," Robbie continued to try and dissuade her.

"What did Kyle say when you told him you didn't know if you'd ever be back?" Markie was worried about her sister. Frankie's whole world had revolved around her home and her husband.

"He said—" Frankie's voice choked off and she pressed her two middle fingertips to the corners of her eyes. "He said that I could do whatever suited me and to communicate with him through our attorney."

"That cold-blooded reptile," Robbie spat. "I say, skin him alive. Take him for every dime he's got."

"Robbie, hush!" Markie said. "The last thing Frankie needs is that kind of talk."

"Maybe it is exactly what she needs! Sometimes a woman has just got to get her back up and fight!"

"Shh!" Frankie silenced their arguing with a flapping hand. "I hear the boys getting up." She dried her weepy eyes and went to the fridge to take out orange juice and milk for their breakfast.

"We'll talk about this later," Robbie promised with steely determination in her voice. "All of it."

CHAPTER TWELVE

NOW THAT THE KILGORES were back from their honeymoon, Zack wasted no time in taking care of the other business he'd had on his mind. After his twelve-hour shift, he drove out to meet with Justin Kilgore late in the evening.

A long drive in the country always set his soul free and his mind to running.

The stunted trees stood like black cutouts against the lavender band of twilight that separated the dark sky from the even darker landscape. To his left the moon rose high and hard, a lone companion over the endless rolling landscape as Zack barreled down the narrow country road.

The repetitive sound of gravel spitting against the pickup's undercarriage like shotgun pellets took him back in time with hypnotic power, while the flicker of his sidelights on the weedy growth in the bar ditches flashed memories across his mind like images scrolling past on a movie screen.

He remembered riding down this very same road in his grandfather's pickup. Out here, with Gramps, things were always set to rights. In town, he always saw himself as kind of an outsider in the closed culture of Five Points. Though he eventually evolved into the typical high school football jock with the handsome smile and the charming wit, in his heart he carried the knowledge that his mother had given birth to him when she was far too young, and that his father, an oil field roughneck, never wanted anything to do with Five Points...or with raising a kid.

It was funny, Zack thought, how things worked out. Though his mother had been forced to work long hours as a nurse, making it necessary for Zack to spend many a weekend out on his grandfather's farm, it had ended up being a blessing for young Zack. Working in his grandfather's vast wheat fields alongside the steady older man, Zack eventually became aware that his masculinity and personality had been well-formed.

Even if his father had left the family when Zack was still an infant, Zack had ended up being a man who was grateful for many things in his life: having his grandfather as a mentor, learning to be hardworking and honorable, the exposure to his mother's medical skills that made him immune to squeamishness, his ability to handle emergencies with amazing calm, his compassion for "ordinary folks" and their problems.

When he joined the Navy shortly after high school graduation, he counted himself lucky because he got his training as a firefighter and paramedic, even if it was in the high-anxiety environment of an aircraft carrier. He was glad he'd learned how to kick some butt, too, if he had to. He was also grateful that he'd seen a good chunk of the real world.

He was glad that when his stint in the Navy was over, he had returned to Texas to spend time with his grandfather before the old man had passed on. The ways of his Texas grandfather—driving a pickup, wearing cowboy boots and a Stetson, helping the downtrodden—had been the reason Zack had decided to put down roots in Five Points. And now his long-held goal to live in peace and someday raise a family in the way that his grandfather had raised him seemed near at hand, even if he did still have a streak of the wild boy left in him.

He smirked as he hooked an arm out the truck window so the night air could beat at it. He wondered what Miss Robbie would think of the tattoo high on his biceps that he had acquired in the Navy. But maybe she would understand why he had wanted an eagle. He eased up on the gas. He still liked to drive too fast on remote country roads, one of many bad habits he'd have to break now that there were going to be people, little people to boot, dependent on him.

The shock and hurt he'd seen in Robbie's eyes this morning weighed heavily on his mind behind all these lighter thoughts. But he hoped he was about to fix everything for her.

He made a slow turn under the ranch gates that met in the Kilgore brand at the center.

The operation known as The Light at Five Points was way out on the Kilgore property, at the end of a dusty ranch road, housed primarily in the old limestone mansion, which, even in the dark, looked impressively restored since the last time Zack had seen it.

Justin Kilgore and Zack Trueblood established a rapport immediately. Men of the range, both had the cut-to-the-chase, plain-spoken way that let them get business done with little fuss and much honor.

"I don't know what my old man's deal is with holding on to that little farm," Justin said ruefully as he led Zack to his sparsely furnished office at the back of the big Kilgore house. "Have a seat."

They sat in two spindle-backed chairs in front of a cold hearth. "Every downstairs room in this old mausoleum has a fireplace," Justin explained as he propped a boot against the stone. "But we don't burn them much. Although I've got plenty of help to clear cedar for firewood out here."

"The migrants," Zack confirmed.

"Yes. Hardworking people. My goal is to help them become citizens and gain the confidence to move up to more highly skilled jobs," Justin explained. "Some of the men are excellent stone masons, coming from a very long Mayan tradition. I wanted to quarry more limestone out near those caves and let them get practical experience restoring some of the abandoned ranch buildings. God knows we could use the living quarters. But my own father won't let me near those caves."

Zack frowned. "If he's letting the farm just sit there, why do you suppose he's hanging on to it?"

"Anybody's guess. For a while I thought he might want to get in on this Trans-Texas thing—"

"The communications and transportation corridor?"

"Yep. But that's not it. This area is too far out of the way, and most of those deals are done. I think he's just mad about what I'm doing out here. But sometimes I can reason with him, and I haven't asked a favor in a long time. If I can get my father to sell you the farm, or at least let you start to work it, will you agree to give me access to the limestone?"

"Absolutely," Zack said, seizing upon this idea. He had no use for the limestone. "And tell your father I'll pay top dollar—more than top dollar—for that land."

They shook on it, and their deal was struck.

Within days, Justin had convinced the congressman to sell Zack the area of the farm where Robbie's old house was located and some acres around it but, strangely, Kurt insisted on retaining the land where the limestone formations and caves were embedded.

"I would assume it's because the *congressman* doesn't want me to use the limestone to restore the ranch buildings," Justin explained after the deal had been made, "because he resents the fact that I'm using my part of the property to help illegal aliens. But there's something else—I just haven't figured out what."

"Something else?"

"Yeah. Years ago—back when Markie and I were kids—we saw Dad out by those caves. His Cadillac was just parked out there, on the rock mound, in the middle of the night. And then last summer—right before the primary—my son followed Dad into the caves one night. It was a bizarre night, let me tell you. We never did figure out what Dad was doing in there. And at the time, some concerns about my son took precedence."

"Your son?"

"Brandon. I shouldn't call him my son, actually. He's got parents. Good ones who adopted him at birth."

"Oh. I see." Zack realized this was the child Robbie had told him about. Sensing that Justin did not really want to talk about this sensitive subject, Zack returned to the more immediate concern. "You ever had a look around in those caves?"

"Oh, yeah. I've crawled back in there a time or two. Didn't find a thing. Those caves go on forever. That is one stipulation." Justin seemed uncomfortable saying this. "Dad demanded that you absolutely stay away from those caves. He claims they're dangerous. Claims he doesn't want to get sued."

"I see. Well, in any case, I'm sorry about the limestone," Zack said, "and about your old man's attitude toward your work." He'd always been mildly envious of people with fathers—of any kind. But looking at Justin Kilgore's downcast face, he realized maybe there were worse things than having no father—like having a really bad one.

"I'm used to it." Justin shrugged. "I was just glad I could help you."

"I really appreciate what you've done. For Robbie's sake."

"For Robbie?"

"I'm getting the place for her. But don't tell her. I want it to be a surprise."

"So you're really that serious about her?"

"Ah. I see the sisters have been talking."

"Let me tell you something, my friend. If you are going to get serious about a McBride chick, you might as well face facts. There are *no* secrets."

Both men chuckled.

"Well, let's you and I see if we can keep this one for a while. It will mean a lot to Robbie to get even part of that farm back, but I'd like time to fix up the place a little bit before she sees it again. My goal is to be done by Christmas."

"By Christmas?" Justin echoed.

"Yeah. This'll make as good a present as any—to give the lady her farm back. Don't you think?"

As soon as Zack had the papers in hand, he went out to the farm. He put his pickup in four-wheel drive and drove as much of the place as he could. When he almost got stuck crossing a low creek, he decided he'd eventually need a beat-up old Jeep for navigating the place, maybe even a horse. His mind filled with happy plans until he came upon the burnt-out barn site. He got out and walked that half-acre space, then made up his mind to plant something there, something to help her forget.

As troubling as the charred grounds around the barn were, the brand-new fence and pad-locked ranch gates he found at the western edge of the property was more troubling. Kilgore had sure acted fast.

He parked the truck on a rise in the road and got out. It was a perfectly clear day, and in the distance he could see the rock formations under which the caves lay. In the broad light of day, they looked bluish-gray, but when he'd seen them before, at sunset, the reflected light had brought out the more colorful tones of the pink granite and yellow limestone. It was a beautiful spot, but strangely remote and ominous. Native peoples—his father's people—attached supernatural properties to these Hill Country rock formations. Superstitions notwithstanding, Zack had never cared for caves.

He got back in the truck and before long found what was sure to become his favorite spot on the farm. Atop a high hill, an old square limestone house sat perched with hollowed out windows and viney overgrowth. Zack loved it immediately. He stood on that hill, looking out over the endless rolling land that seemed almost prehistorically untouched and knew that at last, he was home.

He started to work on the place that very day. By sundown he was sweating bullets from clearing brush along the drive but he wanted to keep going until the last glimmer of light had faded. He wouldn't have another day off for four days.

He thought he was seeing things in the dusk, when he noticed the headlights of a vehicle winking in and out of the low live oaks and cedar breaks in the distance. He wiped his brow and stared. They were headed out to where Kilgore had erected the new fence in the area of the caves.

Trespassers already? Though he'd agreed to stay away from there, Zack got in his truck to go check it out. He bumped off into the trees and doused his own headlights well in advance of his approach. He stayed hidden while he watched some men moving items out of the caves into an expensive SUV. He pulled his binoculars out of his glove box and honed in for a closer look.

The men were definitely Hispanic—dark skin, slicked-back black hair, goatees, heavy chains and crosses around their necks. He even heard them yelling an occasional Spanish expletive.

Well, Miss Robbie, he thought, *looks like you've got good reason to be suspicious.*

Robbie. The hardest part of fixing up the farm was going to be making lame excuses to Robbie about his absences.

CHAPTER THIRTEEN

I WAS LYING IN BED just now and had a revelation so startling, it caused me to sit up so fast I was afraid I'd wake the baby.

Zack is covering something up. What or why, I can't imagine. But I can sense some secretiveness in him whenever I see him lately. After all, he hid the results of the investigation from me for quite a while, didn't he?

All I know is, I can tell when a man is hiding something. I had enough of that crap with Danny. I keep thinking about the night before he died. How he came into our bedroom and looked sort of white around the gills, but bright-eyed and overexcited. He changed out of his muddy clothes and told me he had to go to town, and when I pressed him about what was wrong, he got mad and had another one of his weird outbursts. He said didn't I have enough to worry about with making babies and all?

But now I'm getting the same vibes from Zack. Like he's keeping something from me. More stuff about the investigation, perhaps? Or am I just being paranoid? All I know is, I won't rest until I know the real story of what happened in that barn fire. And if Zack Trueblood needs his space, I'll be happy to give it to him. I'm going to be busy anyway. The old Henkel drug store is up for sale. And I've got ideas for it.

WHEN ROBBIE TELLCHICK flew into action, she flew into action full tilt, and when she started to snoop, she started to snoop in earnest.

She contacted the state medical examiner and asked for the autopsy right away. When she got stonewalled there, she contacted a man in the office of the district attorney, who pointed her to a criminal investigator.

His name was Luke Driscoll, a former Texas Ranger who specialized in cold cases. Although Danny's case wasn't exactly cold, because it wasn't exactly murder, in Robbie's mind it wasn't exactly closed, either.

"Mrs. Tellchick. What can I do for you?" Driscoll's laconic west Texas drawl reminded Robbie of the hero in some old Louis L'Amour Western.

"I am trying to get some answers in the investigation of my husband's death."

"And your husband was?"

"Daniel Tellchick. He died in a barn fire last May."

"Doesn't ring a bell," Luke said in his mellow, gravelly voice. "If it was a fire, the local fire marshal would handle that."

"He is. Or was. I mean, the local fire marshal recently informed me of his findings. After quite a delay, I might add. He ruled the fire itself arson, but said my husband's death was an accident. He thinks my husband set the fire, then got bumped on the head by a falling pulley before he could get out."

"And you don't think that?"

"No, I do not. I think my husband's case has been swept under the rug for some reason."

"Why's that?"

"There were some Mexican illegals skulking around some caves on our property right before the fire happened."

"Say again?"

She could sense the investigator was suddenly listening more intently. "I said, there are some underground caverns on our property—well, it's not ours anymore. I let the land go back to its original owner, Kurt Kilgore."

"Congressman Kurt Kilgore?" There was something sharp and predatory in Driscoll's tone now.

"Yes. Anyway, some men, Danny said they were Mexicans, probably illegals—we get a lot of them trespassing in this part of the country, and they were speaking Spanish—who were sneaking around in those old caves the night before the fire. He shot at them. What if they set the fire and just made it look like arson so Danny would be blamed?"

"Whereabouts did you say this fire took place?"

"Outside Five Points. That's a town southwest of Austin."

"I know where it is. Could you hold on one minute, ma'am? I am going to record this." Robbie heard a click, then a soft squealing noise, followed by Driscoll's voice repeating her name and the facts illuminated so far in a low monotone.

"Now, ma'am, could you tell me again what kind of Mexican illegals these were?"

"What do you mean what *kind?* How many kinds are there?"

"They are not all alike, ma'am. Some are just simple migrant workers, basically honest people trying to make their way to a better life. But some are involved in truly illegal activities like smuggling. Narcotics. Humans. We call those types 'coyotes'. They are the worst of the bad hombres."

"I don't know anything except what my husband told me. When he caught them trespassing on our farm, he took some potshots at them with his rifle, and they shot back. I think that is significant, Mr. Driscoll. Isn't it possible they came back and harmed him out of revenge or whatever? Why are these people not being tracked down?"

There was a long silence, and then Driscoll's bounty-hunter voice drawled, "Where did you get my name, Mrs. Tellchick?"

"I looked up the district attorney in the phone book. When I got a receptionist on the line, I asked her who I could talk to about a cold case—a homicide. Danny's isn't one, but I've been watching a lot of TV lately."

"The receptionist, huh?" He sounded mildly annoyed.

"Yes, sir." Robbie thought the young woman had been a little chatty, but most helpful, most sympathetic. "She said you were the guy I needed to talk to—said they called you the Longest Arm of the Law or something like that."

"Oh, man." Driscoll groaned. "Listen. This isn't a cold case, Mrs. Tellchick. From what you tell me, it sounds like your husband's death has already been ruled on. As an accident."

"With no smoke in his lungs?" Robbie argued, her voice rising. "You think it was possible for him to start that fire, get bonked on the head, then not draw one more single breath?"

"Who told you there was no smoke in his lungs?"

"The firefighter who carried my husband out of that barn. He's…he's been checking up on me since Danny died."

"I see. His name?"

"Zack Trueblood." Just saying Zack's name gave Robbie a pang because she knew he would not approve of her snooping like this.

Luke Driscoll asked Robbie a few more routine questions—did Danny smoke? Had there ever been a fire on their property before? Finally he said he'd get back to her, if need be.

Three days later a copy of the autopsy came in the mail with a note and Luke's card attached.

"If I can be of further assistance," Frankie read the note out loud, "please do not hesitate to contact me. Luke Driscoll, Texas Ranger."

"What kind of guy follows his signature with, 'Texas Ranger'?" Frankie pulled a sour face. It was Saturday morning and they were having coffee in Robbie's kitchen. The baby was sleeping and the boys were peaceful for the moment, mesmerized by cartoons.

"One who's proud of the fact, I guess." Robbie was already trying to decipher the autopsy. The first thing that gave her a chill was the X beside the entry for "Violent or unnatural death."

When Robbie got to the picture of a body diagram, front and back, with areas marked to show where Danny had been burned, she had to stop.

Frankie sat down at the table next to her and gently lifted the pages from her fingers. "I'm not promising anything, sweetie."

After Frankie read it through, she said, "Traumatic head injury. Undetermined origins."

"Exactly what I said." Zack's voice from the doorway made both Robbie and Frankie jump.

"Where did you come from?" Frankie said with her hand on her heart.

"The boys let me in." Zack stepped into the kitchen.

"Some guy name Luke Driscoll called me yesterday," Zack told Robbie as he crossed the room. "May I?" He held his hand out to Frankie for the autopsy.

"Driscoll called *you?*" Robbie said.

"I was the first firefighter at the scene." Zack leafed through the pages.

"What did he say?"

"Well, for one thing, he said you asked him for a copy of this autopsy."

"I did. And now I've read it. Or Frankie has anyway."

"Were you planning to let me read it?" Zack's voice was impatient, perhaps even a little angry, but also disappointed and sad. "Listen, Robbie, even if you start digging around in law enforcement records and the like, you wouldn't have any idea what they meant. You wouldn't understand how they reached their conclusions. Why aren't you letting me help you?"

"I have to do this myself, Zack," Robbie defended. "For Danny. And if you don't understand that, then maybe it would be better if you didn't come around here for a while, at least until I get a few things settled in my own heart and mind." She was thinking he'd been keeping to himself too much lately anyway. Maybe he was getting sick of playing family man.

But Zack looked as stunned as if somebody had gut-punched him.

"You mean, not see you? Not even see…the children?"

Robbie lifted the autopsy pages out of his hands. Then she clutched them to her chest and nodded.

Without another word Zack turned and stomped from the room. His rapid bootfalls on the hardwood floor rang with anger.

"Why on earth did you do that?" Frankie accused after the front door slammed. "It sounded like you don't trust him."

"You wouldn't understand."

"Well, you're right about that! Zack's a great guy. He didn't deserve to be just…just sent away like that."

"I am not about to start letting some man tell me what I can and cannot do." Robbie stood up, fists clenched on the pages of the autopsy. "Especially when it comes to looking into the circumstances of my own husband's death. I owe Danny this much! He did not start that fire!"

"What has gotten into you?" Frankie shrank back from her.

"Nothing." Robbie's shoulders slumped. "But Zack Trueblood has no business trying to control me, either. He's already made it plain he believes this fire marshal's lies. But I know Danny would never endanger his family that way."

But Robbie knew this wasn't really about Zack. Or even Danny. This was about *her*. "Look. The truth is, I am just now becoming an independent woman after a lifetime of letting our mother and Danny dominate me. Oh, forget it." She aborted her own weak-sounding explanation. "You wouldn't understand."

"Why do you think I wouldn't understand that?" Frankie reached for her as if to console. "Don't you think I'm going through the same thing? Trying to get my bearings after the way Kyle has treated me? Trying to protect myself, my heart?"

"Oh, sissy. I'm sorry for treating you like you're insensitive or something. I know you've been doing your best to help me. And I know what you're going through is hard, heartbreaking. I just want to get on my feet and make a go of my own life before I start leaning on a man. I guess I'm not really sure of my own feelings. My attachment to Zack happened so fast and it was all so emotional."

"That's what falling in love is all about, Robbie— emotions."

"No. I'm talking about the fact that I was still grieving and my postpartum emotions were running high. I guess I just don't want to get right back into a relationship with a man after…after…"

"After what?"

Robbie said nothing but her eyes went wide.

"It's okay, Robbie. You can tell me. I'm not a judgmental person, despite what you may think. Just ask Markie."

Robbie swallowed. Markie had told her how Frankie, young though she was, had done her best to help Markie as a pregnant teenager. How strong she had been for her sister, despite pressure from that jerk Kyle. Robbie and her older sister had never been close, but maybe it was high time they started trying. They needed each other now.

"I was going to say after the mistake I made with Danny."

"What mistake?"

"Marrying him."

"Oh, Sissy." Frankie reached out a hand. "That must be so painful for you to say now."

Robbie gripped Frankie's fingers. "Even if Danny was a failure as a husband in some ways," she admitted and then her voice dropped to a whisper, "I still loved him. I think I may still have some grieving to do, some sorting out of my feelings. I'm changing. I guess I'm no longer the dutiful farm wife, or the dutiful daughter, so I don't know who I am. Does that make sense?"

"Of course it does. I think we're kind of in the same boat right now. If you think you can stand my picky ways I'd like to come back and stay on here to help you take care of the boys and baby. Maybe I can even help you launch this new shop you're thinking about. I kind of like the sound of restoring Henkel's."

"Are you sure, sissy? It's so crowded here. And I

know this drafty old house is a dump compared to what you're used to."

"Please. I'd rather live anywhere besides that damned luxurious tomb back in Austin. I think what I haven't admitted until now, even to myself, is that for a long time I've been looking for an excuse to escape from Kyle, affair or no affair. And staying here to help you is as good as any. I should have come to help right after Danny died. Will you forgive me for that? For being so self-centered?"

"Oh, sissy!" Robbie was astonished to hear such words from her sister. Frankie had always been so stiff-necked, always maintaining an air of righteousness, just like their mother. "There's nothing to forgive. Besides, Markie came out to the farm and helped me."

"I'm glad somebody did. And I'm glad all of that worked out—that she and Justin found each other again and everything, after all those years."

Robbie smiled. "Sometimes love really does conquer all."

"And sometimes miracles really do happen." Frankie hooked her finger in the baby's tiny hand. "Just look at this little darling. I adore my new baby niece." She looked up at Robbie with misty eyes. "Let me stay. You'll be doing me a favor. I can't go back to Austin, and I can't take one more day out at Mother's."

FRANKIE WENT BACK to the McBride farm to pack her things that very day. Marynell came up to the attic room when she was partway done.

"What are you doing?"

"Going back to Robbie's."

"Whatever on earth for? It's an unholy mess over there."

Marynell, Frankie knew, would never tolerate any environment that wasn't aseptically clean. She was ashamed to admit that she had been that way herself until recently. "It's a house full of children, and I happen to like it."

"Have you lost your mind, Frankie? You had a beautiful life in Austin and now it seems like you are just hell-bent on throwing it away with both hands."

Frankie ignored her mother's goading. "Mother, I'm going for a long walk. I'll be back in time to say goodbye to Daddy when he gets home from the fields."

Frankie's long walks, the only way to escape from her mother out here, had gotten longer and longer in recent days. She was to the point where she wasn't even winded by the time she reached the limestone formations on Tellchick farm. There were plenty of snakes in these rocks so she always carried along one of her father's old revolvers. Like all Texas girls, she had learned how to shoot straight early on in life. With the gun and a cell phone, she felt safe enough.

But when she came around a low bolder and saw the figure of a man, her heart lurched. He spotted her immediately, too, and when he started striding toward her, Frankie raised the gun, aiming at his heart.

"Whoa, lady." The trespasser frowned as he came up short. "I'm the law."

"Prove it." Frankie kept the gun steady.

"You Hill Country people," he said as he dug inside his jean jacket.

"Slowly," Frankie warned, holding her body rigid in a firing stance.

He slowly withdrew his hand as instructed, shaking his head. "I guess out here, even the women pack heat."

"And we know how to use it," Frankie said as she squinted at the badge he held up. "So you can just quit talking like a chauvinist." She lowered the gun. The badge was a Texas Ranger's. This was undoubtedly the man Robbie had contacted. He looked like some kind of stereotype from a B-grade movie. Jeans. Boots. Even a tan Stetson. She wondered if he had a pickup with an old dog in it waiting somewhere.

"Luke Driscoll," he confirmed, giving her a sweeping up-and-down look that sent a chill along Frankie's arms despite the southwest sun.

Luke Driscoll was thinking that here was someone fairly interesting. He quickly filed away the details of her person. Very pretty face. Sleek dark hair. Knockout figure. Expensive jeans and boots. Manicured nails. Big diamond ring. But this was not your typical farm wife.

"Frankie McBride…Hostler," she said, lowering the gun, but she didn't offer him her manicured hand. "Ranger or not, you're still trespassing."

"I'm a criminal investigator from Austin."

"I figured that out. What are you doing out here?"

She was certainly tenacious, Luke would give her that. Then he made the connection. "Are you related to a Robbie McBride Tellchick?" he asked, instead of answering her question.

"I'm her sister. What are you hoping to find out here on Robbie's old place?" She jabbed the barrel of the gun toward the rocky formations they stood on.

"Caves." Luke could see no reason to bullshit this one and he sure didn't want her to raise that gun again.

"Caves," she said, then without warning she fired off a shot near his feet.

Luke jumped back. "Whoa, woman!"

"Snake." With the gun barrel she pointed at a long copperhead that was now missing his head.

"Thanks." Luke pushed his hat back and wiped at a fresh sheen of sweat.

"They like it out here on sunny days," this Frankie creature explained, "and they like it up in the trees, too."

Luke edged away from the low live oak to his left. "About the caves—" He swallowed and focused on his task. "Are you familiar with them?"

"I know they're there. I've never been in them."

"You don't know where the entrance is?"

"Nope. Sorry."

"Look out here." They were standing on a rise and Luke stepped to the edge of an outcropping of rock. Frankie followed.

He pointed and in the distance she could see the long line of new barbed-wire fencing, and the outlines of a sizable ranch gate.

"It's padlocked. But I'm convinced there's another entrance to the caves on this side."

"Why are you so interested in these caves?" Frankie said.

Luke studied her, trying to decide how much to tell her. She was very attractive. He wondered, fleetingly, if she were married. When she raised the gun, the diamond that had winked in the sun had been on her left hand. Their eyes met and he felt an excitement, an emotional jolt, he hadn't felt in a long time. "I think those caves have some connection to your brother-in-law's death."

Frankie McBride sucked in a breath. "Robbie keeps talking about some trespassers Danny saw out here."

"I believe those trespassers are very dangerous men, ma'am."

"So does my sister," Frankie answered levelly. "And I'll do anything to help her sort it out. I've been staying at my parents'." She pointed at the white McBride farmhouse in the distance. "But I'm in the process of moving back to town. Why don't I ask around about the caves, and then I'll get back to you." She took out her cell phone.

Luke recited his number while the pretty lady punched it into her phone, thinking that he wouldn't mind having *her* number as well.

MARYNELL SHOWED UP at Robbie's a few days later. Robbie kept expecting her mother to be changed, humbled, to at least be somewhat more meek in the wake of last summer's humiliating revelations. Attempting to blackmail Congressman Kurt Kilgore! Robbie still couldn't get over it, nor the fact that her mother claimed she did it all for Robbie's sake. Unbelievable.

Robbie didn't need that kind of help. But if anything, Marynell had grown worse—more strident, more critical—since her self-imposed exile. She had stayed in the attic room of the McBride farmhouse for days after her daughters confronted her about what she'd done, and it was clear she had emerged unchanged.

"I've come to spend some quality time with my granddaughter," Marynell announced defensively at Robbie's front door. She had stopped coming around the second morning Zack had shown up.

"Come in, Mother." The door creaked miserably as Robbie opened it.

"Oh! How can you stand that hideous noise! Can't your firefighter handyman fix that?"

It was bait, but Robbie refused to bite. She knew, from talking to Frankie, that Marynell was dying of curiosity about Zack. "Danielle's in her infant seat, in the kitchen," she replied, deflecting the question.

Marynell followed Robbie into the kitchen. It was funny—when she was with Marynell now, Robbie could sense her mother's moods as acutely as ever, but now she seemed to have lived away from her influence long enough to not be affected by them. She realized she should have gotten off that farm next door to her parents a long time ago, should have never gone there, in fact.

Today, Robbie sensed that Marynell was looking for a victim, brewing for a fight.

"Oh, aren't you the little cutie pie." Marynell rushed across the room, gushing over the baby.

"She looks like Danny, doesn't she?" Marynell

twisted her neck and looked back at Robbie gaily. "Does that Zack man think she looks like Danny?"

"I think Zack only sees Danielle when he looks at her."

"I like that name. Did I tell you that? You were wise, to name her after her daddy."

Why Marynell had always been so all-fired fond of Danny was a mystery to Robbie. Perhaps it was because he had been so lackadaisical that he had let the woman control him, and thus Robbie, from the get-go.

"It was Zack who came up with the idea of naming the baby Dan—" Robbie bit her lip. She had gone and played into mother's hands. Too late, she realized Marynell had already obtained that information from Frankie, and the woman had only brought up Danielle's name in order to turn the conversation back to Zack, and Robbie had obliged her as easily as a dumb cow going down a chute.

"He did! My goodness. Now isn't that incredibly thoughtful? Tell me more about this Zack man, Robbie. He's quite a bit younger than you, is he not?"

"Only four years. You want some coffee, mother?" Robbie went to the coffeemaker.

"I wouldn't mind some. That is, if you were going to make it anyway."

Robbie took down the filters and the coffee, and kept her back to Marynell, hoping that left alone beside Danielle, her mother would focus her attention on the baby and forget about Zack.

"I hope you're not getting all hung up on some younger man, Robbie. Sometimes widows make fools of themselves, you know. Sometimes men take advantage." Marynell stood and sidled up beside Robbie confidentially. "You know, just wanting to sleep with a woman and refusing to commit and all that. I hear it's a real problem with younger men these days."

"Did you and Daddy enjoy your visit with Frankie?" Maybe, Robbie hoped, if she made these diversions blatant enough, her mother would take the hint. A spray of coffee grounds missed the drip basket.

"Oh, Frankie was somewhat short-tempered while she was out at the farm, I'm afraid." Marynell walked over and scooped the dry grounds into her palm. "But I understand it. Anybody can see that Frankie's heart is breaking over being childless. And for the life of me, I don't know why she thinks it will solve her problems to separate from Kyle. She needs to go home and confront her problems head-on."

"Mother." Robbie faced her squarely. "I know for a fact that Frankie told you Kyle is having an affair. It wouldn't be healthy for Frankie to go slinking back to him. Besides, I'm going to enjoy having her here with me. We're starting a craft business together."

"Ardella Brown told me all about that." Marynell dusted the grounds into the sink.

"She did?"

"Uh-huh. She said you two had some idea to redo the old Henkel dry goods store and sell…Lone Star runners?" Marynell said it like she'd never heard of such a thing as a table runner. She picked up a sponge and turned on the tap.

"Yes. Runners. And place mats," Robbie informed her defiantly, knowing the wet blanket was sure to descend, "and napkins, and wall hangings, and baby quilts. And anything else I can sew up quickly with a Lone Star theme. The fabrics and colors will have a pioneer feel. Rustic and homey, but artistic and—" Robbie stopped herself because her mother had finished wringing the sponge and was glaring at her over the wire rims of her little spectacles.

"You are missing the point. That musty old store was built a hundred years ago, honey." Her mother's voice was over-patient, as if Robbie were a recalcitrant child that Marynell was only trying to help. But, of course, experience had taught Robbie by now that Marynell had only one agenda—hers. And the current Marynell McBride agenda was to get the boys out on McBride farm and make Texas landowners out of them.

"Ardella says the place is a complete wreck inside." Marynell continued talking while she wiped Robbie's counters with the sponge. "And where on earth are you going to find the time to do all of this sewing, Robbie? You have a new baby. And I can tell by looking at this place that you are overwhelmed already."

Robbie looked around her messy kitchen and firmly dismissed the chaos as temporary, the way Zack had been encouraging her to these past few weeks. Just thinking about the way he always encouraged her gave her a pang of regret over their earlier discord. It had only been a couple of days since her harsh words and his abrupt departure, and she deeply regretted it already. She missed him.

"I don't have to do everything all at once. Right now I'll just need to have one item—my Lone Star ornaments—ready in time for Thanksgiving. I have to make money some way, mother. Being a waitress isn't gonna feed a family of five. And Frankie's going to help me."

"Well, there are plenty of ways to make money besides starting a business. I think you girls could stand to listen to Ardella a little bit. Ardella's been there."

"And who says I have to do it Ardella's way? She has a floral shop, not a craft store. My place is going to be upbeat and simple."

"Nevertheless, Ardella knows all about being a businesswoman out in the cold, cruel world. And she was very skeptical about this scheme of yours. She doesn't think you are temperamentally cut out for this at all, Robbie."

"Ardella doesn't even know me," Robbie countered. "Nobody in this town does anymore. I have changed." And besides, she thought, if working your fingers to the bone out on a godforsaken farm wasn't good training for sticking it out in a self-owned business, what on earth was?

Marynell gave Robbie a sharp look, faintly disapproving. "You haven't changed all that much, young lady. Ardella is only concerned. She just doesn't want you to fail."

"MAYBE ARDELLA doesn't want the competition," Frankie hypothesized when Robbie recounted the conversation to her sister the next day. "Maybe she's afraid the stuff you're making will outshine her little trinkets."

"Or maybe Mother put words in her mouth," Robbie reasoned.

They were in the kitchen, with the fabric cut-outs spread out on the table.

Now that the baby was a month old, Robbie's energy was returning and the two sisters had flown into action, cranking out the first line of Lone Stars ornaments for the upcoming German Fest the weekend after Thanksgiving. They hoped to start a little buzz then and have more star-themed crafts ready for the Rising Star Christmas Festival. Both events would draw thousands of tourists, enough to turn a healthy profit if Robbie's designs caught on.

"I just don't want you to lose your shirt on this deal," Robbie lamented as she skillfully zigzagged a neat line of contrasting thread to the point of a star.

Robbie still didn't understand how willingly Frankie had leaped at the chance to front her the down payment on the Henkel store. She and P.J. had done the deal at the bank quickly, without Marynell's knowledge or approval. With the fall crops in, P.J. was free to haul his tools over to the Henkel store and get to work on it. To Frankie, Marynell complained about the old man's absence from the farm, but the daughters suspected their dad was looking forward to a season away from the place…and the woman who ran it with an iron hand.

The first thing he'd done was paint the siding on the storefront an eye-catching shade of pumpkin-orange with touches of teal and cream highlighting the turned posts and ornate gingerbread trim. Frankie wondered if she should tell Robbie that Zack Trueblood had stopped by to help P.J. with the painting one day, then another. She wondered if knowing such things would make Robbie's decision about Zack more or less complicated. She wondered if she should even tell her sister how famously Zack and P.J. got along.

"I imagine I'll have money to burn after the settlement's done," she said instead. "What are we going to name this place?" She deftly turned her sister's mind away from money worries. "I think it has to be something with the Lone Star in it, since most of the crafts will feature a Lone Star theme. How about Lone Star Lovelies?"

"Too cute." Robbie kept sewing.

Frankie didn't take offense. They had both become very focused on the business, wanting success badly enough to set their egos aside. Frankie was already imagining what life would be like if she just left Kyle for good and permanently relocated to Five Points to help Robbie run the store. "Lone Star Treasures?"

"Hmm. No. Kind of ordinary." Robbie doggedly kept sewing. A mindless task for her. "I know!" Her head came up. "How about The Rising Star?"

"Oh, now that's original." Frankie's tone was sarcastic, but not wholly negative.

Robbie made a face at her sister because the name wasn't original, of course. But it was simple, like her, like her crafts. "It ties in with the Christmas festival, which is when I'll sell the most crafts, and it'll still work all year 'round."

"True. And don't mind me, honey. If you like it, that's

all that matters. Sometimes I think I just get sarcastic out of habit. Too many years of Kyle's toxic ways, don't you know. The Rising Star is actually kind of clever. And the way you're using every last scrap of the fabric over there is clever, too." Frankie pointed to the work Robbie was doing. "And don't listen to the likes of Ardella, either, sissy. You are going to do just fine with this store. I'll bet you're going to discover plenty of business skills you never knew you had along the way."

It was true, Robbie thought as she plucked up the next star in the stack. In taking hold of her new life, she had already discovered a lot of surprising things inside herself—a lot of strengths, a lot of gifts—she never knew she had. And she'd discovered a few things that maybe even shocked her a little. Things like this fierce hunger for Zack Trueblood that simply would not go away.

CHAPTER FOURTEEN

THE NEXT TIME she saw Zack, that hunger assailed Robbie worse than a craving beset an addict.

He hadn't come to her house again, and she knew he wouldn't. All week she had been telling herself she should call him, then telling herself that if he could just stomp off that easily, maybe they needed the space after all. She didn't want a rebound relationship, or one that arose out of *her* dependence and need. This time she wanted to be in love, real love, not clinging to each other out of convenience or habit the way she and Danny had done.

By focusing her attention on starting up the crafts business and her growing family, she had managed to push Zack to the back of her mind…until she actually saw him.

It was her first full day back at work at the Hungry Aggie. Six weeks was a little soon to be back on her feet all day, but she had no choice. Money was still tight, though Markie and Frankie had both helped her out some. And this was the Saturday after Thanksgiving, with the German Fest in full swing. Throngs of people were bustling up and down Main Street looking at crafts and listening to live music, crowding into the Hungry Aggie for Parson's famous burgers and homemade pies. Parson had been forced to hire a part-timer when Robbie dropped out after her sudden delivery, but today he needed all the help he could get, so they were all working.

There Zack stood, suddenly blocking the sunlit square of the glass door up front. The tall, straight silhouette of his athletic frame caught her eye immediately. He was wearing his day uniform—on duty or about to be, she supposed. With such a crowd in town, there were bound to be incidents that required emergency help. He opened the door and a gust of late November air followed him inside as he stepped into the café.

As he peeled off his black leather jacket, Robbie kept herself in profile to him with her eyes trained on her order pad, pretending to finish up the order of the giggling teenagers in the booth where she stood. She felt his energy sweep past her back on his way to his usual booth. The magnetism of the man could have pulled her off her feet. When she couldn't fake scratching with her pencil any longer, she gathered the menus and smiled at the kids.

But as she whirled to make a hasty retreat to the kitchen, Zack was standing there, blocking her path. "Let's talk."

"I…" She swallowed. "I'm working."

"Then why don't you come and take *my* order."

He let her lead him to his usual booth and as he slid in, she put a menu in front of him, unnecessarily, she realized. Zack always ordered the same thing. But he picked it up, considering both sides of the laminated card with a small crease forming between his brows.

Out of the corner of her eye, Robbie saw Nattie Rose wielding a tray of Cokes toward the teens. Bless her. She supposed good old Nattie Rose had an accurate bead on just about everything that had transpired lately. Everything from Zack's attention to her family, to Frankie's unexpected arrival, to the clean-up going on over at Henkel's, to the little booth on the sidewalk outside where Frankie and Mark were selling Robbie's bright five-pointed stars like hot cakes…to the tense tilt of Zack's shoulders right now.

"Okay," he said and made a fake stabbing motion at the menu. "I'll take a slice of this humble pie."

Robbie cocked one hip out and gave him a level, but warm and loving, look. Then she couldn't help but smile. "Humble pie, huh?"

"It turns out you were right." Zack looked in her eyes seriously and lowered his voice. "It took them way too long to report the findings in Danny's death. And now some other things have happened that have made me suspicious."

Robbie's eyes went wide. "Other things. Like what?" Her voice was hushed.

"I can't discuss it here." He looked around the crowded restaurant. "But I will tell you that I've decided to have a look at the fire marshal's records myself."

"Oh, Zack," Robbie breathed, and felt the sting of tears. He believed in her. "Can you do that?"

"One way or the other, I will. But if I do, Robbie, you've got to promise me you won't run around stirring things up yourself. With arson you never know what you might be getting into, and you've got enough on your plate."

"I can't promise you anything, Zack. I'm…I'm just trying to survive right now. And if there's any possible way to do it, I have to prove that Danny didn't start that fire. For Danny's sake. For the boys." She suppressed her tears and raised her chin. "And I need that insurance money more than ever now."

"You mean for your new business?"

She gave a determined nod.

"I'll loan you some money," he offered sincerely.

"I couldn't let you do that. I'm already beholden to my sister. She co-signed the note on the store."

"That's good of her," he said. He examined Robbie's face closely. "I like the pumpkin-colored exterior, by the way."

"Daddy, bless his heart, about killed himself getting that storefront painted in time for German Fest. I don't know how he did it."

The corners of Zack's mouth turned up in a funny, grudging little smile. "The old man's a workhorse, that's for sure. The place is looking good, Robbie. And by the way, so are you."

Instantly, she blushed. She had lost fourteen pounds now since Danielle's birth. She was fixing her hair in a shiny high ponytail these days and she was wearing some new soft shades of an expensive mineral makeup that Frankie had given her. "Zack," her voice dropped. "I—"

"Me, too. Missed you, that is. If that's what you were going to say."

Already, he knew her so well. She had missed him terribly and it had only been a few days. "I keep wondering," she said shyly, "how on earth I got so attached to you so fast, you know? I keep thinking maybe I was on the rebound or just lonely and insecure or something." The tears insisted on welling up again.

"Insecure? You? I keep telling you, girl, you've got guts to spare." His eyes were full of admiration. "I'm so proud of you. I can see how fixing up that old store and starting your craft business has given you new confidence, how it's brought out your creative side. *You* are the rising star, my sweetheart."

Robbie giggled and blushed higher, which only seemed to encourage the tears more. "Yeah." She swiped the corner of her eye with a knuckle. "I guess I am changing. It's been…I can't describe it. Challenging, but exciting."

"Look, maybe I've been rushing you in this relationship." His voice dropped lower also, so low that Robbie had to lean near to hear him. Suddenly the exchange felt close. Intimate. Even in a crowded restaurant. "I promise to take it easy from now on. That is, if I can restrain myself around you. You're not the only one who got overly attached, you know." He admitted this last bit with a wink, but Robbie could tell that his heart was really *out there*.

Tears welled up again, so that she could only nod, encouraging him to keep talking to her, all the while thinking, *Yes, we both got attached too fast, but here we are. Attached. And you have the most beautiful dark eyes in the world, Zack Trueblood.*

Those dark eyes grew serious, seeing her tears. "You. The baby. The boys. I'm not gonna lie, Robbie. I've got all of you, the whole package, in my blood somehow."

She nodded again, this time really fast, trying to counter the misty-eyed feeling that was overwhelming her.

"Look." He grasped her hand. "Can we just start over? Go slower?" His eyes radiated tenderness and sincerity. "I really don't want to mess it up with you." Shielded by her body, where the folks in the restaurant couldn't see, he rubbed her knuckles gently with his thumb, waiting. "Say something," he encouraged.

Nattie Rose went sailing by. "He-e-elp!" she sang near Robbie's ear.

Robbie gulped, swiped away the pesky tears. "I've gotta get to work." She stood straight and tried to draw her hand away, but he wouldn't let go.

"Okay. But listen." He grabbed her other wrist and Robbie felt a jet of yearning at her core. "There's an antique Christmas decorating show coming up in Austin in a couple of weeks. Will you go with me?"

"Yes. Call me." Robbie made to leave but he didn't release her wrist just yet.

"And promise me you'll be careful about the other thing. Let me look into it. If somebody set out to harm Danny, for whatever reason, then they're still at large. You understand?"

She nodded and quickly got back into the swing of work, but for the rest of the day, Robbie worried. What had happened to make Zack suspicious? And if someone arranged the fire and killed Danny, even accidentally, what did that mean? Why would they do that? What did they want?

THE NEXT WEEK sped by with no answers to Robbie's troubling questions. And it didn't help that Robbie had become the object of a weird form of harassment. First it was a strange unsigned letter, delivered with the mail at the Hungry Aggie the following Saturday.

"Huh. This here one's for you." Parson had pulled it out of the stack of his mail, looking puzzled.

Nattie Rose looked over her shoulder as Robbie ripped open the note. "Your dead husband was a loser," she read aloud, "who owed a lot of money to a lot of people…." Robbie's voice grew quavery and trailed off.

Nattie Rose stepped up beside Robbie, frowning. "And he was up to no good," she finished reading the note aloud for her.

"Now that is just plain weird," Parson said angrily. "Reminds me of those nasty notes us black business folks used to get back in the sixties."

"You were in the middle of the ocean on a ship in the sixties," Nattie Rose reminded him. "And this is beyond weird. It's sick, bringing up Danny in a note to Robbie that way, calling him a loser."

"I refuse to believe that Danny would do anything—" Robbie's voice broke as she stared hard at the note "—no good."

"Why, of course he wouldn't, honey." Nattie Rose patted Robbie's hand as she lifted the note from her fingers. "Everybody in this town knows that. Hmm.

Looks like it was done on a computer. No way to trace that, I guess. But even so we'd better take it to the sheriff."

Robbie snatched the note back, angry now. "You can bet I will. If it's the last thing I do, I am going to find out what happened on the night of that fire. And soon. This mess has dragged on too long already."

SHE TOOK THE NOTE to Zack first, of course. Practically ran to him with it. He was at the fire station, an ancient two-story limestone structure at the bend of Main Street.

"I can't leave in the middle of a shift," Zack explained as he gathered her into his arms for a comforting hug between their vehicles in the back parking lot. "But meet me after. Oh, by the way, that guy in Austin, the one you called, who called me?"

"Luke Driscoll?"

"We're going to meet with him this weekend, while we're in Austin."

WHEN ZACK finished work, they went to the photocopy store and copied the note, then took the original to the sheriff. And got nowhere.

He frowned at the paper and said, "I'm sorry, Mrs. Tellchick. Apparently your husband made some enemies while he was alive. And you are well aware that you all were having financial problems. I'll keep this if you don't mind, but by itself it isn't reason enough to reopen this case. Your husband's death was an accident. You've got to accept that."

But then only a few days later a rock was thrown through the window of Robbie's new craft shop. The place was nearly empty, still being slowly cleaned and decorated and stocked as Robbie and Frankie could get to it. At first it looked like an accident, or simple vandalism, a prank.

But Robbie knew better. And Zack knew better. They talked about it until Robbie was emotionally exhausted and Zack was hoarse. The key, Zack felt, was to talk to the fire marshal in person, to elicit his help on a personal level. If the man could meet Robbie, could understand her dilemma about the insurance, he might be persuaded to reopen the case. Zack knew the man, from way back when. He was a good cop. A good firefighter. He had a lot of connections.

They went the next day, together. At Fire Station No. 2, not Zack's station—he was at the other end of town, near the historic district—they sat down in two vinyl-covered chairs facing a gunmetal-gray desk behind which a heavyset man sat blinking his sympathetic blue eyes repeatedly at them.

"Thanks for seeing us, Roy. Mrs. Tellchick here is still very disturbed about the findings in her husband's death." Zack took her hand.

"I imagine so." Roy Graves tightened his lower lip. "What's it been, now? Only six months?" He was also looking pointedly at their joined hands, but Zack refused to let go.

"About that," Zack went on. "The main thing that bothers her is the fact that her husband told her he had an altercation with some Mexican illegals the night before he died, and now she's getting harassed."

"The sheriff and me looked into that Mexican bit. Came up short. No bearing on the fire, that I could see. Same with that rock through the window of your new store. Could have been kids. The cops talked to Ardella across the street. She's had the same kind of trouble before. Somebody tore down a bunch of her windsocks once. I *am* a cop, Zack."

"What about that weird note?"

"All that means is, Danny Tellchick had…" A tense moment followed, seemed to stretch too long before the fire marshal spoke again. "Zack, aren't you letting your emotions get in the way a little bit in this case?"

"What does that mean?"

"People have talked, Zack. Pardon, ma'am, if it upsets you." The blue eyes cut to Robbie briefly. "But facts are facts." The eyes skewered Zack again. "You tried to save her husband. You delivered her baby. You all have been keeping company, isn't that right?"

Robbie looked at Zack. Zack looked at Robbie. Realization dawning on both faces that this man could not be relied upon to help, after all.

Roy shifted sideways, crossed his legs. "Let's get to the point here. You just never get tired of rescuing people, Zack. That's your schtick, I guess. So now you're trying to coerce me into changing my findings so your girlfriend can get her insurance money. Isn't that the real issue?"

"Why you—" Zack thrust a shoulder forward, but before he could go on, Robbie clutched at his biceps.

"No," she said forcefully, "That is *not* the issue. And I don't need *rescuing,* Mr. Graves." She stood. "But I do want justice. And, by God, one way or another, I will have it." She turned and left, and Zack was right behind her.

When Zack grabbed her shoulders out on the sidewalk, Robbie was shaking. "Sweetheart," he whispered, and pulled her to his chest.

He heard her choking back tears. "Oh, crap," she said as a sob broke loose. She swiped at her cheeks. "I'm going to cry, right out here on the street with you hugging me, so all those people Graves claims have been talking about us will have one more thing to… to—" She broke down in sobs.

"Shh. It's all right, sweetheart." Zack wrapped his arms firmly around her, rocking her against him. "To hell with them. What do we care what anybody thinks?" He held her tight and cradled her head with his big palm tangled in her soft, curly hair. "If I want to help you, it's because I love you, pure and simple. You understand that?"

Robbie gave a trusting nod against his chest and his heart swelled with gratitude.

"I am going to do everything in my power to keep you safe," he promised as he held her even closer. "You and the kids."

BUT EVERYTHING in his power wasn't enough when a Mexican worker approached Mark as he got on his bike in the alley behind the still-empty Henkel store.

"Hey, kid." The man, thin and filthy, smelled really bad. "You want a smoke?" Mark recognized him. This was the same Mexican who had first offered him a cigarette back when Aunt Markie's husband had some migrants working on the Tellchick farm before Markie and Justin got married.

"No, thanks."

"You don't like the smokes all of a sudden?"

Mark regretted that he had accepted cigarettes from the guy out on the farm. Zack would never smoke, he was sure. "I…I've decided to be a firefighter now and it wouldn't be a good example, and all. See ya."

Mark jerked his bike upright and started to pedal away.

But the Mexican grabbed the handlebars and Mark lurched off the seat, banging his crotch against the crossbar. "Ow!" he cried.

"Hurts like *sheet,* don't it?" Without releasing the bike, the Mexican grabbed Mark's shirtfront up in one fist. "But you gonna hurt a whole lot more, little man, you and your whole familee, if your mama don't mind her own beesness." He thrust the boy away then.

Mark pedaled straight to his mother, who was working at the Hungry Aggie.

Robbie took one look at her son's face, gone white under his freckles, and immediately called Zack. After that, Zack dropped his projects at the farm so he could watch over Robbie and her kids even more closely.

He also did something he thought he would never do in a million years. He sneaked into the fire marshal's office.

He had been careful to come at night when the guys on that shift should have been sawing logs in their bunks, but one yahoo must have been on his way to the john.

"Trueblood," the guy said, coming up short. "What're you doing here?"

He had come prepared to think on his feet. "We ran out of training forms for the class tomorrow. I'm just gonna run up and grab a couple off the chief's desk."

"Now?" The guy looked at his watch. "Long day."

"Yeah. Long day."

At the top of the stairs, Zack didn't turn into the chief's office. Instead, he slipped into the fire marshal's. Inside Roy Graves's office, he shut the door and rifled through the desk and the file cabinet until he found the Tellchick file. Quickly, he scanned the EMT, medical examiner and fire marshal's reports.

What the hell? This paperwork—too neat, as if it had all been rewritten—reflected a whitewashed, flawed investigation to Zack's thinking. Some pertinent stuff was missing. Like the statement of the insomniac neighbor who'd looked out the window the night before the fire and seen a plume of dust in the moonlight, trailing behind a vehicle she didn't recognize, leaving the Tellchick farm at a hell-bent speed. Like those drag marks outside the barn. Zack knew he'd told Graves about them.

He tried to remember when it had come up. During the critical incident review? A type of group therapy, anything and everything could come up during those sessions. Zack cringed as he remembered how the psychologist had kept focusing on the fact that Zack had done CPR on an obviously burned corpse. He said firefighters sometimes have an overblown rescuer complex.

Zack wasn't about to sit there and admit he'd had a thing for the guy's wife ever since they were kids. How that had messed with his head, and just for that one instant he had panicked, thinking if he'd acted faster, he might have saved the man. It was as if Zack had been trying to turn back the hands on a giant clock.

For days after that the guys had sat around the station and told stories about the fire, speculating about the whole thing. Arson happened in patterns, they all knew that, so they always talked about every case that was a possible arson until they'd run it into the ground.

Some of the guys knew Danny Tellchick, knew what a slob he was, didn't doubt for a minute that he might burn his old barn, didn't doubt that a loose pulley could have dropped on his head. Months passed, and more fires happened and the talk died down. And now, of course, they were all talking again, this time about how Danny Tellchick had gone and caused his own death by torching his own barn.

He heard a noise, heavy steps on the stair treads. Hurriedly he put everything back the way it was and slipped out into the hall just as Mr. Potty Break's head appeared above the stairwell.

"You still here, Trueblood?" This guy was a big German-looking kid with a loud personality and a penchant for running his gums.

"Couldn't find the damned forms," Zack lied. "Guess I'll have to check back tomorrow. 'Night, Felderhoff." Zack squeezed past the other firefighter, clumped down the stairs and got out of there.

Maybe, Zack thought—hoped—as he fired up his truck, that Texas Ranger in Austin would have some insights.

CHAPTER FIFTEEN

"TRUEBLOOD was going through your office?"

Roy Graves had dreaded this call. Every time he spoke with the congressman lately, he could feel an explosion coming. The old man was wound up pretty tight about something these days. But Roy was no pantywaist. He propped his boot against an open desk drawer and faced the music. "Yessir. Snuck in here at night. And according to Felderhoff he stood right here in the hallway and lied about it."

"Who the hell is Felderhoff?" The ire in Kilgore's voice rose.

"Another firefighter."

"Why would he come to you with this? How much does *he* know?"

"Felderhoff knows nothin'. He's just trying to undermine Trueblood. There's a lot of jealousy between the stations. These boys up here think the guys downtown get all the goodies. And Trueblood got a big state award last month that Felderhoff thought he should have gotten."

"Trueblood again. I should never have sold that guy the land."

"Why did you?" Roy regretted the question the

second it passed his lips. Nobody questioned Kurt Kilgore's decisions.

But to Roy's surprise the congressman only sighed as if he did indeed regret that particular decision. "It was more suspicious not to. He went to my son, was willing to pay far more than the property was worth. I shouldn't have done it. I see that now. But I thought it would get Justin off my case. Trueblood's seen the coyotes out there, is my guess."

"There's a lot of things all of us shouldn't have done, congressman," Graves pressed in on the sudden familiarity, the budding alliance. "I should have gone to the widow myself with my findings instead of letting Trueblood be the one. That's another thing we need to worry about here. Trueblood's seeing that little widow. When they came to my office, they were holding hands and the like."

"Great. A team now, are they?" A silence stretched. "Shit. I need some time. That's all. Just a *little* more time. There has to be some way to distract them, to throw them off the scent. I've only got that one last thing left in there."

"Can't you get it out? Hide it somewhere else?"

"That's actually the best place for it. No one's going to find the deepest cavern without a map. The mural came up from Mexico in pieces, but I need to know the pattern. It has to all be there before I sell it."

"Can't you just sell it in pieces?" To Roy's mind, the people who wanted the Mayan wall carvings that were hidden in the caves should be the ones to worry about assembling them.

"No." Kilgore's voice betrayed a sudden impatience. "The individual pieces are practically worthless without the pattern. And if I can show that I have every piece, it'll bring ten times as much. Once I get the last piece and the damned pattern, I can sell the carvings in Europe. I am this close to getting that pattern from one family of Mexicans now. Once I get it out of there I'll blow up the entrance to those caves."

"Now that *will* get Trueblood's attention."

"But it's gotta be done. I'm not about to start moving bones. I've already made a big deal about of how dangerous and unstable the rock formations are. Those rocks are always creaking and groaning at night."

"Temperature changes." Roy knew this fact about that area.

"I've got 'Posted' and 'Keep Out' signs everywhere out there. I tell you, I just need a little more time."

"Okay then. But we'll need a stronger distraction. If one of the Mexicans roughing up her kid didn't deter her—"

"Her *kid?*"

"No big deal. The kid runs around town like a little wild man anyways. Smokin' cigarettes and gettin' in scrapes at the school and the like." Even so, Roy had not approved of the coyote's plan to scare the boy. "I guess we could employ our old fire starter again."

"The landlord? Mestor? To set yet another fire? I don't like this if there's any chance he'll get caught."

"Nah. Mestor's good. He likes to use a slow match."

"Come again?"

"You take a book of matches and you wedge a cigarette in the book and light it. Cigarette's a fuse. You stick the whole rig in something real flammable, like a polyester pillow. You're long gone when the place goes up, and all the arson evidence goes up in smoke. I suspect he's done it before, on one of his rental houses."

"You're not going to have him do the woman's *house?*"

"With children living there and all? Trueblood surely would be out for somebody's hide then." Roy's shoulders tensed at the thought of the massive firefighter coming after him in a rage.

"Then what?"

"Leave it to me. I've got an idea that'll slow her down but good, and nobody'll get hurt."

"You don't contact Mestor yourself, you hear? I don't want anything that could be traced back to me. There's some cold-case investigator from Austin sniffing around now. He was a Texas Ranger. Has a reputation for getting to the bottom of things."

"We'll use the coyotes again. Then, even if Mestor gets caught and squeals, the people who paid him will be impossible to trace. And even if Trueblood does eventually figure out what happened to Tellchick, the Mexicans will get the blame in the end."

"You're a real asset, Graves."

Roy's shoulders relaxed. He had never heard words like that from Kilgore before. Now was the time to press his demands. "Just be sure *my* land gets included in that corridor."

"I'll do it if it harelips the governor."

ZACK WAS CLEAR about the fact that he considered the excursion to Austin a real date, even if it included a more serious purpose. He had reasoned to Robbie that if people are going to talk, they sure didn't want them saying the two of them had traipsed down to Austin to see a state investigator.

He called Robbie three times to confirm the plans: leave early in the day, meet with Luke Driscoll first thing, brunch at that famous old Hotel on Sixth Street, then a relaxed tour of the decorating show and a slow drive home.

"What about Danielle's feedings?" he had asked during the last call, and his thoughtfulness made Robbie smile. "Bring her if you want," he added quickly. "I'd love to hold both of my babies."

Frankie assured Robbie she could make do with bottles, but in the end Robbie decided it would be simpler to take the baby. Zack, she knew, would help her manage all the infant paraphernalia as well as any real father would.

The day of the date Robbie was so nervous it was silly. She was delighted to find that she could squeeze back into her slim-cut jeans. Frankie insisted she wear her new cream-colored cashmere sweater set.

"I'll never have occasion to wear it anytime soon," the slimmer sister claimed.

Robbie had to admit the soft candlelit color set off her reddish hair and green eyes perfectly. And she really glowed when they accessorized it with some of Frankie's better gold jewelry.

ZACK PICKED UP Robbie and the baby right on time. Together they loaded the baby's things, and when Zack secured Danielle in her car seat in the back of his double cab pickup, he gave the child a little kiss on the cheek. Baby Danielle favored him with one of her newly learned smiles and a little starry-eyed cooing.

"I've missed that little angel, and I've missed *you*." He smiled at Robbie as he slid into the driver's seat.

Robbie couldn't help herself. She pressed close against him and gave *him* a kiss on the cheek. "I've missed you, too, Zack."

"Me? Or just my body?" Zack teased as he gave her a light kiss on the lips and cranked up the engine.

"Both," Robbie said, smiling.

After that the level of arousal between them seemed to build in waves. The bouncing rhythm of the truck lulled the baby to sleep and they were free to touch and hold hands the rest of the way down the long highway. As a result, Robbie was feeling slightly euphoric and very aroused before they ever pulled into Austin.

But she came back down to earth when they arrived at the bureaucratic-looking building where they had a meeting with Luke Driscoll.

Robbie and Zack sat in two generic office chairs again, facing another government-issue desk. Only this time Robbie had the baby on her shoulder, patting her back because she was fussy. And this time the man facing them did not stare back with falsely sincere blue eyes.

Luke Driscoll's eyes were dark, piercing. He was

frowning. His looks matched his voice. He was older than Zack—in his early forties, maybe—with a receding hairline and streaks of gray in his goatee, but his eyebrows were still dark and his jaw was still firm. He and Zack had shaken hands like two guys cut from the same cloth and Luke started right in.

"Mrs. Tellchick, when you contacted me about your husband's autopsy, I immediately made a connection to another case I've been working on." He flipped a folder open. "A friend of mine put some wetbacks in touch with me a while back. These people claimed they all had relatives who had crossed to the U.S., then disappeared 'at the star'—their exact words. I believe 'the star' refers to the town of Five Points."

"Oh!" Robbie said and her head swiveled to Zack.

"These people—" Luke glanced down at his papers "—claim their relatives smuggled Mayan artifacts into Texas in exchange for hiding places and safe passage further north."

"Mayan artifacts?"

"These." Luke slid some pictures across the desk.

Robbie took the photos and Zack leaned to look over her shoulder. The first was a panoramic shot of a low gray-green scrub forest and rough limestone hills that reminded Robbie, somehow, of the Texas Hill Country.

"That's the area in Mexico these folks came from, the jungles of the northern Yucatán, the Puuc," Luke said.

"The Puuc," Robbie echoed as she flipped to the next

picture, a low tunnel-like wedge cut into one of the rocky hills, with jungle overgrowth crowding the steep walls.

"A looter's trench," Luke explained. "leading into a tomb."

Robbie frowned and flipped to the next photo. Some men, squatting in a dark, cavelike stone room. One was looking at the camera; one was aiming a flashlight at a flat piece of stone on his palm.

"A Harvard researcher and his partner," Luke explained. "That is a piece of a Mayan mural in his hand. It's one of the most important finds in Mayan archeology in decades."

"What does this have to do with me?" Robbie said.

"Go ahead and look at the next picture."

Robbie did. It showed a jagged rock mural of half-clothed women and a black-faced male kneeling before what Robbie assumed was a Mayan god.

"That's all they have of it." Luke sighed. "It's so early that they're not even sure how to interpret it. They need the rest of the pattern to figure out what it means. But looters, probably locals, dug the trench a long time before the Harvard guy got there. The majority of the mural is missing."

"But I still don't understand, what has all of this…research got to do with me or my husband?"

"That is what I intend to find out." Luke's dark eyes hardened with determination. "Don't forget we are talking about more than missing artifacts here. We're talking about missing persons. You told me that your husband saw some Mexican illegals near some caves on your land—"

"The caves," Zack said flatly, as if he'd suddenly come to some conclusion in his mind.

"You know about them?" Luke asked them both. "How to get into them?"

"I know about the caves, and I think I could find the entrance, but that's not my land anymore," Robbie was quick to point out.

"I—uh." For a moment Zack seemed like he was going to swallow his tongue.

"The land, uh—" He looked at Luke meaningfully and cleared his throat. "The land has a new owner, and the area around the caves is sealed off behind locked ranch gates now."

"Really? How did you know that?" Robbie asked.

"I, uh, Justin Kilgore and I talked about it."

"I'll want to talk to the new owner."

"I'll, uh, I'll put you in touch with him," Zack said.

"Good. I'm going to try to have another look around out there. I'll be coming back to Five Points soon," Luke promised, "and I *will* get to the bottom of this, Mrs. Tellchick."

While Robbie found it immensely consoling that someone was finally listening to her, she also wondered what they could do in the meantime.

"Nothing," Driscoll said. "Sit tight. The worst thing you can do in a case like this is spook the bad guys."

EVEN AFTER GETTING that disappointing and disturbing news, they still ended up having a wonderful day. The two of them discovered that if left alone to focus only on each other, with no kids except for a contented and mostly cooing baby, with no relatives or townsfolk sticking their noses in everywhere, they had a lot to talk about, a lot to laugh about.

And a whole lot of chemistry, as Zack had suspected they would.

The antiquated Driskill Hotel and the red granite Texas statehouse were both done up elaborately for Christmas. Around the capitol grounds were heated tents featuring stunning decorating ideas and wares. All that artistry and creativity worked like a drug on Robbie. She was like the proverbial kid in a candy store. Several times she fairly squeaked with delight as she held up some beautiful or clever item featuring a Lone Star. "Oh! Look! I could make this! And *this!*"

Once, as they pushed the stroller along in the chilly sunlit air, Zack came to a dead stop in the middle of the sidewalk, staring at Robbie.

"What?" she said.

"I think you are the most beautiful woman God ever made." He smiled at her. "You know that, don't you?"

Her cheeks flushed an attractive shade of sun-kissed peach. "Oh, my gosh. What are you trying to do to me, Zack Trueblood?"

"I'm making you fall in love with me, remember?" he answered honestly.

He couldn't resist taking her in his arms for a kiss then. The passion it unleashed was instant, fierce, undeniable. But Robbie resisted it. She broke off and backed up a fraction, looking stunned.

"What's wrong?" he said.

"Nothing," she lied, and gripped the handle of the stroller way too tightly as she took command of it. "I'll push the baby for a while."

"No." Zack grabbed the handle and halted her progress. "Tell me why you hold back from me like that sometimes."

Robbie looked down at the sidewalk, and Zack waited while the winter sun shimmered through the bare trees and the baby blinked and stretched in her blankets.

By the time Robbie raised her eyes to him, he saw a sheen of sudden tears he couldn't have anticipated. Robbie closed her eyes and swallowed. "Remember when I told you that I knew something was holding me back, but I just didn't know what it was?"

"Yes." His heart started to hammer. For one instant, something in him hearkened back to the day his faithless wife had left him a note that read, *I don't love you anymore.*

"Well, I figured out what it was," Robbie went on as her tears spilled over.

Zack reached up and brushed at the path of a tear on her cheek. "Just tell me, sweetheart."

"I…" Robbie choked up. "At first I thought it was because I was feeling disloyal to Danny, you know? I mean, I think I am falling in love with you."

"Oh, sweetheart." At that he leaned in to claim her mouth.

"But!" She put up a palm to stop him. "I can't…I can't commit to you until…there are two things I have to do before we can be together, Zack. I have to clear

Danny's name," she rushed on, "and I have to become my own woman. I have to make my own way. Otherwise, I'll never know if I fell for *you*, Zack, or if I just ran to the arms of a man for safety."

He didn't wait for her permission this time. He assaulted her mouth in earnest. And this time, Robbie did not hold back, even though they were standing on a sidewalk in front of the Texas state capitol.

When they broke off from the kiss, Robbie, still breathless from it, still teary-eyed, said, "Does any of that make sense?"

Zack smiled. "Everything you say makes sense to me, Robbie. When are you going to learn that?"

As they walked on, his heart was suddenly light. He knew everything he needed to know now. She had been as rocked by the strength and rightness of their physical response to each other as he had. Soon, he suspected, her heart would finally be ready. And her body was ready, already, to be loved like a woman again. And soon, very soon, he would make her more than glad that she was a woman.

ON THE LONG drive down the winding highway back to Five Points, they couldn't keep from touching each other. Finally, Zack pulled onto a ranch road that he knew led out to a remote, starlit plateau.

"Where are we going?"

"To give you a little more inspiration." He smiled.

"What?" Her giggle was nervous.

"Stars."

"Oh."

But out on the plateau, neither one thought much about the stars, at least not the ones in the sky.

Zack parked and turned off the engine without a word. Simultaneously, he and Robbie looked back to check the baby's sleeping face. Then their eyes met and slowly he twisted and folded Robbie in his arms.

They kissed. Again. And then again. The thrill building with each new fitting of mouths. Until finally they were locked in one prolonged kiss, only shifting long enough to gasp for air or to change the fit and increase the access, the passion. No talking. No words. Only this ravenous consuming of mouths, this fierce clutching of bodies, taking their fill of each other after their recent deprivation.

Finally, Zack broke it off and braced a hand at her jaw, ran it down her neck, held a thumb lightly over the pounding pulse there. "If only you knew how much I love you," he whispered. "And want you."

"And I want you, too. But like I told you I…I need a little more time," Robbie stammered. "I think maybe…maybe my hormones are still running riot, making me too emotional, too needy, right now."

Her hormones were running riot all right, but not for the reasons she thought. But he reminded himself of his promise not to rush her. This was only their first date, in actual fact—because their other so-called first date had had a slight interruption.

"You don't ever have to worry about being emotional or needy with me. I don't operate like that. When a woman's with me, I *want* her to need me. I *want* to take care of her, protect her. It's the way I'm made. But I know you've been through a lot and I realize I have to be patient. And I will be," he murmured as he drew her closer to himself. "Everything will work out, Robbie." He held her tightly. "I told you. I can be patient."

BUT IT WAS GETTING harder for Zack to be patient when his heart was bursting with more love for this woman than he'd ever imagined possible. It was hard to be patient when it looked like this woman that he'd always loved—this woman he'd adored from afar ever since he was a kid—could really possibly become his at last.

He fell right back into the pattern of coming around to Robbie's on a daily basis, trying to make himself useful, bringing the family small gifts and luxuries. And Robbie fell right back into the pattern of depending on Zack for everything from being an example for the boys to providing a shoulder to lean on.

And as naturally as breathing, Zack and Robbie fell into the same easy physical intimacy they'd shared in the early days right after Danielle's birth. Only now it had become much more intense. Even in full sight of the children they couldn't hide it. He would pull her onto his lap or wrap an arm around her waist. She would hook her hands behind his neck or rest her cheek against his shoulder.

"We're scandalizing these children," Zack teased. "And Frankie, too, I think. Maybe I'd better go ahead and make an honest woman of you."

But every time he made an oblique reference to getting married, Robbie squirmed. Zack repeatedly told himself to be patient. He told himself that she would realize sooner or later that what they had couldn't be denied. He told himself he wasn't forever going to be a stand-in for Danny Tellchick. The night when he'd read her diary he'd seen with his own eyes how she felt about him. And whenever they were alone together, he could feel just how powerfully he affected her. If she admitted it on the pages of her diary, sooner or later she would admit it to *him*.

Still the illusion of being a couple set in quickly and the days stacked up faster than Robbie's handmade crafts. Suddenly it was mid-December.

The Rising Star had scheduled its grand opening, appropriately, on the opening night of The Rising Star Christmas Festival, a weekend-long affair that featured crafts, music and, of course, old-fashioned German food. Robbie had spent some of Frankie's money on newspaper and radio advertising, and she wasn't about to let it go to waste.

The hours Robbie had been putting in over at the store had gotten longer and longer. But here it was the night before the grand opening and The Rising Star still wasn't nearly ready.

"No getting around it, baby doll," Robbie cooed to Danielle as she got the baby dressed to go with her for another long evening at the store. "You have a working mommy." Thank God, Frankie had taken the boys out to Mother and Daddy's for dinner. What was she going to do when—*if*—Frankie went back to Austin?

Just take it one day at a time, she told herself as she lugged the baby's things out to her van. But even so, Robbie couldn't shake the uneasy feeling that with all that was going on in her life, she had really been pushing the envelope lately.

CHAPTER SIXTEEN

THE BABY was getting fussy. Robbie put the staple gun down on the tray of the ladder and climbed down. She hated to stop her project, but she was glad that she'd brought Danielle with her to the shop. Having her here in the playpen was more convenient than running home to nurse her. At two months, Danielle could roll over, smile, grasp at her toys and guide them to her mouth. But she was a baby who did not tolerate being ignored, even for a second. She had hardly spent a moment of her waking life without someone hovering over her, cooing at her. Her brothers constantly played with her, and stimulated her, and coached her to do cute things, and toted her around the house. Danielle started to cry. Robbie wished the boys were here to distract the baby now.

"Hold on! Mommy's coming, sweet baby!" Robbie sang out. She checked her watch when her feet touched the floor. Wow. Nine o'clock. Danielle had lasted over three hours since the last feeding.

She picked up the baby and Danielle made impatient little sounds and clutching motions at Robbie's front with her fat little fists. "Is Mommy's little baby doll hungry?" Robbie said as she unbuttoned. A responding sweet baby grin and avid little green eyes told her *yes*.

Danielle was such a smart baby, Robbie's pride and joy. Robbie had no idea how strongly having a daughter would affect her. She took pride in everything about her. Every toothless little smile. Her little black cap of curls. Her perfect smooth skin. Her perfect chubby little body. People constantly commented on her beauty. Only yesterday an older woman out in front of Ardella's shop had said, "Why, Robbie, she's the spitting image of you, only with dark hair."

The baby was sweet and precious, as all her baby boys had been, but her baby girl, it seemed, had a special hold on Robbie's heart. Maybe it was because of the circumstances of her birth. Danielle would always be the child Robbie would associate with her moment of greatest grief, and her moment of greatest joy. The little rosebud mouth latched on and as Robbie stroked the child's downy head, her thoughts turned to Zack.

He would be here helping her right now, she knew, if he weren't on duty at the fire station down the street. With Zack, she knew she would never feel like she was pulling the load alone.

He had made it so obvious he wanted to get married, but Robbie was still scared. She thought of how it had been with Danny, at the start. Between the end of high school and their wedding day. The ideals. The romance. Like Zack, Danny had seemed crazy about her, had been anxious to seal the deal, to make her his own, to settle down.

They had settled down, all right. Way down. Once he had her out on that farm, all that attention and romance had dried up as if Danny had just been going through the motions before the wedding.

She wasn't sure she could ever go through that slow, killing disappointment again. The death of love was, in fact, far worse than the death of a loved one. And with Danny, she had felt the pain of both.

Now here was Zack, central to her life so suddenly, so overwhelmingly. Here was Zack, everything that Danny was not. Zack seemed—her hand stilled on the baby's head—too good to be true. Could she make herself wait to marry him? She looked at the baby. She would have to, for her children's sake. This time she was going to get married as a mature, independent woman.

A surge of feeling washed through her as the lulling sensation from the hormones produced during nursing overcame her body. She was so very tired. She wanted to lean her head back and rest, but she was sitting upright in a cold folding chair. *Come on, baby, finish,* she thought. *Mommy's got a lot of work to do.*

She felt guilty, rushing a feeding so she could get back to her decorating, but what would Danielle's life be like if her mother had no livelihood? Even if the timing was inconvenient, this was an opportunity Robbie couldn't afford to miss. If she hadn't taken over the Henkel store now, while it was briefly empty, some other smart businessperson would have. Historic Five Points was rapidly turning into a profitable hotspot, and the price of real estate there was climbing.

She looked around the store space. Was all this work going to be worth it? How much money had she spent so far, just getting started? She was starting to lose track, but Frankie didn't seem to care. Her big sister actually seemed as excited about this venture as Robbie.

The old plaster walls in the building were so cracked that Robbie had come up with an inexpensive plan to cover the defects with softly patterned fabric. To further soften the effect, she had layered thin polyester batting underneath.

The baby dropped off to sleep and finally fell away from her suckling with her little pink mouth gone slack in a soft, lopsided O. Robbie kissed her pudgy cheek then gently carried her to the playpen, laid her on her side and tucked soft blankets around her tiny body.

Back up on the ladder, Robbie pushed herself to finish the stapling, which took her another thirty minutes. Then she climbed down and gathered up the remaining batting and fabric and stuffed the discards in a corner of the back storeroom. She hurried back into the middle of the main room and took a second, only a second, to admire her handiwork. The shelving she'd found on sale at the Wal-Mart was draped with a red-and-white star-patterned bunting that disguised its cheapness.

She and Frankie had congratulated themselves for all their clever decorating tricks—bringing a dark green outdoor umbrella inside and making it look Christmassy with tinsel and colored lights, setting up a little "forest" of artificial trees in one corner for displaying the ornaments, the mixed collection of starfish, yellow roses and pinecones on the newly varnished mantel. And spray paint. *My heavens,* Robbie thought as she admired the colorful display pieces, *they'd sprayed enough tacky odds and ends of furniture to choke a horse.*

The high ceilings and one exposed brick interior wall lent coziness and class, and the old wood floor gleamed, thanks to Zack. She sniffed, worrying that the space was too fumey from the floor refinishing for Danielle to be sleeping here. She'd have to hurry and get done.

Which meant she couldn't stand here and admire her handiwork for long. She still had lots of stuff to carry in from her van. The large oak front door had an automatic lock that Robbie left tripped because she wanted it to slam behind her after each trip inside, locked for safety. When she went outside to the van, she stuck a wood chock in the door to keep it unlocked and also because she wouldn't have a free hand for turning the knob on the way back inside. Back and forth she trudged from curbside to storefront, carrying large plastic bins loaded with her wares.

ARLEN MESTOR waited until ten o'clock. Main Street, Five Points America, was dead as a doornail after ten o'clock. He parked in the alley, but down a ways, behind the Hungry Aggie, and walked unsteadily to the back door of old Henkel's dry goods. There, he listened intently. Nothing.

He tried the knob. Locked. No problem. His ring of master keys opened almost anything and ten to one that woman hadn't bothered to change the locks. Drunkenly he fumbled with his key ring. With a little jimmying the third key did the trick.

Though it was cold outside, he was sweating as he slid the door open and crept inside. He hated to do this, but the place was empty, of course, not even open for business yet. The money the Mexican had slipped him was outrageous, considering that what he was about to do was no hardship for Arlen, once he got up his nerve with enough hootch.

The door creaked shut behind him. He listened again, biting his lip. Silence.

Across the black space, he could see a thin trail of light under a door. All of the merchants left theft deterrent lights on at night.

He flicked on his flashlight, panned around the storeroom and nearly had apoplexy over his good fortune when the beam revealed the pile of discarded polyester and fabric in the corner.

He picked the perfect spot for his slow match in the flammable nest, lit a cigarette and sucked on it until it gave off a satisfying glow. His hands were surprisingly steady as he wedged the cigarette tightly in the matchbook. Then he aimed the flashlight at it and watched smoke curl up from it for a full ten seconds. Finally, he secured the whole works in the pile of dry goods.

As he was sneaking back out the door, he halted, thinking he heard something. His ears were bad old things but for a second it had sounded like a baby crying. His flashlight caught the motion of something in the alley. Ah. Only a cat. "Scat!" He stomped his foot at the thing and it slinked away. And then so did Arlen.

WHEN ROBBIE came back in with her next load, Danielle was mewing fussily. She set the boxes on the floor and scooped the baby up. Wet diaper. She bent over the playpen, changed the baby, then walked her and patted her little back until she was once again asleep. She bundled her up tightly in a receiving blanket, even wrapping it over the baby's head because she was worried about the cold air coming in and out. She covered her with a bigger blanket for good measure.

Robbie stretched, longing to go home and get off her feet, but there was more stuff to unload in the van. And there were only so many hours between now and the 9:00 a.m. opening. She'd just have to hurry.

She went back outside and in her haste forgot to put the chock in the door. When she discovered her mistake on the return trip, she balanced the flat plastic bin on her knee and pulled at the knob in frustration. She banged the box down on the sidewalk and cupped her hands around her eyes to peer into the display window.

In the dimly lit store, she spied her purse—with the keys in it—on the table under the umbrella. She thought about calling Frankie, who was seven miles out in the country with a spare key, then realized her cell phone was in her purse, too.

She tried to see Danielle, but couldn't because a blanket was draped over the near side of the playpen. But surely the baby was still asleep. This was her prime sleeping time. Robbie had a key hidden behind a loose brick on the alley side of the store, but she'd have to walk to the end of the block and around the wall-to-wall buildings. She looked up and down the block. Weak lights shone in every store, but no sign of people, not even a car. She gave the playpen a last look and a prayer and dashed off.

INSIDE THE STORE ROOM the cigarette did its flagitious work. With a *pfft* the matches caught. In seconds the polyester batting melted into flame and some nearby cardboard boxes quickly ignited. The mineral spirits and wood stain Zack had used on the floor went up with a *whoosh* next and then the whole room caught.

By the time Robbie used her key to open the door, she was met with a roaring wall of flame and black billowing smoke. She screamed and fell backward, then charged at the door, only to be knocked back again by hideous heat.

"Help!" she screamed into the dark, deserted alley. "My baby!" She looked around for anything that might get her past the fire. Nothing. Not even a trash-can lid. The flames had engulfed the back door and were licking up the side of the brick. She ran, screaming all the way, desperate to get back around the wall of buildings, planning her attack on the plateglass window in front as she went.

Even as she came barreling out of the alley she heard the sirens. Who had called them? The fire engine turned to go down the alley but she charged at it, waving her arms.

"No! Go to the front!" she cried, but above the noise, they didn't seem to hear her. Finally she saw Zack hanging on the side in full regalia.

"Zack! Zack!" she screamed at him as he hopped off the truck to grab her. "Danielle's in there!"

"Oh my God." He turned and headed for the alley door, but Robbie clawed at the back of his turnouts. "No! Up front!"

Waving his arm, Zack bellowed to the men to follow him and together he and Robbie ran for the storefront. The truck backed out of the alley entrance onto Main Street.

Zack was aiming to jerk open the door, but Robbie clutched his turnout coat again. "It's locked!"

He dashed to the rolling truck, ran around and hitched himself up on the side and came down with an ax. In three mighty blows the display window was gone. The interior of the store, eerily still lit, was filling with smoke, swirling up in the high ceilings.

Zack crawled in the window, with Robbie right behind him. When she coughed at the smoke he turned. "Go back!"

But Robbie plunged past him, toward the playpen, near the back of the store. Just as she scooped Danielle up, the old batten and plaster wall at the back, now covered with flammable polyester and nylon fabric, exploded, then buckled as if to collapse.

Zack grabbed Robbie and the baby and threw them to the floor, covering them with his body as the flaming wall collapsed around them.

Underneath Zack's weight, Robbie found she suddenly couldn't breathe, but all she could think about was getting Danielle out of the inferno.

She finally found enough air to cry out "Zack!" as she struggled to push him off of them. But he didn't move.

"Zack!" she screamed again, then twisted her head enough to get a look at his face in the flicker of firelight. He was unconscious.

A rain of water had started inside the building, so loud that Robbie was sure the other firefighters wouldn't hear her screams. It was beating back the fire, but creating suffocating steam and smoke. Fear for her child and the man she loved driving her, with all her might Robbie rolled Zack's weight away, landing him on his side.

She kicked away some burning refuse and struggled to her knees. With Danielle tucked under one arm, she hooked the other under Zack's armpit and tugged. His body moved, but bare inches. She tugged again. She had…to…get…him…away…from…these flames…out…of…this…smoke. She had dragged him only a few feet when she heard the firefighters calling for them.

"Here!" she screamed, "Over here!"

The next thing she felt were rough hands jerking her up, then strong arms lifting her and carrying her, her and her baby, through the black smoke to safety.

Outside, Robbie gulped at the night air as if it were water in the desert. Danielle was screaming her head off. Ardella Brown, of all people, came rushing forward. "Come on, honey," she yelled. Robbie ran with her to an ambulance, which stood open at the ready.

"Zack's hurt bad," she told the firefighter who ran along on the other side of her.

"We got him," he said. "We got him."

The baby was, miraculously, fine. Not even so much as a blister. Robbie's hands had steam burns on the backs, her face had second-degree flash burns and her hair was singed. Her throat was sore. But she could only think about Zack.

They laid him out in the ambulance, peeling off his turnouts, slapping on an oxygen mask, checking his pupils and the nasty bump on his head all at once. He was already waking up, calling for her, for Danielle, under the mask.

"I'm here." She crawled up and perched on her knees beside him. "Danielle is fine. She was down low in the playpen, away from the smoke, and bundled up so tight in flame-retardant blankets that nothing touched her. They're checking her over now."

The baby's protesting cries, even muffled by a tiny oxygen mask, were, in fact, filling the ambulance. Robbie squeezed Zack's hand and was gratified when he raised his head. "Go back to her," he croaked.

They were all transported to the small hospital three blocks away, where the cops were waiting in the emergency room to talk to Robbie. She told them what she knew and asked who had called the fire station.

"Ardella called in the alarm," a young officer who seemed to know Zack explained. "She was working late in the back room of her store getting ready for the festival, too, and she thought she heard someone go screaming past her door. She stuck her head out and smelled the smoke, then saw the flames. She also reported that she saw Arlen Mestor staggering down the alley a few minutes before the fire started, claims he scared her cat."

"I hope you've already arrested him."

"He's in the next cubicle, ma'am. Had some chest pains and brought himself in. We'll hold him for questioning."

But Mestor didn't need to be questioned. He was already talking, ranting, so loudly that Robbie and everybody in the ER could hear him.

"I didn't know there was no baby in there!" he bellowed.

And then it seemed Mestor got confused and was no longer talking about this most recent fire.

"Some Mexican with a diamond stud earring in his ear gave me cash money to do it. I thought I was just burning up a sorry old barn." Behind the curtain, Arlen Mestor had actually started to sob.

CHAPTER SEVENTEEN

I LOOK BACK on all of it now, the whole thing beginning to end, and I see that somehow Zack Trueblood has always been there, right from the very start of this terrible journey. He came out to my farm one time after the fire, to console me, I guess. But I was in my robe and couldn't bring myself to face him. Markie went out and talked to him in the driveway. I can still see him standing there. Something about the way the man moves, about the way he looks, haunted me, even then.

The night of the barn fire. I can't forget the way his face looked, as he stood there, facing me. Mother, I think, was trying to guide me away, to get me to go back in the house. But I couldn't tear myself away from his eyes. Zack Trueblood was just standing there, looking at me like his heart had broken in half. His face was black with soot and steam was still rolling off his turnouts from when they'd hosed him down after he dragged Danny out. As long as I live, I'll never forget the sound of him, choking back emotion as he kept saying, "I'm sorry," over and over again.

But now the man responsible for the fire has been caught. I try not to hate Arlen Mestor. He claims he did not know Danny was in there. The Mexican coyotes did that. But why? I'll try not to hate them, either, although something inside of me will always burn for justice. My hope is that Luke Driscoll will hunt those men down like dogs someday. If anybody can do it, I bet he can. In the meantime, I'm going to try to go on with my life now and be happy. I'll try for Zack's sake, for my children's sake. They don't deserve an angry, bitter woman in their lives.

It looks like I can finally make a new start now that I will get the insurance money, not only for the barn but for the store as well. I'm going to use that money wisely. I'm excited, actually, about getting the store up and running again.

In the meantime, Zack is still here. Zack, I think, will always be here.

AFTER ARLEN MESTOR was caught setting the Henkel store fire, and after he confessed to starting the fire that killed Danny, he was ruled an unstable arson risk and locked in jail without bail.

"The police have charged him with involuntary manslaughter," Zack told Luke Driscoll as Luke was preparing to leave Five Points a couple of days later. The Texas Ranger had come to town when he got word of the second fire.

"I know. I did get a chance to swing by the jail and interview him. Mestor keeps insisting he had no idea

Danny was in there at the time. The sheriff's theory is that Mexican coyote-types who paid Mestor dragged Danny into the barn first."

"Because Danny took potshots at them at the caves?"

"I take it you don't buy that?"

"Do you?"

"I wouldn't be exactly swallowing it whole," Luke drawled. "It's a nice, neat little theory, because the bad guys are conveniently out of reach."

"Hightailed it back to Mexico," Zack confirmed. "Won't ever be found, likely."

"And the Morales brothers are long gone as well."

"Maybe not for good, though. According to Justin Kilgore, a girl out at The Light at Five Points is pregnant by one of the brothers. Baby's due pretty soon. That might bring the boy back. Until then, there's not much chance of finding them, either. That family's Huichol. And I understand the Huichol villages in the mountains are remote indeed."

"But if the daddy of that girl's baby comes back, I'm hoping those boys can help me piece together an explanation for why the coyotes were in those caves out on the Tellchick property in the first place. That's too far off the beaten path to be any kind of regular stopover for crossers."

"I agree."

"I'm coming back to check out those caves." Luke held out a card between two fingers. "You call me if you see anymore activity on your land."

His land—Zack still had to get used to the idea. He

took Luke's card. "I'll do it. At least now Robbie will get her insurance money, and she can make a decent start in her business. I'd like to thank you for helping us accomplish that."

"Don't thank me just yet. Like I said, I'm not done here."

Zack didn't know if that was a threat or a promise. But either way, he was pretty sure Luke Driscoll wouldn't rest until he had discovered what was ultimately behind Danny's murder.

For his part, Zack had his land. And a plan.

ON CHRISTMAS DAY, one of those bright, clear Hill Country days when the horizon seemed to stretch forever, Zack drove Robbie, the boys and the baby out to their old homestead.

As they came over the rise on the narrow gravel road, Zack started checking Robbie's face anxiously, but he kept on driving as they passed the house. He wanted to be parked in a certain place before he announced to the family that he'd bought the farm as a Christmas present for them.

"It's changed so much," Robbie breathed, as her eyes took in one improvement after another. The large new green mailbox. Shiny black shutters. Fresh paint on the outbuildings. Bushes trimmed. Even a rain barrel at the side of the house. "Surely Kilgore didn't do all of this?"

"Nope." Zack braked the truck at the top of the hill, where a stiff wind was buffeting the cedar trees. "He surely did not."

"Then who did?"

"The new owner."

"Wow!" Mark cried from the back seat of the double cab. "Looky at that!"

Zack turned in the seat, purposely focusing on the boys and avoiding Robbie's eyes. "This is your place, now, fellas. And when spring comes, I'm going to take you guys hunting and fishing out here and we can come and camp out up in this old house."

"Whatever you say, man!" Rob hollered. The three Tellchick boys had developed an unabashed case of hero worship for Zack.

"Can we go look at it?" Mark said.

"Sure."

The boys piled out to run toward the sign Zack had erected.

Robbie stared first at Zack and then again at the large sign at the crest of the hill next to the old stone house. But even as the boys let out whoops of joy and went charging toward it, she maintained a solemn silence, though Zack had caught a quick sheen of tears forming in her eyes.

A frown creased his brow as he said, "I hope that's okay. I mean, that I surprised you like this."

"It's not about the sign, Zack. Or the farm." She swallowed dryly.

"Then what is it?"

"I was thinking about when you nearly died in that fire—"

"Don't. I did *not* nearly die. I got knocked on the head, is all. It was a little goose egg that went away the next day."

Robbie just ignored that. He would forever be this way, she supposed. Minimizing his natural heroism, and the risks he took to exercise it. "When I almost lost you, I realized I cannot waste another day living in the past," she went on, "living without *you*, Zack, the man I probably always should have been with."

His heart swelled to hear her admit it. "Then why so sad, sweetheart? When I've just bought your farm back for you?"

"I...I'm—" Her head swiveled to him quickly. "That's kind of the problem. What are *your* intentions, Zack?"

"My intentions? Good ones, I expect. To make you happy. To make these children happy."

"Then, do you really think I can be happy living out on this farm?"

His heart hammered. Was his plan going to fail? "Can't you?"

Robbie looked at Zack, then out the windshield as she considered it. She really considered it. Sitting right there in the cab of that pickup, silent except for the hiss of the heater that was running for the baby's benefit. Could she be happy out on this farm again? The man deserved an honest answer. "No," she finally said.

"*No?* What do you mean, no? After I spent my life savings buying this thing? After I worked my butt off, using every minute of my spare time to turn it into something decent, into a decent place to live? After all that, you are telling me, woman, that your answer is just flat *no?* I thought you'd be happy to have your farm back."

"I don't know where you got that idea. You certainly didn't ask me, or you would have known that living on this farm just about sucked the life right out of me."

His cheeks puffed out with a forced breath. Now it was his turn to stare out the windshield.

"I want to keep my store, Zack," she went on, "I like it. You didn't ask me about that, did you?"

Finally he said, "The store? Is that all that's bothering you?"

"Is that *all?* That store is going to make it, and you know it. Frankie had good insurance and when she collects, she wants to rebuild, to start over. And now I've got my insurance money to contribute. I was very proud of my designs. I want to give it a shot."

"I agree. You should have your business. We can work all that stuff out, Robbie. I thought you were saying you couldn't live out here because of…"

"Because of Danny? Because of how he died out here?"

Zack nodded, hung his head.

"I am not going to let Danny Tellchick, or anybody else, come between us, ever."

He gave her a sideways glance, hopeful. "I needed to hear you say that."

"I just do not want to move back out here on this farm and be some kind of…slave to the land."

"Do you really think that would happen, with me being the man of the place?"

Of course she didn't. She didn't even have to answer that one out loud. Everything would be different with Zack. Hadn't he already proved that to her a hundred times? And when you loved somebody as much as she loved Zack, you made sacrifices. This was his dream, and she wasn't going to be the one to deny it to him. She looked at the sign and said, "I suppose we'll be running the tires right off that minivan."

His head came up, his eyes went wide.

"So," she said abruptly, "are you still wanting us to get married?"

"You know that I do." His voice was hushed, as a person's might become, Robbie imagined, when their lifelong dreams were about to come true.

"Well, me, too."

He actually got tears in his eyes, which for some paradoxical reason made Robbie smile bigger than Dallas. "I want to have a decent, respectable engagement," she said as he took her in his arms. "There's still a whole lot we don't know about each other, Zack Trueblood. And I take marriage very seriously."

"Me, too." Zack smiled the teary, dawning smile of a man reborn, right before he kissed her.

"Look out there, Robbie," he said when they broke apart. He pointed at the valley below them. "I'm getting ready to plant blue bonnet seed out there. And Indian blanket. Black-eyed Susans. Even tickseed. This will be a beautiful spot for a wedding, once everything comes up."

Robbie turned to him, awestruck, with her own emotional tears coming on as she understood his meaning. He had already intended to wait 'til spring. "How did you know I always dreamed of that valley blooming with wildflowers?"

"I read it. In your diary," Zack answered, and there was no shame in his expression. "One night when you fell asleep with Danielle, back when she was a newborn."

Robbie couldn't hide her shock. And of course, with this man, she didn't have to. "You read my *diary?* How much of it did you read?"

Zack started to actually blush, something Robbie had never seen him do. "Enough to know I'd be a fool if I didn't marry you. Enough to know that—" he took her hand and kissed it tenderly "—we'd both be fools if we didn't get married out there…when the wildflowers bloom."

Robbie realized Zack had read for himself exactly how deeply and passionately her feelings for him ran. But she wanted to tell him anyway.

"I love you so much, Zack," she whispered. "More than I've ever loved anyone in my whole life." For this man, she knew she would do anything.

"And I will find a way to come back to this farm and be happy here, if that's what will make you happy." She swallowed down tears as she whispered, "Because I will always love you."

They kissed again, the deepest, tenderest kiss a man and woman could give one another, at least while three young boys were looking on.

"Come on," Zack said, when they finished. "I want to record this day."

He had brought his digital camera and they bundled up the baby and climbed out of the pickup to snap the boys' pictures as they stood before the sign, beaming with pride.

Then Mark wanted to take a picture of his mother alone with Zack. Frank took baby Danielle from Robbie's arms.

Zack and Robbie stood close and then Zack bent and kissed Robbie again, happily and soundly this time, as the camera clicked, capturing them, braced against the winter wind in front of a sign with bold black Victorian lettering that proudly proclaimed Tellchick-Trueblood Farm.

Turn the page for an excerpt from the third book in Darlene Graham's trilogy. LONE STAR DIARY will be available in July 2006 from Signature Saga.

CHAPTER ONE

LUKE DRISCOLL fought down a clutch of nausea as his boots thudded along the dusty moonlit path. Even with the desert's cooling night breezes, the landscape around him reeked worse than an outhouse.

Little wonder. The place was a virtual garbage dump. His flashlight illuminated an arid terrain littered with bottles, cans, trash bags, foam cartons, soiled disposable diapers, sanitary napkins, discarded clothes, ripped backpacks, even used toilet paper and human feces.

But it was the sight of a syringe with an exposed needle near his boot that angered Luke the most. The coyotes and drug runners shot their veins full of stimulants to stay high enough to endure the torturous journeys. Their human cargo was prodded along with no such chemical help.

Out of the moonlit shadows a figure wearing a U.S. Border Patrol uniform emerged. He flicked a flashlight up into Luke's face and strode toward him.

Luke squinted at the glare as he fished his badge out of the hip pocket of his jeans and flipped open the leather cover. "Luke Driscoll."

The light flashed off the badge then the guard aimed

the cone at the ground as he approached. "Nobody said anything about you being a Texas Ranger."

"More like former." There was no *former,* truth be told. In Luke's mind once a Ranger, always one. But these days Luke kept his badge in his pocket instead of pinned to his shirt for all the world to see. And he no longer covered the span of a couple of Texas-sized counties the way most Rangers did. These days he worked indoors with the hard-bitten crew of the Unsolved Crimes Investigation Team out of Austin, where, he imagined, it had been quietly arranged for the powers that be to keep an eye on him. Long Arm Luke had become Loose Cannon Luke after his wife and daughter were killed.

"Chuck Medina," the border guard said. He extended his hand and the two men shook. "I'm in charge of this case, at least for now." The youngish agent, who looked part Hispanic, studied Luke's face in the off-glow of his flashlight. "Driscoll? Where have I heard that name before?"

"Beats me." Luke kept his expression impassive and his tone neutral. He had long cultivated the habit of sidestepping his history. "Thanks for meeting me."

"No problem. But I'm confused. What does the OAG want with this case?"

"Nothing." And Luke was glad of it. He preferred to work alone. And while the Office of the Attorney General would tackle near-most anything—murder, money laundering, child porn—they would never step on local law enforcement's toes. And Luke had a feeling some pretty big toes were going to get stepped on in this deal. He had already delved into one murder that appeared to be part of some linked criminal transactions. "This one's my personal deal."

"Personal?" Again Medina studied him so closely that Luke decided he'd better throw the kid off the scent.

"I'm sort of a cold-case investigator." He made his involvement sound detached, remote. "We think this murder is related to some old trouble up north." He started walking toward the crime-scene tape stretched between two mesquite bushes.

The guard kept pace with him. "Whereabouts up north?"

"The Hill Country." Luke had already made two trips down the winding backcountry roads to Five Points, Texas, a town that was beginning to devil his mind for a lot of reasons.

"How'd you get wind of this?" the guard asked as Luke raised the stretchy yellow tape to duck under.

"A couple of brothers came to me." Luke was surprised but gratified that the Morales boys had talked to him. He supposed the fallout from his history wasn't all bad. "The young woman you guys found out here in this dung heap—" he straightened and surveyed the surrounding area with disgust "—was their sister."

Medina shook his head. "Oh, *man.*"

Far back in the mesquite bushes, they came to a shallow depression, freshly dug in the hard-packed desert. "He buried her?"

"Yeah. In a shallow grave. Very shallow. Almost like

he didn't care if she got found. I guess even if she was, he knew he'd never get caught. The coyotes aren't scared of us."

Luke's own words, spoken to a most feminine woman with a somewhat unfeminine name—Frankie— only a few weeks earlier, echoed in his mind now.

"These are very dangerous men, ma'am," he had warned the tall, hauntingly beautiful brunette.

He shook off the weird sense of enchantment that overcame him every time his thoughts strayed to this Frankie woman. Right now he didn't have time to dwell on unbidden feelings.

He panned his flashlight over the area, which was un-naturally clean, stripped of all debris. "I see you boys got everything."

"Every last little bobby pin. A freaking waste of time," Medina pronounced.

"Ah, now," Luke drawled, "I've never found catching a killer a waste of time."

Medina grunted as if unconvinced. Luke figured he knew what the guy was thinking: if these people wanted to break the law and trust their lives to coyote types, they got what they paid for. After an uncomfortable silence in which the two men stared at the scene and adjusted to the likelihood that they stood on different sides of the issue of undocumented aliens, Luke said, "What do you know about the victim?"

The guard shrugged. "One more pretty Mexican girl on the run."

The victim's brothers had told him, tearfully, that

their sister was pretty. And the Texas State Police Luke interviewed before he came out here had confirmed that indeed, the victim had a pretty face—what was left of it. Sixty-five stab wounds. Coyotes were rightly named. They were no better than mad dogs, vicious animals that devoured the innocent.

When the Five Points police had shown up at a compound called The Light at Five Points looking for Maria's brothers, Luke was already there talking to Justin Kilgore, the man who ran the relief organization, and—this interested Luke more than it should have— Frankie McBride's brother-in-law. Kilgore said the Morales boys—the same Morales boys, it turned out, who had originally come to Luke with a bizarre story about some Mayan carvings—had disappeared.

The brothers would never come out of hiding, Kilgore told the cops, even to claim their sister's body. Luke knew that was right. Whoever killed the sister was trying to draw the brothers out. While Luke had convinced the brothers to tell him about Maria, about their home town in Jalisco, about their family history, he couldn't convince the boys to come down to the border, though they had begged *him* to go. Luke was the only Anglo they trusted, they said. And Luke intended to keep that trust.

The crime-scene tape, looking defeated as it sagged into the sand, was about all that was left to indicate a murder had occurred here yesterday. Maria's body, after a routine autopsy, would be shipped back to Mexico where her aging, widowed mother and large extended family would bury their baby girl with an elaborate funeral they could ill afford. The men who killed her were undoubtedly long gone, too—possibly back to Mexico as well.

Now Maria Morales's murder would lie unsolved, lost in a morass of paperwork and foggy legalities. Of no more consequence than the litter on this desert. Something ugly, something to wash your hands of. Waste. But for reasons all his own, Luke wouldn't rest until he'd hunted down the dog who killed this girl. Nor would he rest until he had an answer, one way or another, to the ultimate question in this deal. *Why?*

"The girl we took in for questioning described the killer. A coyote in his early twenties." The agent dug something out of his flak jacket. "We mooched this picture off the Houston police. The guy operates over that way as well."

They were standing just inside the border, on the U.S. side of the Rio Grande River, south-southwest of San Antonio, far, far away from the Houston side of Texas.

"Busy hombre," Luke muttered.

"Yeah." The Federal handed Luke a grainy black-and-white photo that looked like it had been down-loaded off the Internet. "According to our sources, the guy has relatives on both sides of the state, *and* in Arizona, *and* as far south as Chiapas. He could be anywhere between here and Central America."

"Can I get a copy of this?"

"Keep that one. And here's another. You know, it's a damn shame. The more the illegals come, the more the coyotes prey on them," the guard explained what everybody already knew while he dug around for another picture. "Sometimes I feel like we're spittin' in a fire. They're like roaches, you know? Scuttling across the border in the night. But we have to try, right?"

"You in your way, me in mine," Luke said. He had heard another agent compare crossers to ants. If you smashed one, twenty more took his place. He gave the skinny guard a pitiless glance. But he couldn't find it in his heart to judge him too harshly. So young. Seemed like they all were. Luke himself was only forty-three and yet he always felt like an old geezer in the subterranean world of the border.

Whether it was the wetbacks or the patrol or the coyotes, the people down here all seemed like scared children caught up in a dangerous game. This one was no exception, no older than your average college student. Doing the best that he could. Patrolling miles and miles of impossibly vast Texas terrain in his four-wheel-drive vehicle searching for illegals that flooded across in numbers that staggered the imagination. Carrying around obscene photos in his flak vest.

Medina finally produced a paper and handed it over. A photograph of the body. A mangled young female form, half-dressed.

"Did she have any personal effects?" Luke said as he looked at it.

The border guard gave him an annoyed squint. "You're kiddin', right?"

The coyote who killed her had, of course, robbed her as well.

"The brothers believe she was wearing a vest covered in Huichol beadwork. It had great...*sentimental* value. She was also supposedly carrying an object in her backpack. Did anybody find said backpack, or perhaps a chunk of carved stone in the vicinity?"

Luke suspected there was more to this chunk of rock and this vest than sentimental value. The Morales brothers were withholding something here, but they would come straight with him or find themselves hugging jail bars.

"No sign of any backpack," the kid said. "Or any carving. But I know the kind of thing you're talking about. Occasionally we'll hear tell of crossers smuggling over artifacts. Mayan stuff, mostly. My guess is they sell them in El Norte for a fortune. And a beaded vest?" The guard eyed Luke sarcastically. "Crossers wear rags. And knock-offs of Nikes when they can get 'em."

Indeed. No one in their right mind would dress in precious ceremonial garb for this journey. Crossers snaked along in unbroken lines over dusty well-beaten paths like this one, cutting through the underbrush, winding their way down canyon floors, sneaking along arroyo bottoms.

Luke pushed his Stetson back on his head and rubbed his forehead, thinking for the millionth time that there had to be a humane solution for these people. Did Maria's brothers blame themselves for not going back to Mexico to get the vest themselves instead of having their sister wear it on her person? But it was Luke's understanding that no man was supposed to touch the feminine half of the pattern. He wondered if evil would befall the coyote who'd stolen it, part of him longing to believe these ancient superstitions were true.

"Maybe her friend knows something about the backpack, but my guess is it's long gone, down the trail with that coyote."

"You mean the girl you took into custody?"

"Yeah. Yolonda Reyes. She burrowed down in the sand behind the bushes while they raped and killed this one. They were traveling together. That little *chica*'s lucky she's alive." The guard spat in the dust. "You know what she said? She said that at least this time the Morales family would have a body."

Luke frowned. "This time?"

The guard hitched at his belt, suddenly self-important with the knowledge that he had information a Texas Ranger didn't.

"She said the dad disappeared years ago."

"Yeah." Luke knew this.

"She said he sent their mother the sign, but they never heard from him again."

"The sign?" Luke squinted at Medina.

"The Lone Star. They'll send it on a postcard or a trinket or something back home to Mexico. It's the sign that they've made it as far as a place called Five Points. I do not know why these people bother with such secrecy." Medina shook his head. "Everybody knows Five Points is a key stopping place for crossers headed north. Five highways in every direction. Just a hop-step to I-10."

"I see," Luke said. The sign for Five Points. He could

practically see a puzzle piece locking in place. The Morales boys had failed to tell him this little detail. Suddenly he knew exactly what he was going to do with this girl. Offer her asylum if she would tell him everything. He could take her out to The Light at Five Points.

Luke thought of the people out there and others he'd met when he'd gone to check out another murder in the small town, and like a rubber band, his mind snapped back to the woman named Frankie.

Frankie McBride Hostler, she'd said. Although the last name hadn't rolled out evenly with the first two. As if she wasn't so sure her name really was Hostler. He'd looked at her left hand then, its slender fingers entangled with the other hand around the grip of a heavy revolver. A diamond the size of Dallas had winked in the blazing southwest sun.

He'd never met a woman that way, while she held a gun on him in a firm firing stance. When she shot the head off the copperhead snake less than a yard from his boot, he had decided this particular woman was something else.

Too bad this Frankie McBride...*Hostler* was married.

Five Points. He was headed back there for sure. Back to the home of Frankie McBride.

HARLEQUIN *Super*ROMANCE®

Home to Loveless County...
because Texas is where the heart is.

Introducing an exciting new five-book series set in
the rugged Hill Country of Texas.

Desperate times call for desperate measures. That's why
the dying town of Homestead, Texas, established the
Home Free program, offering land grants in exchange
for the much-needed professional services modern
homesteaders bring with them.

Starting in October 2005 with

BACK IN TEXAS
by Roxanne Rustand
(Harlequin Superromance #1302)

WATCH FOR:

AS BIG AS TEXAS
K.N. Casper (#1308, on sale November 2005)

ALL ROADS LEAD TO TEXAS
Linda Warren (#1314, on sale December 2005)

MORE TO TEXAS THAN COWBOYS
Roz Denny Fox (#1320, on sale January 2006)

THE PRODIGAL TEXAN
Lynnette Kent (#1326, on sale February 2006)

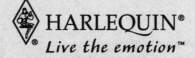

HARLEQUIN®
Live the emotion™

Since when did life ever tell you were going?

Sometimes you just have to dip your oar into the water and start to paddle.

THE
SUNSHINE
COAST
NEWS

KATE AUSTIN

National bestselling author

Janice Kay Johnson

A new and memorable tale of
Patton's Daughters…

Dead Wrong

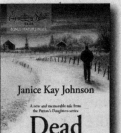

After many years of estrangement, Ed Patton's oldest grandchild, Will, returns home. Now a prosecutor, Will finds himself embroiled in a murder case that mirrors one from eight years before involving his then girlfriend. With the help of Trina, a policewoman, Will must solve the murder and prove his innocence.

"Janice Kay Johnson wins our hearts with appealing characters…"—*Romantic Times*

Look for *Dead Wrong* in February.